MUN[illegible]
KEEP

Brian C. Austin

A Novel

MUNINN'S KEEP

Quotations draw from *The Latin Vulgate,* 405 A.D., which is in the public domain. Paraphrases draw from the Old English style of *The Geneva Bible,* 560 A.D., which is in the public domain, and from *The King James Bible,* 1611 Edition (Hendrickson Publishers, Inc., 2003, 1-56563-160-9).

Map of Muninn's Keep and surrounding area by author. Parchments and drawings by author. All rights reserved.

Historical Fiction, Northern Britain, 892 A.D.

ISBN-13: 978-1-926676-66-1

Printed in Canada

Printed by Word Alive Press
131 Cordite Road, Winnipeg, MB R3W 1S1
www.wordalivepress.ca

FOR CAROLYN

One ring given.
Twice broken from the finger
that wore it—twice repaired.
Once lost at spring flood
in an icy, muddy river—
all but buried in the mud
as the floodwaters receded—
yet found again.
Once cut from a severed finger—
but repaired and worn yet once again.

THE SAME RING—NOT A COPY.

This book is dedicated to the one
who gave me that ring
and still puts up with me
all these years later.

Acknowledgements

This work owes a great debt to historians through the ages who have preserved tantalizing tidbits of a time and place in history fascinating for its very elusiveness. As Christianity moved north, Woden worship (frequently called 'Odin' worship) and many other ancient pagan practices conflicted and blended in strange and often contradictory ways. Woden worship became less visible, but continued to hold a strong grip on the minds of people. Small city-state kingdoms struggled for survival in an unforgiving culture. Bits and pieces of that history are preserved in songs, nursery rhymes, children's games, and wedding and funeral traditions.

Thanks also to The Word Writers Writing group, a Fiction Intensive Workshop at Write Canada, and to Ray Wiseman and Mary Lou Cornish for invaluable feedback and professional critiquing. To the extent that I have taken their advice to heart, this manuscript has improved.

Nikki Braun deserves thanks as well for a dynamic cover design, and Evan Braun for typesetting, while Word Alive Press as a whole has made this project both possible and practical.

Two books proved of particular value for the insights and research, though are never quoted directly in this novel:

King Arthur's Place in Prehistory: The Great Age of Stonehenge, W. E. Cummins, 1992 Bramley Books. ISBN 1-8583-3769-0

A Street Through Time: A 12000 Year Journey Along the Same Street, Dr. Anne Millard, 1998 Dorling Kindersley Ltd. ISBN 0-7513-5535-6

Countless other books from a lifetime of reading have doubtless influenced this work in ways even I am unaware of.

Table of Contents

Muninn's Keep

Illustrations

Characters

KEY CHARACTERS (IN ALPHABETICAL ORDER)

With literal meaning of name and age at first appearance in story.

Bertrm *(glorious raven)* 48 years old. Twisted and crippled from being thrown by a horse. Bertrm is Theodoric's instructor with horses.

Dierdre *(sorrow, wanderer)* 15 years old. The young 'wench' of Mr. Gerhardt's household, pregnant when Theodoric first becomes aware of her. A hard worker resigned to her lot in life.

Erhard *(strong resolution)* Early 60's make him a great age. White streaks the little hair he has left. A self-taught scrivener, (scribe) he has skills his master needs, but despises.

Holt Gerhardt *(from the forest / spearhard)* 42 years old. Theodoric's master. A harsh, powerful man with hands seemingly made to clutch a sword.

Muninn's Keep

Theodoric Thorvæld *(powerful people / ruler of the people)* 15 years old. Disjointed memories, yet skilled in languages and with weapons. No beard when first introduced. Scarred from a flogging and a brand. *This story is told from Theodoric's point of view.*

Other Characters (in alphabetical order)

With literal meaning of name and age at first appearance in story.

Æthëlrd *(foolish one)* 35 years old. Deceptive in size, in appearance much like Mr. Gerhardt. A cruel man with too much love for beer and ale. He has a deep, slow voice.

Burleigh *(a field with knotted tree trunks)* 26 years old. Idle drinker who later becomes a skilled blacksmith.

Cameron *(Hooked nose)* 68 years old. A wise old man Theodoric finds himself drawn to.

Chapman *(Merchant)* 25 years old. One of Theodoric's men-at-arms.

Chester Tnsmith *(from the fortified camp / Tinsmith)* 31 years old. A tinsmith.

Durward Morton *(gatekeeper / from the town near the moor)* 18 years old. A young, highly skilled warrior.

Erskine *(from the height of the cliff)* 26 years old. One of Mr. Gerhardt's Men-at-arms. A completely loyal man, strong and skillful with arms, courageous in battle. He has a strangely broken voice.

Finlay *(light-haired soldier)* Dark-haired with a ruddy complexion—in marked contrast with his name. Finlay is the "watcher" who knows something of Theodoric's past.

Glenine *(from the valley or glen)* 22 years old. Wife of Burleigh. Timid, starved, afraid, grieving the loss of an infant daughter.

Guinevére *(white wave)* Infant daughter of Burleigh and Glenine—died within hours of birth.

Hamil *(from the proud estate)* One of the prisoners in lockup the night of Theodoric's confrontation with Æthëlred.

Harlan *(from the long field)* 28 years old. Runaway slave. Physically frail. A poet whose verses do not celebrate battle and warfare.

Ilsa *(noble)* Dierdre's infant daughter.

Kenyon *(white-haired, blond)* 26 years old. One of Mr. Gerhardt's Men-at-Arms.

Kïncaid ap Tïrrèll *(battle chief / belonging to Thor)* 28 years old. Leader of the Pict army.

Oöna *(united one)* Relina's nurse/teacher and Mr. Gerhardt's whore, though only rarely summoned to his bed.

Pollard *(cropped hair)* 24 years old. Runaway slave. A blacksmith with great muscled arms, a deep chest and broad shoulders.

Ralina *(doe)* 8 years old. The daughter of Mr. Gerhardt. Her mother died in childbirth.

Sheridan *(wild man)* 70+ years old. A bard and harpist. A man of great age and great wisdom.

Spittin' Sheffield *(from the crooked field)* 14 years old. Tall, gangly and arrogant.

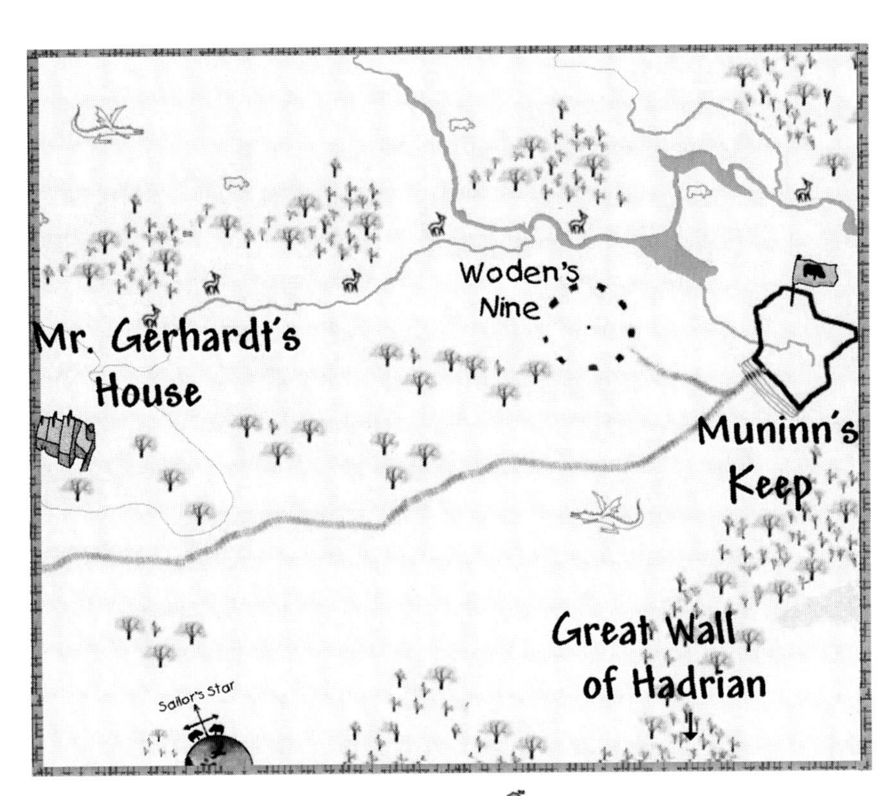
Woden's
Nine
Mr. Gerhardt's
House
Muninn's
Keep
Great Wall
of Hadrian
Sailor's Star

Britannia
Hadrian's
Wall

Chapter One
MEMORIES LOST

4 Janus, in the 773rd year after the Emperor Hadrian began construction on the Great Wall. As the present generation would measure time, January 4, 892.

BLACKNESS! BLACKNESS TO MAKE EYES ACHE. Stale air. Something hard and cold beneath me. Streaks of fire across my back and shoulders. A pounding inside my skull.

I raised a hand to see what covered my eyes, gasping at the pain, then stared into—blackness. The groan that escaped echoed, like I lay in a room little bigger than the latrine. No memories—just an aching emptiness. No past—only the blinding, empty now.

Woden's Hall. My mind grasped the thought. *I've fallen in battle and been carried to Valhalla.* Bitter laughter rose within me. *But I've been found unworthy.*

I fought to awaken, to escape the nightmare. The pounding in my head intensified. Tortured hinges groaned. *A door?* Flickering torch-light danced. The rustle of clothes and hiss of harsh breath sounded.

"Ga. You stink like a dead pole cat." The deep, slow voice somehow brought to mind a bull.

Cold water shattered the remnants of the dream. I stared through bleary eyes, aware of an intense burning on my left arm, a more extreme pain in a body that felt on fire.

"Master says you've rotted here long enough." The bull's voice mocked. "Smells like he's right."

I searched for names, memories, understanding, but found nothing, my head throbbing with the effort. Two faces loomed through the torch-light.

"Get on your feet and out to the stable. At least you're closer to the dung-hill there. Mayhap Bertrm will throw you on." The same bull's voice.

Clean air found its way past them into the tiny room. I sucked it into my lungs, aching as they expanded. I tried to rise but only managed to drag myself forward, every movement an agony. A boot struck me in the face.

"I said get up, witless, stupid horse-killer," the words rumbled deeply.

Cruel hands dragged me into a corridor. I coughed and spit blood. A boot dug into my chest and rolled me onto my back.

"Æthëlrd! Kick him again and Master will take his worth outta you. You'll be lucky you don't get the lash anyway, letting him git this close to dead." The second man spoke in a strangely broken voice.

I fought myself to hands and knees. The world spun, a world of greys and blacks. A dark door squatted in a low opening in the stone wall on my right. On the left a steel gate enclosed another cell. Another door stood open in front of me, more cells beyond it. The men crowded the corridor.

"Get on your feet. I ain't about to carry something stinks as bad as you." The one called Æthëlrd flung contempt at me, slowly, deliberately, like he was piling dung.

It took all my strength to force my body up. I felt sick and dizzy. The rattle of keys and the thump of an iron gate sounded as I stumbled into a larger room. A torch gave smoky, flickering light. Climbing the stairs wrung a groan from me.

"The stable, Fool! Where the four legged animals live." Æthëlrd's voice vibrated in my bones, but told me nothing.

"Go easy Æthëlrd. He don't know which way is up yet. Show him, but keep your boots off him." The broken voice spoke in my defense again.

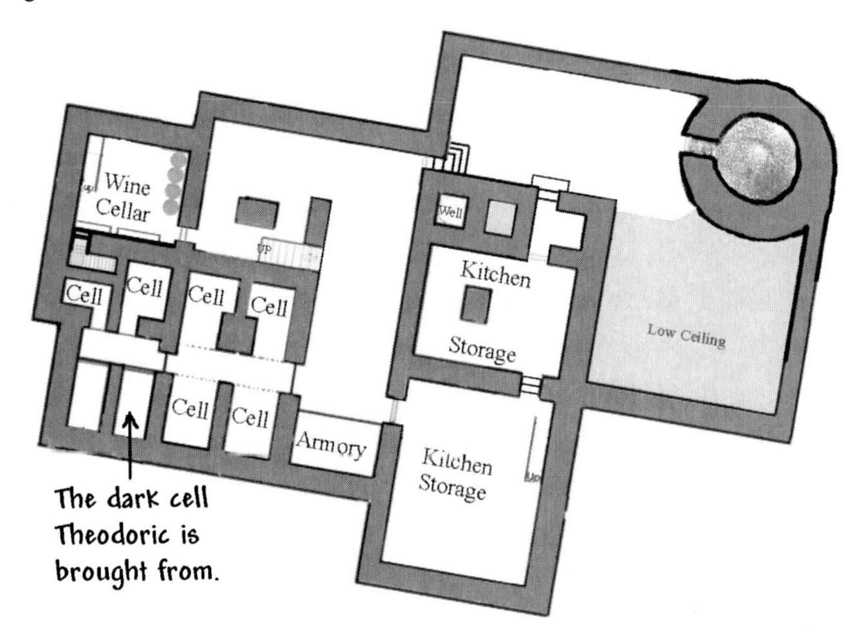

Æthëlrd stomped across the room, flung back a door and jerked his head to the right. The outside light blinded me as I swayed in the doorway. "Get!" Æthëlrd spat the word, then gave me a shove. I fell forward, stone steps with their dusting of snow pounded my already tortured body.

At the base of the stairs my breath came in sobbing gasps. I pressed my face into the thin, dirty snow and sucked some of it into my mouth. I struggled to rise, but slumped forward again.

The cold had lost its bite when a boot thrust against my shoulder.

"Curse Woden. Be this what they send me? Already dead? And I git to dig his grave." The boot pressed harder. "Git up. You don't die at my stable door. Jist try it and I'll kill you." A man bent over me, then got a hand under my arm and threatened to pull it off. I don't know how I got my feet under me, but I stood, swaying, staring at the short, twisted man before me. I knew the voice and the face, but couldn't put a name to him.

"You!" he burst out. "The beardless horse killer? Again? By all the gods! What have I done to deserve this?"

"Where? What?" I questioned stupidly. "Why—can't—I remember?" I stared around me. We stood in a walled courtyard covered in snow. A beaten path led to a tiny building set against an old fortress wall. The stone walls of a large house towered behind me and to my right. Dark and gloomy under a grey sky, it seemed to tease some memory, but I could make nothing of it.

"It talks," the voice mocked, then continued. "Theodoric. That's what they calls you ain't it? And horse killer." He snorted. "A half-grown whelp but already a horse killer." He spat on the ground beside my feet. "Git yourself inside then. I'm stuck with you and you're stuck with me. Two bleeding thræls who git as much say as pigs fattened for slaughter."

I stumbled beside him, his hand tight on my arm. He was rough and coarse, but in a strange way comforting. The stable door opened and then closed behind us. The dimmer light soothed my eyes. We walked between heaps of fodder and straw.

"There's steps here. You don't need no more falls," the man warned just before we descended two steps to stand among horse stalls.

At the closest water bucket I fell to my knees, cupped water and drew it up to my face. I sucked it from filthy hands, then scrubbed my face.

"No water in the dark hole? Someday Æthëlrd will get his." The man shoved me aside and grabbed the bucket. "No horse will wanna drink from that now. Woden's beard, but you stink. Did they not give you a bucket in the dark hole?" He carried the bucket to the doorway and pitched the remaining water outside. "Stretch yourself in the straw. You're no good to nobody till you can work."

Questions churned in my mind, but my tongue seemed thick, words weighty and cumbersome. The next thing I knew a hand roughly grabbed my shoulder. "Here. The lassie brought you something to eat. Something fitting to drink too—better'n the horse bucket. They won't let you to board, the way you stink."

I tried to rub the sleep from my eyes and stared up to a young wench carrying a trencher of food and a jug. "Where am I?" I questioned. "Who are you?"

"You that daft?" The man beside the wench spat on the floor. "Dierdre here, worked in the kitchens afore you killed Mr. Gerhardt's best horse and got the whipping post for your troubles. You worked for me afore that too." He snorted. "She had eyes for you, though you was too sick to see."

"Stow it, Bertrm. Unless you want to wear this." The girl raised the jug toward him.

"Ha!" Bertrm snorted. "You wouldn't dare." But he backed away, grinning.

"Wanna try me?" she shot back at him.

"Na. Don't waste it on me. The laddie here is the one what needs a bath."

I struggled to my feet. "Why—can't I remember things?" I hurt, bad, like someone had ridden a threshing sledge over me. I wore old patched pants made of some heavy woven stuff. High boots covered my feet. I wore a sark of wool covered by a leather coat. Some kind of hat pulled at my scalp.

"I'm Bertrm, stable-hand, thræl, jist like you, 'cept I hope I still have some sense." The man shoved me down in the straw and yanked the hat away from my head. Caked with dried blood, it tore hair and skin out with it.

"What the. . ." I burst out. A gasp sounded from Dierdre.

"I shouldda guessed it," Bertrm muttered. "Got no business being alive, head beat in like that."

"Well sorry to disappoint you," I spat the words at him. "I'll try harder to die next time." Sickness washed over me. I pressed my hand against the wound and felt the stickiness of blood.

Bertrm muttered something as he stomped away, limping, then came back with a dirty rag. "Mop up the blood and see can you keep out of trouble till it heals," he said gruffly. He turned to Dierdre.

"Shouldda let him eat first," he said, half apologetically.

"Aye," she agreed, then knelt in the straw beside me. "Eat." She thrust the trencher into my hands. "It'll give you something to think about while I try to clean the crud from your scalp." She drew in a sharp breath. "Bertrm got one thing right. Don't know why you're still alive."

The food didn't do it. Only stupid, stubborn pride kept me from screaming while Dierdre clipped away matted hair and scrubbed at caked blood. I gulped the small jug of ale when she finished and sank back into the straw.

Frost covered scraped animal skins stretched over the windows when I awoke. A bit of snow made a line beside the door. A big gelding stood in the aisle, sides heaving and steam coming off its coat.

"Theodoric! Master's gonna be back soon. Git up and git the saddle off that horse," Bertrm hollered at me. Thrown by horses too many times, he was strangely twisted. I staggered as I walked to the gelding. "Buck up laddie," Bertrm added more gently. "You'd best have his saddle on a fresh horse when he gits back."

I stared at the saddle, trying to figure how to get the thing off. With the buckles and straps, I didn't know where to start. I had weird, half-memories: a steaming horse and a bucket of water, shouting voices, something that whistled and cracked, and a dark, dark room where no voices reached—just pain.

"What in the name of all the gods you doing?" Bertrm challenged me. "You act like you've never seen a saddle afore." When he got close to me he burst out with, "Ga! You stink!" He shoved me aside. I couldn't quite stop a groan.

"Pretty buckered up ain't you? Still not thinking too clear neither." His voice dropped to a mutter. "Fools! If you ever had any sense, which I doubt, they beat it outta you." He spat on the floor. "Another beating will kill you, but he'll only think of that afterwards. And Theodoric!" His voice got hard. "Don't even think about watering this horse for the next half hour."

Bertrm had another horse saddled and ready when the stable door banged back. The man who barged in had a head thrust forward from broad shoulders. Cold eyes stared at me. It had to be the master, 'Mr. Gerhardt,' Bertrm had called him. His dark hair, drawn together with a twist of rope at the back of his head, showed grey streaks. White dominated his crudely trimmed beard. A hard looking, powerful man, he wore leather breeches, a dark stained coat and a hat made from sheep skin. A sword and purse hung from his belt. He held a short horsewhip in one hand. His face twisted and he sniffed as he stared at me. "By the gods, Bertrm! Dig a hole and bury him."

"Aye, Sir. He sure enough smells over-ripe for burying."

"Where do they breed this kind?" the master asked. I didn't know you could put a sneer in the sound of a voice.

"Well, Sir, this'n seen hard work, but don't know nothing about horses. Ain't been time to teach him, only here two days and still sick from the brand when it happened. I don't reckon I'm telling you nothing you ain't already seen, but he'd been whipped afore, and not yet healed up. His head beat in too and he hardly didn't know his own name. Woden's beard, Sir! Another week and I'd tie him to the post myself if he pulled such a stunt. But he was doing the best he knowed for the horse."

"You'd defend a thief and horse killer?" The master's voice dropped to a low growl.

"That was a braw horse he ruint, Sir. I was powerful fond of that horse. I most wanted to git in a few licks myself." Bertrm paused as he checked the saddle. "No Sir. I ain't defending nobody. It comes nigh to being a hanging crime by my reckoning. But if lads be like horses there be two kinds. I've seen the look this laddie had under the whip jist five times in my day."

"And what look is that?" The master's voice sounded his contempt.

"You sees it in their eyes first time you drop a rope round their neck, Sir. The young whelps are all hell-bent for riding them, cause they're beautiful to look on. But they'll die afore they bend to the whip and the spur."

I could feel the master's gaze on me again. He reached across the saddle, grabbed an arrow from the quiver and pulled his bow free. I felt my whole body go sick, then somehow hard. I stood stiff and straight, staring at the master, just daring him to plug a hole in my chest.

He notched the arrow. "So it's shoot him or cut him loose so he'll breed more of the same. Don't think I want a whole litter of the like." He drew back on the string and I stared death in the eye.

"Aye, Sir. Three of them horses died fighting the rope." Bertrm prattled on. "But I watched a man who loved horses better'n his own bairns. He got ahold of that beastie after three young lads had been dragged away to let their broke ribs heal. I never seen a ride like that one, Sir!"

Bertram sighed, savouring some special memory. "I swear he'd glued hisself to the saddle. Time that horse quit bucking he couldn't walk. But he'd won hisself the best piece of horseflesh a man might see in two lifetimes. More'n one horse been named Llewellyn, but I don't guess there's ever been one earned the name so afore. He was sure enough lightning."

A story—while I waited to die. I wished I had an arrow aimed at Bertrm. Sweat ran down my face.

"And the other one?" The master prompted.

"The other was a braw horse. Name of Rolf. But not the match of that grey. . ." Bertrm's voice fell silent for a moment, then he continued. "I rode him out." He paused again. "He throwed me. But he bucked clean under me again. I come down with my chest acrost the hard part of the saddle." His glance swept the stable, coming to rest on me. "I don't remember the rest of the ride. I mustta stuck, somehow. I ain't done much riding since, or drawed a breath that don't hurt."

"And the horse?" The master kept shifting the arrow, aiming it at my gut or my chest.

"Nobody else couldn't sit him, but I'd rode him out so they give me some say. He's the granddaddy of the one this lad ruint."

"So I bury this whelp, or whip him till one of us drops?" The aim rose to my throat.

"I don't rightly know about laddies, Sir, but I seen his eyes at the whipping, and I seen his eyes jist now with that arrow aimed at his gizzard. I guess it's a long shot that he's worth the extra trouble, Sir, so shootings prob'ly the thing, cause I reckon there ain't no in between."

I just stood there and waited. I wanted to kill Bertrm. The master grunted. He slacked the bow and stuck the arrow back in his bag. He swung onto the horse, leaning low under the beams. Bertrm swung the door back and Mr. Gerhardt spurred the horse out into the stormy evening.

"I wasn't in the mood for digging your grave tonight." Bertrm spoke harshly, his breath coming in quick gasps.

"You told him to kill me." I spat the words back at him.

"You still so blind? His pride wouldda made him think he'd gotta stick you. I saved your neck, boy, and I stuck mine out a long way to do it." He glared across the back of the gelding. "And you killed a braw horse."

"I didn't kill any horse."

"You killed it sure as if you'd hamstrung it and cut its throat." He ducked under the horse's head and grabbed me by the front of my coat. "I aughtta have let him put a arrow in you. No sense and no 'preciation."

He shoved me back. I stumbled and cried out when my back hit the wall. I lunged forward, my hands spread to break my fall. My head started pounding and spinning again. When I could focus I looked up at Bertrm. He stared at my hand like he had seen a wraith.

"You gots—nine fingers?" He spoke in a slow and broken voice.

I got back on my feet and waited until the stable stopped spinning. "Nine?" I spoke disdainfully. "That's what's left if one is missing."

The stump of a finger showed just short of the knuckle on my left hand. I could have told him the toe on my left foot was the same.

Bertrm propelled me out of the stable. I didn't know where he was taking me, or what got his crippled legs going so fast. He pounded on the door of a small cottage. An old man opened it.

"Ah, Bertrm. Come in. Set ye and bide." His glance swept me, then ignored me. I stood there, waiting for the dizziness to pass.

"Well?" Bertrm questioned me. "You jist going to stand there while the house gits cold?" I stamped the snow off my boots and came inside. Bertrm reached past me and pulled the door closed.

The old man stared at me with obvious disgust. "Not a bucket in the darkroom, or did you roll this laddie in the latrine, Bertrm? Take him to the horse trough first and take the stink off."

Bertrm pulled the old man aside and they mumbled in low voices. "Thunder 'n damnation!" the old man burst out. I could feel his gaze sweep me, coming to the stump on my left hand.

A peat fire glowed in the fireplace along one wall. A pair of candles flickered at a small table with a scroll spread across it. Round clay jars held more scrolls. I could see inkpots and quills. A map hung from pegs on one wall. The only window wore a thick rim of frost. With a crude bed and the small table, three of us crowded the room. Hands stained by the ink he worked with contrasted with the man's pale flesh. A bit of chalky white hair still clung to his bony scalp. A shrunken man, very old, yet fully alive.

"Erhard, this be Theodoric," Bertrm said. "Already famous for killing Patton, Master Gerhardt's fav'rit horse."

Erhard stared at me a bit, then poured some dark liquid into earthenware jugs. He passed one to me. I couldn't make sense of why he served me first. "To your health and long life, Surra." He pronounced 'Sir' strangely, accenting the "rr's" and ending with an "ah." He held his cup up to mine, then sipped a few drops.

"And to yours," I stammered, astonished that he had called me

"Sir."

Erhard, my mind rolled the name around. *Strong Resolution.* He searched among clay jars, muttering to himself. "Thunder 'n damnation! Never thought it'd happen in my cabin, or he'd stink like they'd dug him outta a grave when they found him." He pulled a jar from among the others. Smaller than most, this one had an old look about it.

He closed his inkpot and put his quills away, then rolled the scroll he'd been working on. He polished the table with a rag. He wiped his own hands, then opened the door, stood there and breathed deeply a number of times.

Erhard closed the door again and thrust the bolt across. Then he spread a dry and brittle parchment, yellowed with age. "Can you read this?" he asked me. Candlelight flickered across it.

Chapter Two
PARCHMENTS AND PROPHECIES

"IT'S AN OLD SCRIPT WITH UNCOUTH SPELLING," I said. "But it's plain enough—except that middle part in runes."

"Well?" Erhard demanded.

A stabbing headache forced me to close my eyes for a moment. Then, with my finger marking the spot, I read, slowly translating the ancient script into recognizable language. "It's something about '*feared the steed he*'—but it's cut off. Then,

> *Feared the nine fingers that wield weapons of war yet give no quarter when weapons be broken all.*
>
> *Restored will be the ring. Renewed will be the kingdom.*
>
> *Of old has it been told. By the ancients has it been prophesied. Yet will it be said in his day, Of no importance is it. Neither of any consequence.*

"Then you get this bit in Runes."

ᚾᚢᚾ ᚠᛁᚾᚷᚱᛞ ᛦᛁᛚᚱ ᚨᚠ
ᚺᚨᚱᛋᛚ ᛗᛁᛏᚢ ᛁᚾ ᛒᚨᛏᛚ

"Almost—I think I can read them. Nin—Nine. It's a nine—I think—that first word." I glanced up.

"And below that? Where you can read it?" The old man spoke with a strange blend of restraint and urgency, respect and impatience.

Again I closed my eyes a moment, then searched lower on the parchment. "It's a poor piece of work with the smudged print," I blurted.

He of the nine fingers. With many stripes his back is crossed. Clouded is his memory. Red blood flows from many wounds.

Many the blows of his beating. He the accused. Yet of old is the prophecy. The ring by him found shall give proof of his office. He is a warrior born. His destiny from of old is sealed. Yet few will his title recognize or give the honour due him.

Trials and much wrong will first ensue. Then will be restored to him the ring who alone may rightfully wear it.

Of nine fingers is he. Mighty in battle. Called of old Killer of Horses.

"Killer of horses?" My glance swept from the old man to Bertrm and back again. "Isn't that what I got whipped for?"

"Please to finish the reading, Surra," Erhard urged me.

I lowered my gaze and found my place on the parchment again.

His son perchance will better fare with seemly honour and the tribute of men.

For fierce will be the battle in that day. Many the dead. Loud the weeping. The raven and the vulture feed. Black the smoke of funeral piers.

"And there it is cut off again."

"That's what it really says?" Bertrm questioned Erhard. He stared at the parchment.

Erhard ignored Bertrm's question. He rolled the parchment, wrapped it and returned it to its jar. He asked, "Where got you your training?"

"It's ordinary script with old style spelling." I responded. "There's nothing special about being able to read it."

He brought out several other scrolls in three different languages. I could read two of them easily and laboured through the third. He put them away and then stood and looked at me for the longest time. Then he grabbed my hands and examined them, staring especially at the stump of a finger on my left hand.

"They're working man's hands, not a scholar's hands." Erhard seemed to talk to himself. He pushed my sleeves back and exposed the bruising on my wrists. "How'd this happen?" he asked. I shook my head. I supposed they had tied me for the whippings, but didn't remember.

"And the whippings?" Erhard continued to question me.

"My back feels like it's on fire, but I don't remember the whippings. I just feel like I've been beaten and my head's been used for an anvil."

"What do you remember?"

A thousand memories seemed just out of reach. Nothing was clear before the whipping. I shrugged.

"But you read with skill," Erhard's voice held wonder, as at some rare accomplishment.

"Doesn't everybody?" I questioned.

Bertrm snorted, but Erhard responded. "In the opinion of your owner, Surra, reading be for the feeble and the idle. He reads enough to cipher a bill of sale for buying a thræl, but sees no value in pursuing it no further. I have made myself somewhat useful as a scrivener, but it be a value he holds in contempt. Could I also play the harp and sing like the bards of old, perchance I would be of some worth in his eyes." He fumbled with something in the corner. "The strength of your arm and your skill with a sword—the way you sit a horse and your courage in battle—those now, are things he values." He handed me a sheathed sword.

My hands instantly felt at home as I drew it from the scabbard. I knew in an instant too, that no armourer had made it. "The balance is poor," I said. I ran my finger across the rough edge. "It would not stand against a good sword." Still, it felt good in my hand. I swung it slowly. The small room did not have space to make it sing through the air, if such poor workmanship could sing. Muscles protested, but

I somehow knew how to complete the motion.

I wasn't listening much, enjoying the feel of the sword in my hand. But I heard Erhard respond to some question from Bertrm. "I don't know, Bertrm. It fits and it don't fit."

"So what do we do?" Bertrm asked.

"We wait, and we watch," Erhard responded. "I wish we could get the rest of the scroll, but if I ask after it, it'll get tongues wagging."

"How came you to have that one?" Bertrm asked.

"It has been in my care above forty years." Erhard fixed me with his gaze and I stopped my slow swinging of the sword. "You of no memory. A careless tongue will cost your life as well as ours."

I held the blade and stared at him. I didn't mean disrespect. He lowered his gaze after a moment.

"It was entrusted to me by my grandfather after my father died in the library fire. I'm the fourth of my line to hold it." Erhard seemed to battle with some intense emotion. "A copy was made of the full prophecy. That piece was torn from the original scroll. It be old beyond belief. The copy of the full scroll was in my father's hand when the wall fell on him. The scroll was rescued by one of the Druids."

He reached out and grabbed the sword from me, gripping it by the blade. A trickle of blood flowed over the heel of his hand, down his wrist and forearm. "My father was jist a thræl as his father before him and his son after him. He was nothing to the Druids. The same hand that took the scroll could have pulled him from the fire. It did not." He spat on the floor. "I was flogged—and sold—after I spoke a bit too freely about the high calling of holy men."

He smeared blood the length of the blade. "Mayhap this blade still thirsts for blood." He found the rag he had wiped the table with and crushed it in his bleeding hand, then continued. "I learned to read, no small task for a thræl, for I wished to know what my father died to save. But the script has been beyond my ken all these years." His voice became quieter. "I thought the runes flædg-stafir, deliberately misleading. In time I made myself valuable as a scrivener and began to get other scrolls." His focus drifted away from us.

"Forty years I have waited for him of the nine fingers. This one comes with no memory, but with knowledge of languages and hands that wield a weapon like a warrior born. I dare not assume it be him. I dare not assume it be not."

He clamped his jaws shut as if he would not speak again, then jerked the bolt free and flung back the door.

"I never thought the very air of his coming would be the death of me." He spun on his heel. "Take him to the horse trough. Scald his clothes. Douse him with turpentine. It might stop the rot that grows in wounds. If he be man enough to take that without screaming, maybe he really is our warrior." He turned back inside and threw a block of peat into the fireplace, dismissing us.

An ice-water bath when the skin has been flayed off your back and your hair is matted with blood isn't something to dwell on. I couldn't see the whip cuts, and only part of the brand on my left shoulder, a big "T" Bertrm told me meant "Thief." There was a reason it felt like someone had stuck a piece of red-hot iron on me. They had.

After the turpentine, burned alive should come easy. The clothes Bertrm gave me had a smoky smell, like they had dried too close to a fire. I'd forgotten what clean felt—or smelled like. I don't know who got the job of scalding my clothes. Probably some common thræl.

That's what you are, I reminded myself. The way my whole body ached and burned, it shouldn't have taken any reminders.

At board that night, Dierdre served. Her swollen belly showed her with child. I don't know how I'd missed that before. A hopeless look seemed to cloud her eyes, but there was something more also, a strength, a defiance she didn't quite manage to hide. Still half sick from the turpentine treatment, I could eat little, but she drew my attention. I didn't have many memories, but I hadn't forgotten her hands on my scalp. If a maid's hands are supposed to feel like an eagle's talons tearing a rabbit apart, I don't know why men are so drawn to them.

The Master ate from pewter or silver while trenchers, spoons and cups of a dark stained wood held food and drink for the rest of us.

Fat clung to the pig flesh set before me. The ale in my cup tasted bitter, the biscuit dry and hard. My place was way below the salt-cellar. I couldn't remember why that mattered.

Nine people sat at board. They included the Master, four men and three lads near my age. Dierdre and an older woman who helped serve rarely spoke and did not sit or eat in our presence. No children appeared and none had I heard.

I spent that night on a bit of straw in the big house. Three lads sprawled under smoke-stained oak beams in a small square room with a stone fireplace built in the centre. The tallest one got up when I tried to find a spot. "Stupid horse killer," he sneered. He spit where I prepared to lay, then moved to the other side of the fire, deliberately kicking one of the boys in his way.

Some things can't be let go. He stood taller than me, but had not yet filled out across the chest and shoulders. In the dim light I could not gauge his strength, or if he carried any weapon. Grabbing him under the chin, I shoved him against the corner where stone met oak planks. He started to kick and punch, but I kept squeezing harder, lifting till his feet barely touched the floor. His face got red and his punches got weak awfully fast. He wasn't nearly so tough as I'd expected. I let up a bit, then twisted one arm behind him and got a fistful of hair. I shoved his face into his own spit.

"Okay, Theodoric. That'll do." A hushed urgency sounded in Bertrm's voice. I hadn't known he was still there.

I looked at Bertrm. "Guess you're right," I said and let him go.

The guy threw himself back out of the straw, stumbled and smacked his head on the fireplace stones. Cursing, he kicked one of the lads in the face. The battle-blood still hot in me, I grabbed him by his hair and belt and mashed his face into the corner. "Kick someone else in the face and maybe they'll find a different name for me than Horse Killer," I hurled the words at him.

"Theodoric, keep your voice down," Bertrm cautioned me.

"Sheffield!" he blasted the boy. Then he dropped volume to a strangely subdued voice. "You called that up of your own self. Keep it up and there'll be a flogging tomorrow and a week in lockup—probably the dark hole, and well deserved as I've seen."

An hour later I heard footsteps across the floor above my head. I lay on my right side, avoiding the brand. The stones seemed to probe upward through the straw, reaching hard fingers to claw at my raw back. My mind searched desperately for some hint of my past, an identity, some reason to claim the name everyone called me by.

I woke stiff and sore, but my back didn't burn so badly. The headache, dulled now, still plagued me. Blood had oozed from my scalp wound and I picked the straw out of it. I watched as the others tried to come to life. No sign of a beard showed on the face of the spitter from the night before, so I pegged him at about fourteen. I felt much older than that.

We broke fast with scratchy barley porridge. Little talk broke the dull clunk of spoons on wooden bowls, but the sound of laughter from the kitchens startled me. I realized I had heard none since coming from the dark hole. Dierdre brought food in and took bowls away. I guessed her age at 14 or 15. She wore her hair down like an unmarried lass. A bairn close to its time did nothing for her appearance, but eyes full of laughter, even with her gaze down, transformed her somehow.

Another woman, with hair done up like a matron, helped serve. A pinched faced woman with a sour expression sat at board. A man I had not seen before also shared the meal.

I didn't see or hear any signal, but everyone pushed back from the board and headed out the door. Not knowing where to go, I waited. "You looking for another beating?" Bertrm's voice reached me from the door.

"Nobody told me what to do," I replied.

"They told you yesterday. Master don't believe in telling people something twice."

I went with Bertrm and found I could move a bit more freely today. He shoved a fork into my hands and I made a clumsy attempt at cleaning stalls. My sark pulled and burned where whip cuts still oozed.

A dung pile steamed along the east fortress wall. I stood and worked the kinks out of my back and shoulders. The old stone loomed dark and glowering. The newer buildings showed the mark of centuries, backed against ancient stone walls. The ruins of a tower thrust through a section of the roof at the east end of the house. Big and foreboding, the house, built into the remnants of fortress walls, reached high sullen peaks and smoking chimneys against a grey sky. Narrow windows showed a feeble light, yellowed by the scraped animal skins covering them. Steeply roofed with slate, not thatch, it seemed grown from the rocks it stood upon, and as hard and cold. No vines softened the harsh lines, although moss struggled to cling to the face of some of the stones.

A walled courtyard cowered in the gloom of the house. Stained, hard packed snow showed the passage of men and horses. Smoke drifted from the chimney of Erhard's cottage against the east fortress wall, and also from another cottage and a guard house against the west wall. Thatch covered the cottage roofs, old and grey, but still holding some memory of a warmer, softer gold.

A pair of whipping posts thrust out of the snow between the guard house and the west cottage. A dog sniffed at the stained snow, then lifted its leg against the post. Yellow droplets blended with the pink stain at their base—not yet covered by fresh snow. At least one whipping had followed mine, but the blood drove a sickness into my gut.

Behind the whipping posts, almost against the fortress wall itself, archery targets stood on low posts, the beaten snow showing them well used.

The corner of a latrine showed beyond the second stable. Animal pens with low stone fences completed the courtyard, butting against Erhard's cottage. The pens stood empty, the gates open. A drift of fog seeped from the open stable door. The wheel track of a barrow led to the dung heap I stood beside.

I sighed and forced myself to push the barrow back through the stable door. I finally asked the question churning in my mind. "You said I killed the horse. How'd I do that, put an arrow in it or something?"

"You can't water a horse when it's hot, else you'll founder it." Bertrm spat the words like I should have known it from birth. "You couldn't have picked a worse way to introduce yourself to your new owner."

I ignored what he said about an owner. That didn't bear thinking about just now. "What's founder?" I asked.

"You really don't know nothing do you?" he said with a sigh. "The joints all stiffen up. Sometimes they gits better, but mostly they don't." He looked at me for a long time. "That was a good horse—best on the place. Master Gerhardt will remember you for a long time."

I had started out badly with Bertrm. Destroying a horse did not merit quick forgiveness. A hard taskmaster, he took my ignorance of horses as a personal affront. I learned the parts of a saddle and bridle and how a horse would puff its belly when you cinched up the saddle. I learned the parts of a horse too, from fetlocks to mane. Bertrm knew horses well. I worked hard and learned fast. He did not speak his growing respect, but it began to show in his actions.

Spittin' Sheffield steered a wide path around me. That name stuck like a burr the first time somebody used it. He may have hurried me to a leadership role among the lads by trying to put me in my place that first night. He found he'd grabbed a snake, not a stick. And

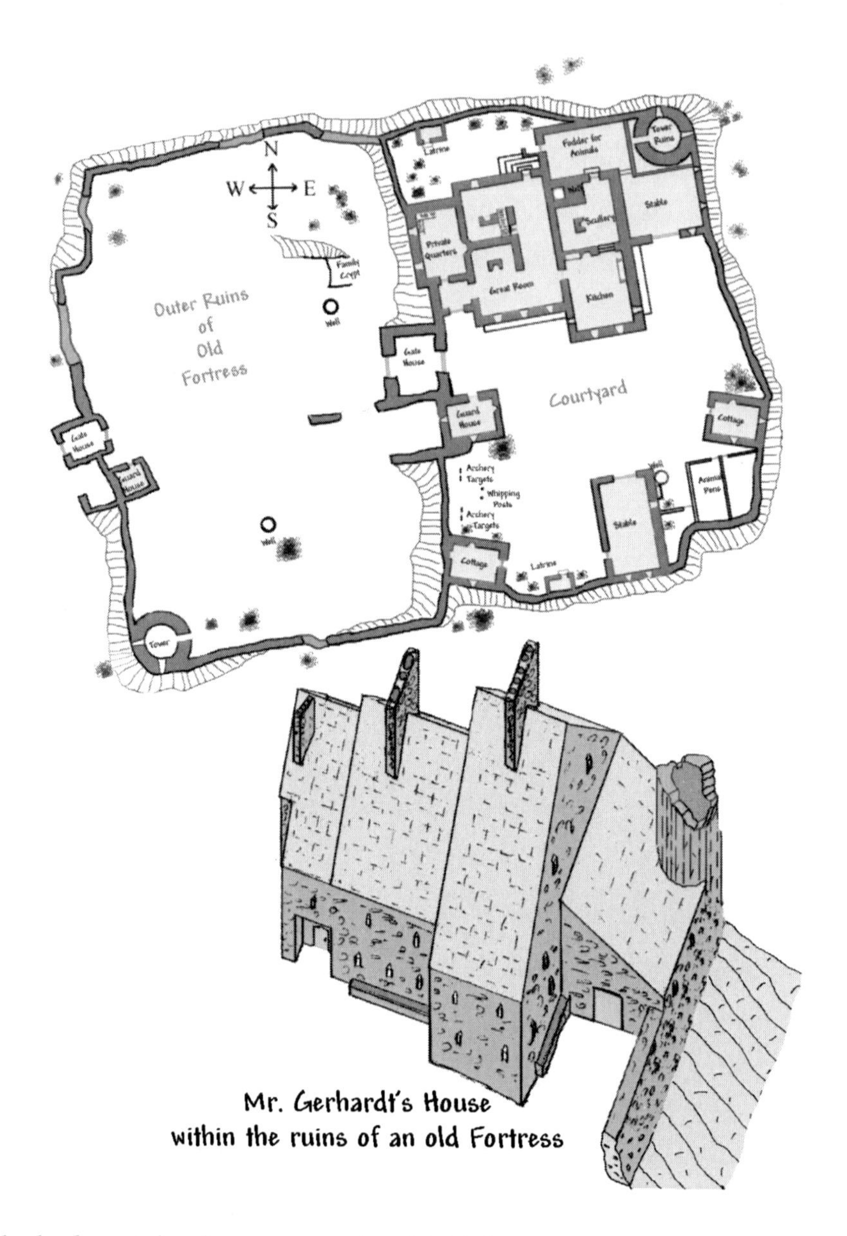

Mr. Gerhardt's House
within the ruins of an old Fortress

he had got it by the wrong end and it bit him.

Mr. Gerhardt still looked at me like something he might scrape off his boots.

Taking food and water down to the lockup and emptying the

night buckets became one of my tasks. You remember fast that you're a slave, a thræl, while you carry someone else's mess to the latrine. Each cell had a shallow wooden bowl for bodily needs, a second one for food. They could just slide under the bottom bars of the doorways. A slide would lift on the doors of the dark holes, but again the bowls would slip through. Dumped in a larger bucket, the stink clung to the stained wood.

I had no clear memories of my time in the lockup. The darkrooms proved a hated punishment for crimes that didn't quite warrant a flogging and the long sickness that would follow. They also added to the punishment for major crimes. No blanket or straw eased the discomfort of cold stone, and the low ceiling did not give height enough to stand. They told me I'd spent five days. Lack of memory has *some* benefits.

I also got the job of drawing water for the stable and the house. The stable well with its old wheel was dug outside the foundation wall. A stone trough took the water through the wall and into a cistern inside. The ice that formed outside during the winter never got too thick because horses, cows and pigs go through a lot of water every day. Fresh water melted any ice, morning and evening.

Drawing water for the house took me to the attic, a strange place to find a well. Yet careful planning showed. Tipping the bucket into a shallow trough of oak planks would feed a reservoir. From there it flowed through multiple reservoirs, each against one of the chimneys from the kitchens below, warming the water. Feeding through five tanks, the final one felt warm to the touch. About waist deep and lined with lead, they also provided a great reserve for times of fire.

Weighted plugs attached to ropes fed warm or cold water to the kitchens or to laundry tubs on the second floor. Spouts overhung troughs set into the ground at the front and back of the house. You could water a horse or fight a fire.

A narrow path between heaps of fodder and straw reached the pigeon cote above the pigs. The small birds fascinated me. However, they fell under Spittin' Sheffield's care. I questioned Bertrm and Erhard, but they could tell me little. I often slipped into the cote area when I had a spare moment and knew Spittin' Sheffield worked elsewhere. I wasn't about to tell him, but his skill with the birds showed.

I often wondered about the ring I had read of that first day. With muddled memories and nobody telling you anything, your mind does its best to fill the blanks. The trouble though, it was all blank. It's like trying to paint the whole sky blue with two hairs from a horse's tail. It's a slow process.

By the end of two weeks I had mostly healed. My scalp and my back itched. The headaches came often still, but not so severe. It's strange how a pitchfork uses the same muscles as swinging a sword, but doesn't appeal the same at all.

I took to the saddle quickly. It took some getting used to handling the reins so the horse knew what I had in mind. A saucy filly by the name of Lorellefue, Little Fool, had dumped most of the lads a time or two. Less than half broke, she had an attitude. I took my time. I didn't suppose two beginners would be great teachers for each other. Most of the men show little interest because she was a small-framed animal. Bertrm figured so far as a thræl can have anything to call his own, she'd be mine if I could make her mind. He said Master would find the name fitting as well.

That thræl word still stuck in my craw, but there seemed no help for it.

Chapter Three

Bloodlines and Boundaries

The lads' sleeping area was similar to the men's although more often disturbed by someone heading out to the latrine. A threshold held straw from spilling into the great room. A large stone hearth consumed peat blocks. Mr. Gerhardt threatened whippings if hot coals ever reached the straw.

Bertrm and I spent many evenings with Erhard. He seemed bound to make up for my lack of memory by making me read every scroll he had—except one. I'd look where that jar had stood, but he had removed it—little room though he had to hide anything. I noticed Bertrm picking up reading too.

I grilled them for clues about my past. "It's only the bloodlines of horses Master cares about," Bertrm finally informed me. "All I know is you was beaten bloody on the auction block. You wasn't bringing a price worth spitting at, so he took a chance on you. When you killed Paton, he had you whipped again, and thrown in the dark hole."

"So I wasn't even a fit thræl to buy," I stopped myself before spitting on the floor.

"Thunder 'n damnation, Surra! You was ready for a hole in the ground. Didn't know your own name. And Bertrm's telling it straight too. Master don't care about your bloodline. You're jist one more piece of horseflesh. Though the stunt you pulled on his horse, he was gonna feed you to the kelpies."

I didn't need reminders of my title. What if I was the thief that deserved the whippings I had gotten? Or what if I was kin to someone like Spittin' Sheffield? It's strange though, having no past. Every time I would get my hands on a sword, it seemed some memory drew painfully close. But it only tormented.

Five weeks I had spent in the house before I knew Mr. Gerhardt had a daughter, though I had sometimes heard sounds I could not account for. Only by chance did I see her then, while climbing the stair to draw water.

The bairn, perhaps eight years old, showed a pale complexion. Startlingly pretty, she had been spared her father's jutting head. Her hair, brushed till it gleamed and falling across her shoulders in bronze waves, gave a softness to her face. Her eyes danced with a blend of fear and mischief when she saw me. Kept so secluded, her caretaker had doubtless taught her to fear men. Still lacking a beard, I may have been young enough to not disturb her.

Her nurse tried to usher her back into her private rooms, chastising me the while. The child teased and tormented. She ran into a room I had never seen opened, then closed the door. The nurse stood outside and wrung her hands. She seemed torn between ridding herself of me and rescuing her charge from this strange room. She feared something. I went about my duties, but could hear her voice pleading with the child, though I could not make out the words.

She was the pinched-face woman who broke fast with us in the morning. She wore her hair tied back severely, pulling her already narrow face even tighter. It drew her eyebrows up in an astonished expression, as if she had bitten into a piece of rotten fruit. She wore a drab garment that hid her form. I knew she sometimes helped in the kitchen, but had not known what other duties she had.

Later I questioned Bertrm, and then Erhard. They knew little, except that the bairn's mother had died in childbirth. Her father would not see the child, blaming her, apparently, for his wife's death. Yet he had not allowed her the common practice of boarding in some other noble's house. Named Ralina, the Doe, she was more a prisoner than anyone else in the household. So far as they knew she had never stepped outside the doors of the house. Her nurse, of necessity her jailer, had become bitter with a sharp, caustic tongue, for the confinement had become hers as well.

The room the child had gone into held a shrine. "I've heard tales," Erhard admitted. "A door to Woden's Hall." He mused a moment. "Tis folly for the lass to play there."

"This lad is a puzzle, Surra," Erhard told Mr. Gerhardt as I laboured on a boring document. He's no braw bard with Latin, but reads it well enough. He's got a working man's hands, but a scholar's mind."

"I'm not much caring about puzzles, Erhard. And Latin is the language of people with nothing better to do than fill minds with fool's tales," Mr. Gerhardt cut in, idly tapping his leg with the horse-whip. "Is this thræl capable of anything 'sides killing horses?"

"Well, Surra, Bertrm tells me nobody kenned less about horses than this laddie when he started, but he already sits the saddle like he was borned to it. He's quicker with numbers than I ever was too, and reads the old spellings from generations gone. That's why I have him at those old land-title documents. Even when my eyes was younger I couldn't cipher all. . ."

"What are you at there, Thræl?" Mr. Gerhardt interrupted Erhard as he hurled his question at me.

I stretched the time a little before answering him. "It's in the old spelling, Sir, and I'm trying to determine if this smudge says the boundary borders the *Grægstan Bourne* from the seventeenth pace north or the seventieth pace north to the old oak tree. With the ink smudged they look much alike." I pointed to the scroll, and the scrap of parchment on which I had begun to write a copy, *'seofontientha pas Nor* or *seofontigotha pas Nor.'*

"And what does it matter?" he challenged me.

"It is the task I was given, Sir. It is the difference of 53 paces in the placement of a boundary. That may have significance to. . ."

"The *Grægstan Burn,* you say." Mr. Gerhardt interrupted. "Is that Greystone Burn?

"Aye, Sir. Tis just the old spelling."

"I wonder . . ." Then his voice fell silent for a long moment. Turning to Erhard, ignoring me now, he commanded, "Have that document copied in full, in the old spelling, then translated into readable language. Inform Bertrm that someone else will muck the stalls tonight. Keep this horse killer at the task till it be done." Mr. Gerhardt's boots thumped on the floor. At the door he turned back to Erhard. "The scroll is to be seen by none."

His hand lifted the latch. Then he turned back. His eyes glared at me. "A word of the contents of this scroll will cost you more than you wish to pay."

"Yes, Sir." I answered quietly. "The scroll holds no significance to me and I speak little to anyone but Erhard and Bertrm." I raised my gaze to meet his. "I ween you speak of a whipping, or worse."

"Aye. And this one you will remember, if you survive it."

"I ken, Sir, but you make one mistake." I tried to keep my voice quiet, but could not hide my anger.

"You challenge me?" His voice dropped dangerously.

"I have no memory of how or why I became a thræl, Sir." I stopped myself before telling how it galled, like a burr under a saddle. I forced myself to speak slowly "I have no memory of the brand or the whippings. I had no reason, beyond doing the task I was given, to take interest in this document. You have given me reason for interest, Sir." I emphasized the last 'Sir' a bit more than necessary.

The latch closed and Mr. Gerhardt walked toward me, his horse whip in his hand, the redness deepening on his face. I heard the hiss of Erhard's strained breathing, the rustle of his clothes as he backed against the wall.

Mr. Gerhardt's boots made almost no sound. I met his angry stare. "You're an insolent whelp, aren't you?" The whip in his hand drew back.

It took all my stubbornness to sit there as his whip arm came forward. The whip struck the writing table, cutting the parchment, spilling the ink jar. The tip caught my right arm, cutting, stinging like fire. Still, I stared at him.

After several seconds he spat on the floor then spoke coldly. "Clean that mess—before it ruins the original. See that your added interest makes your ciphering accurate and complete." As he flung the door back he added, "Do not provoke me again."

He stood in the open doorway, letting a blast of cold air into the cottage. "The scrolls in the shrine room," he paused, then continued with a sneer sounding in his voice. "They've been collecting dust since before my father was killed. They'll have more to say, though most of it will be useless—the rantings of an old bard." He stared at me. "I'll expect you to 'cipher them too, 'stead of killing horses." He slammed the door behind him.

I continued to stare at the door. I heard the soft pat of ink drops striking the floor, the panting breath of Erhard and the swish of a rag wiping up the mess.

A trickle of blood dribbled from my arm and mingled darkly with the ink puddle on the tabletop. A deep sigh rose and escaped. I lifted my arm as Erhard pulled the old scroll away and blotted the ink that had soaked into one edge of it.

"*Man be born to trouble as sparks rise to the sky,*" Erhard quoted the proverb in a soft voice. "And you seem attracted to it like a moth to a flame." He finished wiping up the spilled ink while I sat in silence. "How you got outta that one without a flogging I'll never know."

"Is it ruined?" I asked, reaching for the scroll. "It would serve him well if it was."

"It might serve him well, but you would take the whipping for it. He called you *insolent whelp*. I would say he is not far wrong."

Erhard stared at me for a long moment, started several times to speak, but each time fell silent again. Finally he told me to inform Bertrm that I would be unavailable in the stable that evening, and perhaps for several days. "Wash yourself. So soon as the bleeding be stopped, come back and get at this scroll. Guess you'll get to see what's in that shrine room soon enough."

I pushed back from the table and rose to my feet, surprised at how unsteady I felt. The mid-afternoon sun gleamed coldly in the west. A flew clouds dotted a soft-blue sky, but a raw wind chilled the sweat on my body. Bertrm did not question me, however bare arms and angry words on a winter day tell their own story, even in the shadows of a stable.

I scrubbed myself at the reservoir, flecks of ice floating on the water. Chilled, I returned to Erhard's door.

A dark stain spread across the old oak table. The scroll itself showed no damage anywhere it mattered. Letter by letter I copied the text, the quill slashing the parchment. I forced myself to eat the evening meal, then returned to my work.

Late in the evening I sank into the straw in the big house. My eyes burned and my head ached from hours of staring at the wretched manuscript. The cut on my arm stung. Someone else had cared for the wretches in lockup, at least I hoped someone had.

I stretched myself in the straw, trying to shut out the joking and bickering of the boys. I couldn't shut out the prisoners. Finally, rather disgusted with myself, I brushed the straw off, pulled my boots back on and took the stairs to the cellar.

Æthëlrd stood guard, one of those self-important men with too much love for the beer jug. Even through the fog of my earliest memories, his face and character had burned into my mind. He was built much like Mr. Gerhardt. I suspected they shared blood some generations back. His head too thrust forward from his shoulders. He wore his hair long, and took pride in his carefully trimmed beard. Younger than Mr. Gerhardt, his hair showed no grey, though his beard did. His face belied his character, for he had a gentle face with smile lines around the eyes. I had only seen him smile when inflicting pain. His voice always reminded me of a bull.

"Have these men been fed tonight?" I asked. He just stared at me.

"Have these men been fed tonight?" I asked again, making my voice hard as a lad my age can. Still no answer.

Moving to the barred doorway I spoke to the man in the nearest cell. "Hamil, has anyone brought you food or wat. . . .?"

A hand grabbed my shoulder and spun me around. The naked blade of a long knife gleamed in the torch's glow. "Fool horse killer!" A mouth with foul breath spat the deep-toned words at me. "I'll take the rest of your fingers off, one by one."

"Nobody's brought us nothing," the words reached me from behind the bars.

"Nobody's gonna bring you nothing, 'cept the lash, if you don't shut your gob," Æthëlrd hurled the words back.

His change of focus gave me my chance. I grabbed his knife arm with both hands, one at the wrist and the other below the elbow. My knee came up as I brought that arm down hard and fast. His mouth hung open when the crack of breaking bones echoed. I spun and drove the heel of my boot into his knee. I completed my spin and planted my fist in the soft of his gut. Before he had drawn a single breath I drove my boot into his groin as he sprawled on the floor. It took all of five seconds to disarm and disable him, without a weapon in my hands.

The thump of unbooted feet sounded on the stairs.

"Drawing steel on an unarmed man is a coward's act." I held back nothing of the scorn I felt for the groaning man at my feet. "Drawing steel on a beardless youth and being overcome by him earns you a place among the fools of history."

Æthëlrd's breath came in sobbing gasps. His left arm strained for the knife. The heel of my boot came down on reaching fingers, mashing them into the stone floor. "You were going to take fingers off, and it *is* your knife. I hope you are satisfied with your work this night."

I bent down and grabbed him by the back of the coat, flipping him over. He groaned and cursed me. I grabbed the keys that hung from his neck, lifting him from the floor till the rawhide thong broke. He fell back, his skull cracking against the flagstones.

I glanced up at the thræls who gaped at the two of us, but said nothing as I turned and unlocked the barred door to the lockup.

"Is anyone in the dark hole tonight?" I asked the other prisoners.

They stared at me like I was some kind of avenging fiend before one of them said no. I dragged Æthëlrd in, opened the heavy oak door at the end of the short passage, and the second door into the smaller of the dark rooms. Heaving the big man inside, I slammed the door, turned the lock, and then closed and locked the outer door as well, shutting out his rumbling curses.

"There's nothing for you here," I told the thræls who stared at me when I came back out. "There's liable to be whippings, so you would be wise to be found elsewhere." I felt my shoulders sag as that reality sunk in. The exhaustion that had plagued me returned in greater measure, the headache coming with it.

My strength seemed gone as I brought the water bucket into the lockup. “Hold your cups through the bars,” I told the prisoners, then filled each cup from a dipper. My hands shook, spilling water. I closed and locked the outer door, then sagged against it for a long moment.

“Thank ye, Laddie.” The mocking words came from one of the prisoners.

Laddie! Thanking me and calling me an infant in the same breath. I raised my gaze. “I can’t get you food at this hour.” I didn’t much care after the insult. I turned and stumbled away, avoiding the blood spots blackening on the flagstones.

I lay long in the straw before sleep came. The pounding in my head slowly subsided, the echo of Æthëlrd’s arm breaking seeming to replay ever louder.

I had completed my normal duties in the stable and drawn water for the house before we broke fast. I could hardly force myself to eat my own meal. The headache lingered, dull but inescapable. Approaching Mr. Gerhardt I could almost hear the whistle of the whip.

“Permission to speak, Sir.” I requested quietly.

“What is it, Thræl?”

“It is the prisoners, Sir. There were problems last night. I worked late on the parchment and they were not fed. Æthëlrd threatened me with a knife when I checked them.”

“And you come whining to me over that?”

“No, Sir.” I set the keys on the table before him. “He is in the dark lockup and will have difficulty holding a knife for some time. I believed it my duty to inform you and not put others at risk of punishment, since it was I who put him there.”

"You overstep yourself, Thræl." Mr. Gerhardt spoke the words harshly, but the threat of a chuckle escaped from behind his beard. "I would have given much to see that fight," he mumbled, half to himself. "He was deep in his cups then. Bring him to me."

"I doubt he can walk, Sir, and he is a big man to carry."

"You doubt he can walk," Mr. Gerhardt mused, "and he will have difficulty holding a knife. What did you to him?"

"I did what a man does when threatened with a weapon."

"So you are a warrior now as well as a scholar," Mr. Gerhardt snorted. "Where got you this training, Thræl?"

"I wish I knew, Sir. The lack of memory is at times painful as the whip. Other times I fear what I might find."

"Erskine, Kenyon, bring swords," Mr. Gerhardt shouted. "Clear the great room. Test this thræl's skill with arms. Slay him not." To me he said, "What weapons will you choose?"

While men pushed benches and tables against the wall, I gazed around the great room. The scraping sound seemed to drive the headache deeper. Swords and shields, pikes, daggers, heavy battle-axes, bows, longbows, slings and staves hung on the walls. I knew a locked armoury in the cellar housed newer and better weapons. I chose a short sword. With a nearly perfect balance, it fit my hand well. The shield that matched it had a spike thrusting out of its face so I left it on the wall, choosing a simpler design that would not cause serious injury.

"You demean us, Sir," Kenyon protested.

"Bring Æthëlrd up from the dark lockup. Put him in irons, but look well to his injuries before you too loudly protest." Mr. Gerhardt rebuked Kenyon. "This thræl, unarmed, took the knife from his hand

and put him behind bars. I would know what his skills are."

Moments later they brought Æthëlrd in, scowling and cursing. Shackles on his ankles attached to a ring in the wall. An iron clasp around his neck held him fast. His right arm had swollen grotesquely. The men had carried him up, for he favoured his left leg and could not walk. The fingers of his left hand showed bloody scabs. One twisted at the wrong angle.

Mr. Gerhardt walked up to him and grabbed his chin in his hands. "Drunk last night?" he demanded. "You draw knife on an unarmed thræl—not yet a man—and he leaves you useless as a foundered horse. Bah! You were not much more useful before. If you weren't already whipped as a dead dog I would have you on the post for a flogging." He turned away. "Send for the leech. The bone must be set or this man will be good for nothing."

Chapter Four

A Very Bonnie Lady

"A purse, Erskine, if you defeat this thræl, but injure him not. Look well to your own defense." Mr. Gerhardt dumped a small bag of gold coins out on the table.

Nearly the whole household had gathered. I glanced up to see Dierdre staring fearfully at me. Big with a child no father would claim as his own, her look showed more pity than hope. A kind of sickness raged in me. Yet the sword somehow steadied me. I ran my left thumb along the edge. Sharp and deadly, it was meant for killing. "Is there a blunted weapon used for training, Sir?" I asked.

Erskine stood with a cold sneer, his fingers playing with the hilt of a sword. I knew him only as a man-at-arms completely loyal to Mr. Gerhardt. His broken voice grated on my nerves, but he moved with a fluid grace that had earned my respect even without a sword in his hand.

"You think you're going to git close enough to draw blood?" He mocked, then charged, a long-sword in his hand. It outreached my weapon by two full handbreadths, but overconfidence in the man who carried it rendered that advantage small. I let his rush take the sword past me, twisting my body to the side, then brought the flat of my sword up against his forearm. It could as easily have buried itself in his chest. Even before his weapon had clattered to the floor, my boot drove into the back of his leg behind the knee. Another half turn, and the point of my sword pressed into his neck. A long moment of tense silence followed.

I stepped back, bent and picked up his sword, then stabbed it into the floor beside him. I offered him a hand and helped him to his feet. "Youth does not always mean ignorance and weakness. Don't make such a mistake on the battlefield, else it be your last. Now defend yourself. If the offer of a purse is still good, earn it."

"Aye, Erskine. I took you for a man," Æthëlrd's deep voice rumbled. "Now spill this pup's blood."

Erskine shifted the sword to his left hand, bent down and pulled a knife from his boot. I had raised my shield, but he spun and hurled the blade at Æthëlrd, striking the stone a foot beside his head. "You got nothing to say about this, Æthëlrd. You had your say yesternight and look where it got you."

He turned to me then. Hard-edged anger replaced his overconfidence. I had shamed him and he fought to redeem himself. A skillful swordsman with powerful arms, the long reach of his sword put me at serious disadvantage. I was quicker on my feet however, and handled the sword with ease. Twice the flat of my blade caught his ankle with force that would have severed a foot had I used the edge. A clumsy lunge on his part and my sword point found his chest. It took all my skill to stop the thrust before it killed him.

He stood gasping. His left hand felt the wound in his chest, then came away bloody. I backed away and waited.

A tremor shook his body as he lifted his sword again. His eyes betrayed a mixture of fear, resignation and determination as he stepped toward me.

"NO!" I shouted, louder than necessary. I drove my sword into the floor. "You have fought with courage and skill. A knight would be proud to cross swords with you. If ever I face a real foe in battle, I would count it an honour to fight at your side."

He nodded slightly, wiped his sword on his pant leg, then stumbled back to the table. His glance took in the gold coins beside Mr. Gerhardt. "Pity. My wife wouldda been glad for it." He slumped on the bench and glanced at the blood oozing from his chest wound.

Shallow cuts on my right arm bled slightly. I continued to stand in the middle of the floor, breathing heavily. The throbbing in my skull had seemed to recede during the combat, but came back now with vengeance.

Mr. Gerhardt's glance took in the other armed man, who stood to his feet.

"A blunted sword if I may, Sir," I requested. "I have no desire to kill over a bag of gold."

A grunted order from Mr. Gerhardt sent one of the thræls after a couple of training weapons. I stood, fighting the urge to close my eyes and clutch my skull between my hands.

The second fight stirred small interest. I disarmed the man quickly and ruthlessly, though without drawing blood. He fought with resignation more than skill.

A collective sigh seemed to escape into the room. The exertion, of a few moments only, had left me panting. I caught Dierdre's glance. Her eyes seemed overly bright and her breast rose and fell in a quick catch of breath, then she turned away.

"Theodoric! Thræl." Mr. Gerhardt's voice stopped me as I turned to walk away. "You have won the purse. Does it mean so little to you?"

My mind, razor sharp through the conflict moments ago, seemed slow and sluggish, my judgment clouded by the headache. "It was offered to the men who would defeat me, Sir, not to me." I could hear a slur in my slowly spoken words. "I have no claim on it. Gold is of little value to a thræl, unless. . ." I paused as the reality penetrated, "unless with it he could buy his freedom." My voice dropped to little more than a whisper. All else became silent as other servants and thræls waited the master's response.

"I would earn my freedom, Sir." I heard my voice breaking, that maddening, boy-man break that comes at the most inopportune times. "But I would earn it openly, not by trickery." Again the headache almost overcame my ability to think through my words. "There are fathers with wives and sons. One has today bled to prove my skills. There is also a wench with child of a man who will not fill the role of a man. Divide the gold among them if you will, Sir." I gazed around the room, a great weariness weighing on me.

"Eleven pieces of gold there be here," Mr. Gerhardt's voice broke the lengthening silence. "Two men with wives and families, plus the wench. Three coins to each leaves two extra. Does it meet your approval, Thræl, if one of those be given to Erskine and one to the wench?"

"If my approval is sought, Sir," I raised my gaze and squared my shoulders, "it meets it well."

"So be it." Mr. Gerhardt's gaze swept the room. "You so named, receive the winnings this thræl so quickly surrenders." He snorted. "He is a young fool, for it would indeed have purchased his freedom." Mr. Gerhardt sniffed as Kenyon approached. "Spend it not foolishly, Kenyon, for hardly have you earned a share by your handling of the sword today."

He stared at Dierdre, his gaze sweeping her pregnant form. "Wish you to marry, Wench?" Mr. Gerhardt asked the girl who came last to receive the four coins that fell to her share.

"None will have me, Sir, since one took me. For other things mayhap, but not to wed." Her gaze met mine for a moment, then she clutched the coins in her apron and stared at the floor, her face scarlet.

"No, I suppose not." Mr. Gerhardt stared at her for a moment, then dismissed her with a nod before glancing around the room.

"Where is that leech?"

"He is tending a horse galled by the saddle, else he'd be here, Sir."

"Aye," Mr. Gerhardt grunted. "He is overly fond of blood and would never miss a fight by choice. Get him here as soon as can be."

"Beer for Æthëlrd for the setting of his arm, Sir?"

"No!" Mr. Gerhardt spat the word. "Let the beer he drank last night be sufficient. He deserves no better." Again his gaze swept the room. "Is there no one with tasks to do?" his voice thundered. "Be gone, or there will be floggings." The room emptied with a quick stomping of boots.

I closed the door behind me, though it failed to shut out the sound of voices. An excited buzz sounded as people headed to different tasks. I walked slowly from the house, hating myself for missing the opportunity, yet telling myself, unconvincingly, that freedom earned falsely was simply another kind of slavery. The cold air eased the throbbing in my head.

I got the parchments, ink and quills out while Erhard watched me silently. As I sat to begin my work he finally broke the silence.

"So—Æthëlrd be damning you to Hades while they set the bone without a drop of beer to dull the pain. And Master be asking himself who this thræl be he has purchased, who speaks and acts like a lord born, has trained under the masters, both in languages and with arms, yet can give no account of himself. . ."

I struggled to keep my attention on the scroll. Finally I pushed back from the small table. "I'll take a look in the shrine room." The headache had eased to a dull, distant annoyance.

"Aye, there'll be scrolls there, if rats haven't destroyed them," Erhard informed me after a moment of silence. "That door be rarely opened." His voice betrayed hesitation, some story he was reluctant to share.

"And . . .?" I could not resist the query.

"Master used to give some regard to the gods, though the priests always went away angered. A sham they called him." He paused a moment, then continued. "Since his wife died he has had no use for the gods, though it may be that he fears them more."

"And this room?" I pursued the topic. "It has been made to honour the gods?" I mused. "The lassie plays there sometimes. She seems less afraid of the gods than of me, though her nurse cowers outside the door."

"A bairn's innocence may be beyond the god's reach." Erhard spoke slowly. "Some gods crave innocent blood. Woden at least be a warrior god and looks with favour on no one till they be proved on the battlefield."

"What else can you tell me of the gods I might find there?" I questioned further. "How might I petition them to give me my past?"

"You want your past? You'd best forget it. Beatings and brandings. You're a thræl now, whatever you was before." He stared at me pensively. "Jist get the scrolls. Don't disturb Woden, or whatever other god you find. If the lassie plays there mayhap you can get in and out without waking them."

Three steps led down into the room. Deep shadows accented the narrow slash of light from a crack in the shutters over the one window. A finger of snow reached across the recess of that window, startlingly bright in the dimness. Dark beams brooded over the shadows.

I had not thought of needing a candle. I stood on the second step.

A table stood in a narrow chamber to my right. A broken clay vessel lay on the floor, some crumbled residue spilling from it. Mingled smells of dust, mold, and some hint of the stables reached me.

As my eyes adjusted to the dimness I saw small footprints in the dust and places the cobwebs had been wiped clean. Drawing a deep breath I moved on into the room. The floor beneath the window showed a darker colour, as if damp.

Dead flies crunched beneath my feet. A table of sturdy oak stood between the window and a cold hearth, a three-legged stool beside it.

An ink jar and worn quills lay on the table, beside a scrap of parchment.

Bat droppings formed a small heap in the ashes on the hearth. Long lances and a great broadsword hung on the wall above a boar's skull. Yellowed tusks gleamed wickedly in the faint light.

A latticework of cavities held more scrolls than I had ever before seen. Tall thin jars of pottery stood on the floor and doubtless held more. Mr. Gerhardt might have cared nothing for reading, but someone before him had cared deeply.

The bairn had evidently scratched over the words on the scrap of parchment on the table. I could make out few words and no meaning.

More weapons hung on the wall either side of the window. Ancient and crude, they seemed fitted to the barbaric race known as the Pict. A crude painting covered a panel of whitewashed stone, though water stains and ages of dust had dulled it. A man wore a headdress of antlers and rode an eight-legged horse. Two wolves ran beside. A raven clung to his left shoulder while another flew above him. I took it to be a likeness of Woden.

The form of a cavern appeared along the north wall. Two gnarled oak trees, branches intertwined above, sheltered it. Old and dry, with stone built around them, they seemed rooted in the floor itself. Within the cave mouth I saw the appearance of a well, though without water. A wooden bucket, staves dry and shrunk, formed the bottom of the well.

Little enough I knew of the gods. Cruel and vengeful they were, sometimes placated with sacrifices, sometime scorning them. I dared not take Woden lightly.

The bairn plays here. I shrugged and turned back to the scrolls. I brushed cobwebs away to pull one from the clay jar that held it. The dry musty smell seemed to speak of endless ages. Spreading the scroll across the table I stared at the words in the dim light. Runic letters mingled with recognizable words, though of an ancient spelling.

The scroll crackled, but did not split as I rolled through it. I found little of interest beyond the careless hand that had written it. I returned it to its jar and drew down another.

I had not heard the door open, for a fourth scroll had fully caught my attention. A suppressed giggle arrested me. I looked up to see the lassie staring at me like she had discovered some delightful joke.

I felt the heat rise in my face. "Your father wanted," I began, then stopped. "Your nurse will not be pleased." I blurted out, then leaned back from the scroll.

Straightening myself with an effort, I glanced at the scroll, then back at her. Again she giggled. "Nurse is a'scared of this room. Any time I tire of her I only hafta come in here and I'm free." She pantomimed wringing her hands, then continued. "She'll be outside the door now, but too a'scared of the gods to come after me."

She came a step closer. "Aren't you a'scared? Nurse says these scrolls is full of magic and portents. I wishdt I could read. Can you read? Why aren't you pulling up water, or mucking out the horse stalls?"

"We've never been introduced," I said solemnly to the girl. "You must be the lady Gerhardt."

Again she giggled. "I am a very bonnie lady. And you, Sir, should kiss my hand."

I lifted the offered hand and touched it to my lips.

"Are you really a lord and jist pretending to be a thræl?"

I found myself entering into the spirit of her prattle, however I felt nervous too. Her father would undoubtedly disapprove of our having any contact, much less a private conversation.

"So you gonna kill the dragon what lives in that hole and help me 'scape from this castle? Or will you tame it and hitch it to a plow? Nurse says taming a dragon's lots tougher'n killing one. Though most people who try get stomped, then clobbered by the tail, then ate up, so there ain't been many dragons tamed or killed." With barely a pause to catch her breath she continued. "You ain't wearing no sword. You can't fight a dragon without you gots a sword. I guess you'll jist git ate up an' I'll have to wait till another brave knight comes along."

Again she paused just long enough to draw a breath. "I'd better git. If'n Nurse hears me talking she might git brave enough to open the door. Hope the dragon don't eat you. Leastwise if he does cut out his gizzard from the inside and make soup with it. Nurse says it'd be hot enough to roast a pig if'n you ever got past the gullut of one. If you helped me 'scape I could be your princess. Maybe I'd let you be my prince or maybe you'd hafta be my thræl. Nurse says I should learn to think on things 'afore I speaks them. With nobody to talk to it don't make much nevermind. She wants me to be a fine lady, but there ain't no parties. The father don't wanna see my face. The mens are all animals who will do shameful things so I shouldn't never get near them, so there's jist nurse. She's the father's whore at night. I don't know what that is, but she cries when she thinks I'm not listening. Sits in front of a copper mirr'r and tells it she weren't meant for such a life. Then pulls her hair back even tighter than afore. The father makes her have it down when she goes to his bed. She should leave it down cause she's mostly purty then. She's like to a dragon herself those days. That's when I comes here mostly. Dragons and snakes don't like garlic, Nurse says. She knows most everything, but she's still a'scared to come in here."

The prattling voice suddenly became silent. She tiptoed to the door, listened at it for a moment, giggled again, then opened it, reaching high to the latch. It closed with a dull thump behind her.

For a long moment I stared at the closed door. I rubbed both ears, surprised a bit that they had endured, then grinned as I picked up the scroll, placed it back in its clay jar and returned with it to Erhard's cottage.

Erhard stared at me pensively when I came in. "You didn't tamper with the shrine I hope," he challenged me.

"No, but the bairn came into the room. She can talk faster than a bard or priest. She hides from her nurse in there and about finished me with her noise."

"A bairn often says things wiser people miss. What did she speak of?" Erhard asked.

I thought for a moment, then took an exaggerated deep breath. "Will-I-kill-the-dragon? and how-will-I-since-I-don't-gots-a-sword? and if-he-eats-me-I-should-cut-his-gizzard-out-from-the-inside and a-bunch-more-without-taking-a-breath." I gasped and grinned at Erhard. "If I kill the dragon and help her escape from this *castle* she might let me be her prince, but I might have to be her thræl instead. Her nurse is the father's whore and has to go to his bed with her hair down. But she cries and pulls it back even tighter and is like the dragon herself those days."

I turned my attention to the scroll and for a while the scratching of my quill on a piece of parchment made the only sound.

"The dragon?" Erhard questioned. "Did she say anything else about it?"

"Just that it lived in *that* hole," I responded. "The shrine has what looks like a well, but it only goes down to the floor."

"You're best not knowing more about it." He stared at me for a while, then changed the subject. "Don't speak of Master's whore aloud. Don't suppose he'd take blithesome to the word." Erhard spoke barely above a whisper. Her name's Oöna. Means united one. Suppose that fits for a whore, though she don't look the part."

I had transcribed a good length when I came to a reference of particular interest. I copied and re-wrote it in readable language. The translation read:

> *The words of Riordan the Wise—chief bard to the House of Thorvæld:*
>
> *Where share the ravens the feast of Woden, even there, neath the shadow of nine fingers where bones have dried to dust is the well of old. There sounds the trumpet from Woden's Halls, and flames from the pit do rise.*
>
> *Put not the ax to the trees, lest thy head from thine neck be lifted. Break not the stones, nor from their place remove them, of the number of a man's hands save one. Wrest not from its place the ring, except thou be that called one. Hades beckons the usurper, and craves his blood.*
>
> *When strikes the shadow of summer solstice at the dawn-*

ing from Muninn's Keep—stand where the waters of the burn darkle. Turn thine back to the sailor's star. Linger not, for the shadow moves apace. Lift then thine eyes to the yew tree, which grips the cliff face at the height of nine tall men above you. There in the shadow of the cleft find passage neath the nine fingered rock.

Think not Kings and Jarls, to wrest the treasure. He with the name of infamy must wrest the ring, lest death take one of more seemly birth.

While still the strength of an infant's hand the yew tree could break—even then was the digging of the well of memory old. Then was the time. That the season. Stones to the number of a man's hands save one ringed the ancient waters. Then was builded the Keep. Then was forged the ring. Then was sired one of birth noble, yet not of the blood of kings.

When girdled cannot be the yew by four man's hands, even in that day will corruption unspeakable be drawn from the depths. The thræl shall the ring discover. Beatings and a name of shame will yet a short while follow.

The riddle shall be broken not ere found shall be the ring. Death within its circle lies. Claim thy prize and Hades enter, else bow to one purchased with goodly gold.

Here ends the words of Riordan the Wise

More words proved tedious, lacking interest. I questioned Erhard, but he knew little, although *Muninn's Keep* and the *Feast of Woden* stirred some deep emotion in him.

Another hour passed before the question finally surfaced. "What significance does nine hold?" I asked as Erhard pored over the scroll I had copied.

"I too have wondered," Erhard responded quietly. "Nine stones, the shadow of nine stones, the height of nine men, the nine fingered one with the name of infamy. . ." He mused for a moment. "I would ken the whereabouts of this Muninn's Keep."

I returned to the dull ciphering of ancient text. "There are old, old stories," Erhard broke the silence, speaking slowly. "Sacrifices, animal and human, was made in sacred groves. Rings of stone surrounded a well in a grove of ancient trees. Woden was there worshiped. *Muninn's Keep* be a name lost in legend. I have of times come acrost it in my reading. Muninn was the name given to one of Woden's ravens, and Woden hung for nine days and bartered an eye to gain the wisdom of the runes." He paused a moment. "There be another nine," he interjected.

For long moments he stared at the translated document, mumbling darkly to himself. "The boundary you spoke of," Erhard challenged me again. "What name was given the small burn?"

"The Grægstan or Greystone Burn it was. Reference was also made to the Loch Græg Clif, but the writer assumed knowledge of the area." I looked up at him, longing to probe his thinking.

"There be a ruin that overlooks a burn flowing toward *Loch Græg Clif*. The word *Cepan,* you translate as Keep. I have seen with the word *Hræfn*."

"That could be *Raven's Keep* then," I suggested. "It could be the same as *Muninn's Keep,* if Muninn is the name of one of Woden's ravens."

I did not see the bairn the next two times I went to the room, but on my fourth visit the big door whispered on its old hinges, then thumped softly closed. I heard her giggle before her face appeared around the stone wall.

"I thought you wouldn't come back. You probably shouldn't when I am here," I weakly rebuked her.

"I had to see if the dragon ate you. Somebody else'd hafta draw water if'n that happened. Sides, I haven't seed many knights who wasn't a'scared of it. So I thought maybe I'd let you be my prince, 'stead a jist a thræl, if'n for true you wasn't a'scared."

"Where's the dragon live?" I asked, hoping to draw her out a bit more.

"If'n I telled you that it'd be mad. Then it'd breath fire. I got my hair singed once. Nurse said t'was the candle and I got's to be more careful. But t'wasn't the candle. I didn't got a candle that day." Once again she scampered away, closing the heavy door softly this time, with hardly a thump.

Chapter Five
The Whipping Post

Dierdre bore her infant during a February storm. I knew nothing of childbirth, but the cries that came from the wench's sleeping quarters as we took our evening meal disturbed me deeply. When I first saw the infant three days later, the smallness astounded me. She carried it, bound in a blanket snuggled against her breast.

The lads' talk focused on the fullness of those breasts, the feel and taste of them. I wasn't much impressed with myself for listening, and hungering. It disgusted me to hear the men in the same kind of talk, for surely they had outgrown such. I became much more aware of Dierdre, and ashamed of my awareness. The change in her shape astounded me. She was allowed more rest for a time, and motherhood brought some quality to the surface. It seemed she glowed.

Heavy snows in February lingered and continued to choke trails and hamper travel as late as early April. Banks of soggy snow still lay in the folds of the land. I had transcribed thousands of useless words—and a few of interest. Mr. Gerhardt occasionally grilled me about the boundary or Muninn's Keep. He never asked directly after the ring, but so circled it in his questioning that a blind man could have seen the direction of his interest.

I swept the shrine-room, brushing cobwebs down. I lit a fire in the hearth, driving bats from the chimney. I hesitated to touch the shrine itself, yet the cobwebs spreading between the branches of the dead oak trees seemed somehow shameful. A part of me wished to shame whatever god made this place his dwelling. A part of me feared to do so. The bucket forming the well disturbed me. Could it have been a hlaut-bolla? Did this room bear the taint of blood sacrifices?

The bairn's comments about the dragon continued to stir unrest in my mind. A baffling feature on both the kitchen level and the cellar also stirred half-formed questions. Something about the stone surrounding the well seemed wrong on those two floors.

"Should there not be old cellars, dungeons, cisterns?" I questioned Erhard. "It was an old fortress. There should have been an escape route; a tunnel somewhere." I leaned back from the scroll and rubbed my eyes. "There's a listing of stores here, in some cellar."

"What kind of stores?" Erhard questioned.

"There's barley and corn. There are coins and silver plates. Weapons: swords, bows, spears and shields. A barrel that wouldn't fit down the stair behind the cells."

"What was that? Where was that stair?"

"Behind the cells." I turned my attention to the scroll again. "Ha," I snorted. "There was also a punishment—ah—a whipping—then a hanging." My voice dropped. "The silver had been counted before it went down, but a bunch of coins were missing." I searched the scroll further. "They weren't found, but somebody hanged for it—after he'd been beaten half to death."

"There's always been two laws. Always will be." Erhard bit the words off. "A starving man will hang for stealing a loaf of bread, though he's done all the work to grow the grain. A rich man can beat a starving man and the law will tell him how braw he be. But stealing silver? Only a fool does that."

"Two laws?" I stared hard at Erhard. "Not if I ever become Master."

Erhard mused darkly for a long moment. "Well, mayhap one day we will see." He stared at me pensively, then sighed. "You take food and water down to lockup," he finally commented. "I'll join you tonight. There be one cell I'd like to look at." He paused, then continued. "If my memory be right, one cell—acrost from the dark hole, be half the size of others."

With curiosity roused, the afternoon seemed to drag. While I provided the meager meal to prisoners that night, Erhard took a torch into the second chamber. "Nothing," he said when we returned to his cottage. "The stone be solid as a Keep wall. If there be a stair behind, the door be well hid."

Erhard worried the question like a dog worries a bone. It intrigued me, but I knew nothing of the room on the other side of the cell. Whispered longings among the men to breach the jugs stored there hinted of a wine cellar. A locked door led into the room from below the boys' sleeping area, but I had never seen that door opened.

"Leave the scrolls," Mr. Gerhardt ordered as we pushed back from the board on a May morning. "Every thræl and man-at-arms will earn his crust this day. Put the oxen on the plow. There be fields to prepare."

Little talk sounded around the board that night. Mr. Gerhardt had driven his people hard. Too weary to stare at old manuscripts, I had remained at board. The door banged open and one of the men from the gatehouse rushed in, followed more slowly by a figure heavily wrapped in stained woolen garments.

"A bard Sir. And he carries a harp." The words conveyed excitement and anticipation.

Mr. Gerhardt stared at the figure, bitter recognition playing across his face. "Have we nothing better to do at seed time than listen to the rants of a mindless old man? Let him in then. If he does not too badly bore us, we might throw a crust his way when we break fast in the morning."

The harpist, his face deeply lined and his beard falling wild and white across his chest, stared out of hard, cold eyes at Mr. Gerhardt. "No doubt you play the harp better than I, Sir, and know all the wisdom of the ancients. I would sit and learn at your feet then, for I have not yet gained all the wisdom I would."

"Bah, Sheridan," Mr. Gerhardt responded. "You were old before I was born. Your mindless verse bored me as a lad, though my grandfather and father both spilled good gold at your feet. I thought you had been buried long since. What do you here? For I will not waste gold on your rants."

"You have purchased one who is your master,
steward of a trust bigger than the shoulders it rests upon.

With your own gold,

spuriously spent

you have sealed your downfall,

though he would be your ally did you let him."

"You talk in riddles, old man, and weave verse out of empty air. Throw off then your foul cloak that smells of weeks sleeping with the goats. Blow the dust from your harp." Mr. Gerhardt turned and stared about the room. "Wench!" he shouted at Dierdre. "A jug of ale, that I might easier wash down the groaning this man calls singing. A jug for him as well, that it might mellow his raven's throat. The whipping post has been idle these weeks. Here is punishment enough for all."

A wide leather belt parted to let the cloak fall clear of the man's shoulders. Spare of flesh, he wore brown leather garments. A shrunken purse hung at his waist. A horse's sweat stained his leggings while heavy boots covered his feet. They were big boots for the size of the man. It seemed he had shrunk with aging, all but his feet.

He fingered the deep lines that crossed his face. Heavy brows drew together between his eyes. His scowl, as his gaze swept the room, caused more than one watcher to take a pace backwards. Though he carried no visible weapon, something of his person menaced each one.

"What would you that I should sing, noble and learned sir?" Sheridan asked. "Or, since you so despise my skill, shall I ask your men-at-arms, or even your thræls what they would?"

"Ask," Mr. Gerhardt spat the word. "They think wisdom hides

behind your words. And some small entertainment might bend their backs the quicker tomorrow."

"The Lay of Beowulf, I would hear again." Erskine's voice reached into the troubled silence.

"A noble tale, that, though other worms and closer have been slain." The bard stood before the fire, his harp in his left hand, then thrust his right into his purse. Hazel nuts he drew out and three times clusters of three he threw upon the flames. Each time he passed his hands three times above the fire. He stared long into the embers, then turned and faced us. His fingers ran across the strings of his harp. A plaintive and sad sound filled the room. The voice Mr. Gerhardt had likened to a raven's fell upon my ears like rain on dry sand. Mellow and rich, I had no memory of such music. His voice grew harsh, then soft as a maiden's, while the harp brought thrills upon my spine.

"T'was now, men say, in his sovereign's need

that the Jarl made known his noble strain,

craft and keenness and courage enduring.

Heedless of harm, though his hand was burned,

hardy-hearted, he helped his kinsman.

A little lower

the loathsome beast he smote with sword;

his steel drove in

bright and burnished;

that blaze began to loose and lessen." [i]

The magic of his voice caught me, held me in thrall. The tale itself, I largely missed. The crackle of the fire amplified the silence as harp and voice became still.

"You have gained some in skill since last I was compelled to listen," Mr. Gerhardt rudely broke the silent awe that followed the song. "Almost I hear music in your noise. Yet it does not call men to battle, like the bladder-pipe or the trump. More ale, Wench."

"Battle is not all of life, Sir. And men battle best who hold a dream. The bladder-pipe and the trumpet truly set men's blood afire. But that fire burns longest when a dream is deep-rooted and feeds the flame."

Again he strummed the harp and all voices fell silent. The clip of Dierdre's feet as she bore a pitcher of ale to fill Mr. Gerhardt's jug, and the fire made the only other sounds.

"Ale is for Jarls—an atheling's joy.
A horse's hooves are proud—when heroes sit it.
The wealthy on war steeds—do mighty deeds."

With just a breath, he moved on:

"But new this tale rings—for one purchased with gold,
not got by sea or ship—will to his master be lord."

His gaze swept the household, his eyes fierce and menacing.

"Overly fond of gold is every man.
Dragon's spawn.

Lust has laid them low.

What is fitting?

To enjoy the wife of your youth,

bread for this day,

hoary hairs to crown a head,

a goodly name to pass to a son."

He paused a moment and drank. His gaze met mine and he set the cup down slowly. Foam covered his mustache. He spoke in a softer voice, the harp silent in his hands.

"The land of the raven—ancestral property

so held in trust—which trust betrayed

shall to the rightful heir—restore.

Though strength of sword and spear and bow

and lust for another's wealth

shall fight in wrongful hands to hold it,

that strength shall not prevail."

"Enough, bold fool!" Mr. Gerhardt's voice carried something of fear within the anger. "Bard you may be, and wise in the eyes of many. But words so carelessly spoken will earn a rope upon a gallows."

It seemed that prophecies had been uttered, though I could make no sense of them.

Sheridan returned his harp to its bag, tipped his cup once more, and finding it empty, grunted. His gaze found Dierdre leaning against the wall beside the kitchen door, jar still in her hand. She glanced at Mr. Gerhardt, but met with a stony glare.

Sheridan grunted again, then fixed Mr. Gerhardt with a withering gaze. “A key to the room above, if it still be locked, my worthy host.” His voice held an edge, yet he spoke the words softly.

“It be not locked. The bairn sometimes amuses herself there.” Mr. Gerhardt’s voice sounded weary, apologetic.

“I would not call it wisdom that she plays there. But too much wisdom was never your weakness, was it Holt?” Sheridan spoke as if to a child. “You have one in your company who would wrest the secrets from its scrolls and profit you thereby, if you remembered your station.” He paused before continuing, his gaze again falling on me. “He *will* wrest their secrets and will strive to profit you, though you make his task bitter. The bairn will cause him grief, though he be innocent of wrong in the matter.” His gaze turned again to Mr. Gerhardt. “She dreams of wyverns and a prince to slay them—so empty you have made her life.” He snorted. “Enough. You are at seed time. An old man needs his rest, and the younger, that they might work the better tomorrow, must seek their beds.”

A strange joy filled me. I had thrilled to the bard’s voice and the notes of the harp. His words held some promise I could not comprehend, yet felt myself lifted on. I lay in the straw and stared at the dark beams above me, barely lit by the fire glow.

Sleep slowly claimed me. *Two teachers strove for my attention, one with letters and the other, younger, with a sword. I wore the garments of a nobleman, swung a sword with silver hilt studded with gems. My arms easily bent a great bow, or hurled a spear. I danced a swordsman’s dance as words in three languages were flung at me, parrying them with the sword or impaling them with the spear.*

I woke to the sound of a door opening and closing, then footsteps above me. I rose to another weary day and saw the bard depart shortly after the house broke fast.

Exhausting day followed exhausting day until heavy rain called a halt. I gladly turned my attention to the scrolls once more. The bairn did not appear and I felt a sense of loss.

The bard had left a scroll open on the table. The message seemed more a riddle than before, the spelling of Thorvld noticeably different.

THE LAY OF THORVLD AS TOLD BY RIORDAN THE WISE

PUT TO PARCHMENT BY IVAR,

THRÆL TO THE HUS OF THORVLD

ELEVEN SEASONS AFTER RIORDANS FUNERAL FIRE.

Near The North Tower Gainst The Well

Worship was wont to be Made

A Worms Lair is There.

Enter At Thy Peril.

Beware the Torch

Fire Gives Birth to Fire.

Though The Wyvern Sleep An Endless Age

The Rightful Lord May Waken Her.

Steward To The House Of Thorvld.

Arrows Bite Rotting Flesh

The Woads Blue On The Face Of Thine Enemies

A Trust Betrayed.

Lust For The Wyverns Hoard.

Death That Will Not Complete Its Task

Though Begged For.

A Daughters Death

More swift than The Fathers.

The Worm Sleeps Still.

The Steward is No More.

It was a strange and disturbing document. It seemed it spoke of this house and somehow echoed the bairn's words about a dragon. I stared long at the shrine, my mind grasping for answers. The small peat fire burned with a faint hiss. It sounded the breath of a wyvern, a dragon.

The bairn came into the room, her faint giggle somehow profane, though she was doubtless the closest thing to innocence the room had seen for generations. I stared at her pensively. Her giggle fell silent, then the smile left her face

"Tis a dangerous place to play, Milady. I fear I am the one who will wake the wyvern, though I know not where it sleeps." I glanced down at the scroll spread on the table. "This one may cause grief to your father." I paused, then continued. "And to you."

I covered the missing finger on my left hand. "Has nurse told you tales of a nine-fingered man?" I asked.

She shrugged. "Dull tales 'less I can learn to swing a sword. Nurse tries to beat everything strong outta me. Make me soft and refin'd."

Her voice faltered on a bitter note. "And useless!" she spat the words. "I shouldda been a warrior maid. I'd kill the worm myself. But my hands ain't never even held a sword. They ain't worth telling. Can't remember them nohow, the ones about nine fingers. Jist lots of fighting and killing." She drew a long breath. "You got all the seeds planted, so's we won't starve next winter? Nurse works extra when you're in the fields. She ain't but a scullery maid when things is busy, and the father's whore at night. I gits ignored. But I try to do anythings and I'm told that ain't proper for a lady. What good's a lady? The father won't see me and I can't go near the mens, so I might best to not been borned."

The door burst open. Heavy boots stomped down the three steps. Mr. Gerhardt glared at me. "So Oöna did speak true." His words hissed through clenched teeth. His glance turned to the child. "Get to your room, Wench!" His voice rose to a shout. The back of his hand flung out and struck her across the face. "No. Stay! He would shame you. You will see him shamed." He drew his sword and advanced on me, though the table stood between us.

"She has not been shamed, Sir," I spoke quickly. "She plays here and I do the task I was given."

The bairn had fallen. She crept as far from her father as the room would allow. A trickle of blood stained her face where he had split her lip. An angry welt already began to rise. Her chin and bottom lip trembled.

Mr. Gerhardt grabbed the table and flung it aside. His sword he thrust against my throat, forcing me back against the lattice works. The sword pressed hard. I drew ragged, gasping breaths. I dared not move or speak. "Æthëlrd, get up here," he shouted.

Boots sounded on the stairs, then Æthëlrd's face appeared around the stone wall. "Here be a task you will take pleasure in. The whipping post for this one. Lean into it, but make sure he can work the fields tomorrow."

His right arm was still crudely bound, but a cruel grin lit Æthëlrd's face.

"Strip!" Mr. Gerhardt ordered me. He drew his sword back, but continued to menace me with it. I carried no weapon, though the walls of the room held many. My glance swept across them.

"Aye," Mr. Gerhardt's voice dropped in volume. "Reach for one and you'll die like a gutted pig." His glance took in the scrolls, swept clear of cobwebs. "A waste of time your work in this room anyway. I said strip!" he shouted again, after I pulled my sark over my head. His sword point thrust against my privates. "Make me say it again and I'll see you never father a son, even if my daughter plays the whore."

I doubted neither his word nor his temper. Naked, shame a foul taste in my mouth, I stumbled down the stairs and out to the whipping post. The rain had stopped, but the day remained sodden and grey. A thin mist swirled around the courtyard and drifted from the dung heap, bringing the stink with it. The fresh green of new grass showed in places through the mud. A raven croaked mournfully. Branches of the oak trees rubbed against each other with a strangely dry sound.

Mr. Gerhardt had dragged his daughter down. I heard more shouted words, childish crying and another slap. As with most punishments, everyone was called out to witness. Dierdre too stood in the crowd, her infant in her arms. That she should see me so added to the shame.

They tied me to the post, my hands raised high. The raw, damp wind sucked the warmth from my body. A fly crawled through the trampled grass and mud at the base of the whipping post. Time seemed to crawl as slowly, my flesh puckered with the cold, cringing against the pending lash.

I knew Æthëlrd used his left arm. Still the whip cut like fire across my shoulders, back, buttocks and legs. Nakedness and the whip together heaped shame too deep to bear.

"Put your back into it man," Mr. Gerhardt ordered. "Dierdre's whelp could do as well, and it not yet walking."

"But he busted my arm," Æthëlrd growled.

"Aye. And for your own stupidity he did it. Now show yourself a man or trade him places."

The whip fell harder. I fought the urge to scream. I barely heard the shout, "Enough!" though the lash cut one more time. I sagged against the rope and fell when they released me. The mud felt cool and soothing against me. I struggled to raise myself up, then a pail of cold water struck me.

I should have known to expect it. Standard with whippings, it was usually salt. My back burned, but somehow with cold fire.

Wet grass and mud beneath me. Wind across bloody, sweat-slick welts. Disgrace too deep for words. All sound seemed silenced except the rubbing of branches in the oak trees and the pounding of my own heart-beat.

Chapter Six
To a Greater God

A BLANKET COVERED ME, bringing instant burning against the whip strokes, but gentle warmth as well. "You can't stay longer, else you'll die." Dierdre spoke.

She shook me by the shoulder, demanding that I get on my feet. She bent and drew my arm over her own shoulder and lifted me. The blanket fell and I swayed, leaning against her, naked. Her left hand grasped my arm in a fierce grip as she bent and retrieved the blanket. She half carried me to the stable. It seemed an endless walk, though I leaned heavily against her.

When the stable door closed, Bertrm helped. "You risk much to do this, Wench," I heard him say to Dierdre.

"He didn't do it, did he?" Dierdre asked. "To the lassie? He didn't do nothing to her?"

"If Master truly believed, he'd be hanging on a gibbet now. And he'd have had the flagellum first. The bairn can be but eight seasons.

There be men would take her, but not this one."

They half dragged me up the two steps into the straw and fodder area of the stable, then lay me in the straw.

"I didn't believe it of him." I heard Dierdre's voice again, almost too faint for me to catch.

"Aye. He's a better lad than that." Bertrm's voice sounded clearer. The warmth of the straw surrounded me. The blanket covered me. I cried then, to my shame. Sobs convulsed my body, thought I fought them.

A cup sloshed water beside my face. A voice spoke softly, questioning. "A drink?" Dierdre held the cup to my lips. I raised myself and gulped eagerly, desperately, though I spilled more than I drank.

I caught the hand that held the cup. "Why do you help me?" I questioned. My other hand reached up and touched her cheek, leaving muddy imprints there. "Thank you," I whispered. She broke my grip on her hand and fled the stable.

Stiff and sore I washed, then dragged clothes over my raw back. I ate little at the evening meal and felt sick afterwards. I then returned to the stable. I shunned the other boys that night.

Because the weather remained too wet for field work I returned to the shrine room long enough to get the scroll I had last examined. I left the table lie where Mr. Gerhardt had thrown it. If I had known any god worthy of prayer, I would have petitioned for his downfall. I stared long at the shrine, wondering if Woden might strike him down. But Woden rewards those he slays, letting them feast and battle eternally. I wished no reward for my master, even one so questionable as that. I plotted his death in a thousand ways.

The sun shone again. Work in the fields was honest work, and I healed, at least in body. Twice, a horse and rider appeared at the edge of the field. Each time he quickly withdrew when someone approached him.

We finished planting toward the end of May. Mr. Gerhardt's impatience to be at some other task evidenced itself in countless ways, yet he drove himself relentlessly. Against my will, respect for him increased.

Dierdre worked in the fields as well as the kitchen. I had returned the blanket, but we had rarely spoken since the whipping. She had to despise me. It shouldn't have mattered, but it did. The touch of her cheek had wakened a hunger in me.

I entered the shrine-room only on rainy days and never lingered, returning one scroll and taking another. The table still lay on its side. Mr. Gerhardt could right it or it could rot where it lay. The bairn did not appear.

On the day we dug the last of spring planting into the ground, Mr. Gerhardt rode his horse across the field. "I will see the scrolls tonight and hear your thoughts on them," he informed me. "Ere another sen'night passes, I would know if Muninn's Keep be part of my holdings, and if in truth there be a sacred grove and well there."

The flicker of candles in Erhard's cottage lasted late that night. My eyes burned before we rolled the final scroll and put it away. Even as I stumbled to my place in the straw beside the other boys, I heard Mr. Gerhardt demanding that Dierdre rouse herself and prepare food for our departure. Ilsa fussed a bit, then quieted. Thumping sounded in the kitchen. We were to be up before dawn, and, I presumed, on our way to Muninn's Keep. Mr. Gerhardt had told us almost nothing.

I became aware of a strange itching as I washed my face in the dark of the early morning. I realized with embarrassment and satisfaction that my beard had begun to grow. The burnished copper shield in the great room did not give sufficient reflection to see it by. I guessed it would be a pale, sickly thing like most of the other boys when theirs first started to appear.

We broke fast long before daybreak. I longed to speak to Dierdre as she served us, though I had no words to say.

First light saw a party of four with a burdened packhorse already on the trail. A chill fog settled as the feeble sun climbed higher, giving barely enough glow to mark its passage. We each wore swords and carried bows on our backs. Erskine carried his longbow.

The sun melted through the fog in the mid-morning, but the day remained cool. By the time we stopped at noon to rest the horses, I could scarcely sit, for though I had gained skill in the saddle, I had never taken an extended ride. Erhard, for all his age, seemed to handle the ride better than I.

I walked aside to a grove of small trees I did not recognize, stumbling after the hours in the saddle. A few shriveled berries showed a dull blood red against the opening leaves. Old brown leaves clung stubbornly to some branches. The wood proved surprisingly tough under my blade, but I returned shortly with a stout stave of about two paces in length.

"What have you there, Thræl?" Mr. Gerhardt questioned.

I held the staff out for his inspection. "Do you wish it? I can cut another." I kept my words short and blunt. Since the flogging I did my tasks with the least contact possible between my master and myself.

Mr. Gerhardt drew back, declining to touch the staff.

"It be rowan. With it do the priests hold staff of office," Erhard spoke the words softly. "Bards and prophets of times also carry such a staff."

"Should I then discard it?" I asked, little caring about the answer.

Mr. Gerhardt and Erhard exchanged glances. "Beyond my ken it be, Surra," Erhard finally spoke.

"Keep it then, for something of the bard overshadows you," Mr. Gerhardt said, rising and remounting his horse. "Aye, tis the insolence of the bard, no doubt," he muttered.

As the shadows lengthened we descended a long hill among great oak trees. Their branches showed the pale green blush of leaves beginning to open.

Brooding shadows darkened the forest floor. Conversation had fallen silent some time back. The repeated croaking of a pair of ravens sounded off to our left. Other birdcalls came rarely. Squirrels scolded, and we saw deer and rabbit droppings at times, but little evidence of other life.

Our horse's hooves clipped at times on a surface resembling a cobble-paved highway. Moments later peat that looked centuries old deadened the sound.

"We should cut no wood here, Surra." I heard Erhard's murmured voice urge Mr. Gerhardt. "If I might be so bold, I suggest no blade be drawn. Little I know of the sacred groves and the sacrifices made, yet I would urge no action a watcher might think a threat."

"Someone watches our passage then?" Mr. Gerhardt demanded.

"Someone has been before us, Surra. Mark you not the branches broke, the peat tore from the cobble roadway?" Mr. Gerhardt started, staring about him.

"Since leaving the burn where it last turned sharply, we have followed another rider closely," I confirmed Erhard's words. "And he is over heavy for the animal he rides, that or has ridden long and hard, for the horse stumbles often."

"And you spoke not of this?" Mr. Gerhardt demanded.

"My trail craft is but poor," I stressed. "I was sure you saw far more than I."

"And yet I saw nothing," Mr. Gerhardt spoke as if to himself. "Though it be plain as the hairs on a dog's face when you draw my attention to it."

We made camp on a broad meadow with scattered clumps of oak trees and more of the rowans as well. The land still dropped gently to the east. We could see but a short distance because of the great trees that surrounded us.

My respect for Erhard had deepened as the day progressed, for I ached from the long ride, yet he did his share as we made camp.

"Tis early in the season for the Pict to be a-warring," Mr. Gerhardt observed quietly. "And they would come screaming, blades thirsting for our blood, not skulking in the shadows. Who then is our watcher? Is he the same who would not make himself known while we did spring planting?" He spat on the ground. "I like it not."

No answers did any of us have to offer. Stars began to glimmer. A single wolf howled. Something grunted close by.

Mr. Gerhardt and Erskine played a game of knucklebones. The lads played it sometimes when the work had been easy during the day, but I spent those evenings in Erhard's cottage.

I stood the first watch, walking stiffly, painfully. I wore my sword and carried the rowan staff. The stars had swung around the pole star like spokes around a wheel. My time was nearly up as I paced just beyond the glow of the coals. A dark shadow loomed before me. It stood higher than my head by half. Only the sliver of a moon gave light. The stars hung low and brilliant. I could no longer see the shadows of my sleeping companions, though I had taken only a few paces extra.

I shifted the staff to my left hand. My right hand rested on the hilt of my sword. For a long moment I stood, scanning my surroundings, tasting the night with all my senses fully awake. The squeaky moan of branches rubbing against each other, the rustle of stubborn dry leaves still clinging from last year, the faint whisper of new leaves kissed by the slight breeze sounded. The smell of crushed heather, damp grass and burning peat; the feel of a wind so gentle it was almost a caress, these too I took in. It seemed there was something else, but I could not define it. I raised the staff. *Rowan,* Erhard had called it.

"Theodoric?" The call came in a subdued voice. I stood a moment longer, then walked toward the voice. The fire-glow greeted me after only a few paces.

"All is well, Erhard." I approached him in the shadows east of the fire. "All is well," I repeated. "A finger of stone points to the sky just where I came from. I could not see if a circle of them stood, or if they numbered nine."

"Daylight will be time enough for that. You be foolish to walk alone in this place. There be powers you know nothing of. You give allegiance to no gods, old or new, so all will seek to make you their own."

"What can one of a grandfather's age know of the gods? Much less a youth who has lost his past." I gazed at the stars, so brilliant.

One fell, a white sword slash across the sky, yet the sky was not depleted at all.

"The god who hangs the stars in the heavens, who gives wings to Mercury, who makes the moon wane and wax; the god who from an acorn births an oak tree—to that god will I pledge allegiance if ever I can find him. Though he be too busy for the likes of a thræl called horse killer, I will bow to no lesser god."

"You be wiser than your years in your thinking," Erhard responded to my outburst. "But yet a whelp in your actions. Do not let the whelp lead you to a early death." He stared about him, then continued. "Sleep now, and if the gods should quarrel in the night—and this be the place for such to happen—that one, whose name you know not—may he prove the stronger."

I stared at the stars as I lay on the hard ground, a nameless ache in me. For a fleeting moment I wondered if Dierdre too questioned the gods, then Erhard roused me, shaking my shoulder.

The morning dawned clear and bright, though cold. The dampness from the ground had penetrated my robe and chilled me thoroughly. Muscles ached as I tried to rise. We broke fast on blocks of cheese toasted over the peat coals and hard, heavy biscuit. Erhard had found a tiny burn from which we drew water.

"My grandfather brought me here, or a place near-about, shortly after my father was killed in battle," Mr. Gerhardt spoke softly, with unaccustomed frankness for the company of thræls. "Even then it was a disputed holding, steeped in legend. We stood on an old wall, wide enough that four horses could have walked abreast—or so it seemed to me. I was but a lad." His gaze swept the moor. "We looked over a burn and two small lochs."

Mr. Gerhardt turned the focus of his talk. "What of our watcher? No sign did I see for the last two hours of daylight. Marked you, any of you, his presence in the night?" Mr. Gerhardt stood and stretched.

"Our thræl of no memory made a discovery, Surra, though it seems to bear no connection to the watcher." Erhard informed Mr. Gerhardt as we saddled the horses.

"And what might that be?" he responded, the question addressed not to me, but to Erhard.

"A stone, which fits well one of the nine said to encircle the ancient well," Erhard replied.

"And how far wandered you to find this stone, while we slept without a watch?" Mr. Gerhardt's voice carried suspicion and anger.

"Only three paces beyond the fire-glow." I cut my words short. I checked the sky to get the points of the compass, then pointed. "There. Just beyond a slight dip in the moor."

Leading our horses, we walked to the northwest. An oak tree, juvenile by a century to some we had seen, overshadowed a rowan tree. Heath and heather crowded close. A black finger of rock lifted into the branches of the rowan. "I could not have walked up to this one unaware in the dark. There is another close by." After two more paces, the stone I had found in the night showed, twenty paces to the right. "My trail-craft is poorer than I knew, if I am so much mistaken in direction."

I could scarcely mount my horse to join the search. It seemed I ached as deeply as from the flogging, though in different places.

It soon became clear that the stones formed a great circle. The growth of trees, both within the ring and at its perimeter made finding and counting the stones a weary challenge. The concern about finding the well, one step too late, added to the slowness of our search.

Only six stones still stood, but three showed their form against the ground, though covered with peat and heather. Nine in all we found before stopping for our noon meal. The northern extremity of the circle overlooked a cliff, two small lochs and a burn. Farther east a larger loch showed against the deep green of a peat bog.

Erskine's horse found the well. When he refused to cross a small hollow of old broken stone, Erskine dismounted. The glint of his sword caught my attention. I galloped my horse across the circle toward him, drawing the others to join me. We converged to find he had backed the horse out of the circle and stared around fearfully, gibbering something we could not understand in a voice even more broken than normal. He gripped his sword and seemed on the verge of fleeing in panic. None of us understood Erskine's terror, but we knew he did not cower easily.

A massive stump thrust up from the heath while moss covered the remnants of a fallen tree. I swung down from my horse calling myself a fool. Stepping over the fallen log and kneeling at the edge of the heather, I reached into the small circle and brushed my fingers through the dust. I rolled a tooth out; a human tooth, I believed. I forced myself to stand and tried to walk with steady steps, probing the ground before me with the rowan staff. Where a clump of heath reached out into the ashes and dust, the staff penetrated deeper. Drawing a deep breath and steadying myself, I knelt and parted the stiff low shrub. A hole reached deep into the earth.

"Here is the well." My voice broke. "Here sacrifices have been made—to Woden." The shaft surprised me by its smallness. Lined with stone, it descended straight as a plumb line.

A thorn had stabbed the stump of my finger. I watched as a drop of blood disappeared into the darkness. I heard the faint plink of it hitting water at the bottom. "Blood should not again be spilled here. Not to Woden." I leaned back and looked at my bleeding hand, then stood, glanced at the others and turned back to the well. Intense emotions warred within me, an almost overwhelming need to bow to Woden, but a stubborn and unbending refusal to do so. I raised my arms and my voice.

"There are powers I know little about. I am a thræl with scattered memories. I have little knowledge of the gods. But here, where Woden once was worshiped, I declare allegiance to a greater god, to him who hung the stars, who makes a path for the sun and the moon. I do not know his name or what he requires, but no blood will I offer him except it be my own. With nine fingers I come, called Killer of Horses—a thræl. No prize am I to any god, nor would be if I were king, yet will I offer myself to the one god only, whose name is higher than Woden."

A sense of exultation swept over me. The sun shone warm and no thunderbolt fell from the sky. I lowered my arms and slowly turned to my companions, suddenly embarrassed. Astonishment marked their faces as they nervously backed away.

"Thunder 'n damnation! Know you what you have jist done?" Erhard demanded in a shaky voice. "You would defy Woden while standing on the very ashes of his victims? Killer of Horses? Rather fool and twice fool! What would you. . ?"

"Be still, Erhard!" Mr. Gerhardt broke in. "Fool he may be." He snorted. "Aye, fool he is! But even the gods respect courage. Let us move, however, outside the ring of stones. Though little I believe in Woden or other gods, I have heard stories enough, with some bit of truth in them. Woden has been challenged. If god he be in any measure and in temperament at all like my own, he will have drawn his sword."

We returned to our campsite of the night before where a bit of blowing managed to find a spark of life left in the peat fire. We kept our swords loose in our scabbards and repeatedly scanned our surroundings. Mr. Gerhardt probed our knowledge of the scrolls, though his eyes too made a restless search.

"Somewhere near should be the ruins of the Keep. Did any of the scrolls tell more?" Mr. Gerhardt asked.

"They speak of it overlooking the lochs and the burn," Erhard responded. "The cliff shows steep east of that burn that flows into Grene Loch. A wall built there would give a army the slowdown."

"Then before sundown let us search for a wall," Mr. Gerhardt made his desires known.

We mounted, a painful process for me, and rode slowly around the outside of the stone ring until we approached the cliff at the northeast curve. We followed it as it curved back somewhat to the south. The cliff here could be negotiated in places by a horse, but only with difficulty. Where breaks in the trees gave us a clear view we could see that it became much more rugged farther east and north. A half hour's slow ride took us across several narrow, steep sided ditches. Each one sloped gently to the northeast, then rose steeply to a low wall at the top. Obvious defense works, they had us watching for archers peering over the low walls. We rode for a while down the centre of one, thinking we would come to a roadway leading into the

Keep. We found bridgeworks, long since fallen, and old rusted chains of immense size.

"Every trench included a drawbridge and a wall." Mr. Gerhardt expressed his astonishment. "There would have been sharpened poles in the ditches. With only children to defend the walls this would have been a costly approach. What must the fortress itself be?"

Each wall stood more than the height of a man on horseback higher than the one before, forcing any enemy to make a long uphill attack against great defenses.

Where the cliff face turned sharply northward we found ourselves outside an old stone wall coated by centuries of growth. It quickly drew to the edge of the cliff face. We turned back and rode south, and then southeast until we reached the bridgeworks.

Chapter Seven
Muninn's Keep

With the bridge long gone, this last scramble up a steep slope challenged our horses. A jumble of broken stone lay in the entryway. A ramp led to the top of the wall. For a space, by unspoken agreement, we rode four abreast. But the horses were skittish. I drew back and followed the other three. Small cobbles paved the wall surface and a narrow wall rose more than the height of a man higher, with archery notches at frequent intervals. Vines had entangled and broken much of the higher wall. At times we could see across the valley. Where the wall turned from north to northeast, the narrow wall was gone completely, exposing a dangerous drop. From this angle, with the sun now low, the loch below us showed emerald green.

"It can only be the Grene Loch," Erhard declared. "Farther north will be Long Pond, and the bigger one to the east will be Loch Graeg Cliffs, or Grey Cliffs, if you prefer."

"The size of it," Erskine exclaimed, drawing our attention back to the wall we rode on.

"It was a fortress to rule a kingdom," Mr. Gerhardt agreed. "It be bigger even than my memory as a lad."

The rising hump of rock inside the Keep walls offered natural shelters refined by the tools of a stone worker. We spent little time exploring the interior of the Keep, however.

A drier area of heath and heather reached a finger close to the Greystone Burn. Something about it teased at the back of my mind.

Much of the north and east wall crowned a cliff edge to which a gentle slope descended, giving good footing to horse or man at the edge of a fortress fashioned by nature herself. Lorellefue shifted beneath me, eager to follow the other horses. "How would such walls be breeched?" I asked when I caught up to the others. "I have read of no battle that could defeat such a fortress."

"The walls were never breached." Mr. Gerhardt's voice held contempt. "Treachery from inside be how you take such a fortress. No king or lord ever built walls high enough to protect against that evil. History records the great battles. It does not celebrate the snake that crawls under the wall."

We spoke little as we completed our circuit. "I thought it a ruin," I finally said. "It is unbelievably old, but still the most defensible place I have seen. A hundred men would not provide more lookouts than needed for the length of the wall."

"A thousand men and more it was built for. Most likely it was never fully manned," Mr. Gerhardt responded.

"Thræls by the thousands will have sweat and bled and died in its construction," I said, hearing the bitterness in my own voice.

"Aye, and freedmen, and men-at-arms," Mr. Gerhardt added

bluntly. "It may have been a last retreat. It may never have seen battle. The army may have been cut off before getting back to this final and greatest refuge. Else why so obscure in the ancient tales?" Mr. Gerhardt fell silent again.

We camped that night near a spring that fed the small burn flowing through the Keep. I found my gaze drawn to the peak, now to our east. Foundations could be seen around us, but no complete buildings. A large hollow had the look of a quarry from which rock had been cut. The proximity to the stream suggested the possibility of a reservoir.

"If this be the only source of water, it would have to be tightly rationed under siege or battle conditions," Mr. Gerhardt observed. "Though doubtless there are wells dug and cisterns to be found."

In the waning light we looked again at the scroll from the words of *Riordan the Wise*. One of us would continually rise and sweep the surroundings with our gaze. We had our horses tethered close by and kept our swords strapped to us and our bows by our sides. I read the first section.

"Where share the ravens the feast of Woden, even there, neath the shadow of nine fingers, from oak trees hanged, where bones have dried to dust is the well of old.

Put not the ax to the trees, lest thy head from thine neck be lifted. Break not the stones, nor from their place remove them, of the number of a man's hands save one. Wrest not from its place the ring, except thou be that called one. Hades beckons the usurper, and craves his blood."

"The well and the nine stones be plain enough," Erhard interrupted. "So too the warning against cutting trees or moving the stones. The feast of Woden? I think none of us wishes to dwell long on that. The ring seems to be at the well, but comes with warnings." He spoke quietly. "This next seems to tell where the treasure be. Are the ring and the treasure one and the same, or be they two things we should search for?" He read,

> *"When strikes the shadow of summer solstice at the dawning from Muninn's Keep—stand where the waters of the burn darkle. Turn thine back to the sailor's star. Linger not, for the shadow moves apace. Lift then thine eyes to the yew tree, which grips the cliff face at the height of nine tall men above you. There in the shadow of the cleft find passage neath the nine fingered rock."*

"The shadow will fall aright the morn of the summer solstice. But what be this word, darkle?" Erhard asked.

"It means the edge where the shadow ripples against the water," I answered. "But the wall was higher once than now."

"Turn your back to the sailor's star be plain enough," Erskine declared. "It be the pole star that does not move, so if your back is to it you be looking south."

"Then we look for a yew tree the height of nine tall men above us." Mr. Gerhardt added.

Again Erhard read,

"Think not Kings and Jarls, to wrest the treasure. He with the name of infamy must wrest the ring, lest death take one of more seemly birth."

"Horse killer! Who better fits those words?" Erskine exclaimed, broken voice rising. "Not a king or jarl, so probably not Master, but one with the name of infamy." He snorted. "A fine heap of dung that be. It'll kill the king so the thræl's gotta do it. But not jist any thræl. It's gotta be the one with the name that stinks."

I glared at him. "I like this less as I learn more," I blurted. "Especially with threats of death to the wrong person touching the ring. And how should a thræl outrank his owner?"

"Tis a riddle and we are not meant to know all," Mr. Gerhardt spoke coldly, but his hand rested on the hilt of his sword and his eyes burned as he looked at me.

Erhard moved us farther along in the scroll, trying to relieve the tension.

"While still the strength of a infant's hand the yew tree could break—even then was the digging of the well of memory old. Then was the time. That the season. Stones to the number of a man's hands save one ringed the ancient waters. Then was builded the Keep. Then was forged the ring. Then was sired one of birth noble, yet not of the blood of kings.

When girdled cannot be the yew by four man's hands, even in that day will corruption unspeakable be drawn from the depths. The thræl shall the ring discover. Beatings and a name of shame will yet a short while follow."

"Girdled?" I questioned.

"I think it means four men together cannot reach around it," Erhard answered.

"There will be few trees of that size," Mr. Gerhardt added. "And yew trees are never overly common."

"If we find where the shadow of the wall crosses the burn," Erhard took up the discussion again, "it should not be too difficult to guess where that would happen under a June sun with the higher wall. A yew tree that big should be easy enough to find." He then continued with the reading.

"The riddle shall be broken not ere found shall be the ring. Death within its circle lies. Claim thy prize and Hades enter, else bow to one purchased with goodly gold.

Here ends the words of Riordan the Wise."

"And to me it sounds—and I deeply hate the sound of it," I burst out, "that we will not fully ken the riddle until after the ring is found." I paced near the fire Erskine had lit while we held our discussion. I knew nothing about the ring itself.

"Shall we seek the boundary, Sir?" I questioned. "Or shall we first seek the ring?"

Mr. Gerhardt started at my use of 'Sir'. I had dropped it since the flogging. But since my declaration to a greater god, the pettiness of my master seemed a lesser thing.

We passed another night with no sign of the watcher. "It might be well to confirm whose holdings we search on, lest the ring be disputed." I raised my concerns as we broke fast in the morning.

"Let us seek the yew tree, though the shadow will be far removed from the prophesied location when we reach the burn." Mr. Gerhardt made his plans known. "Failing that—or succeeding—we will seek to prove the boundary ere the day be done. What think you? Will our watcher be found somewhere in the valley below us, himself seeking the boundary?" He paused a moment, then continued. "If more than one yew tree might be that one spoken of in the scroll, we will make our camp close to the burn, that our error be smaller at tomorrow's dawning."

"The best passage I saw leading to the valley was near the ring of stones, though no love for that place do I hold," Erskine said as we saddled our horses.

"Aye. And at any point a watcher hidden in the rocks above and armed with a good bow could take our lives." The sobering reminder came this time from Erhard.

"Think you he is still around?" Mr. Gerhardt questioned.

"Aye, Surra. I smelled the smoke of a peat fire and the flesh of a boar cooking. He be not only close, but feasting this day."

"What direction the wind, yesternight?" Mr. Gerhardt asked.

"It eddies around the walls and heights, Surra," Erhard replied. "I tried to determine myself, but could not with surety. A ride on the great wall might have showed the smoke, though little does a peat fire give."

We picked our way across the trenched defense works and then down the cliff below *Woden's Nine,* as Erhard chose to call it. I thought much of my pledge to the unknown god while we made our slow way, each of us sweeping the surroundings with our gaze, keeping our swords loose in their scabbards.

Was he in truth a more worthy god than Woden? Could a mere youth, a thræl, know him? Knowing him, would there be honour or only fear? My reading showed other gods corrupt as the worst kings. Powerful and much to be feared many of them were, as a savage and brutal enemy is to be feared. Was this god other, or only bigger and more savage?

We crossed the burn about noon. It ran narrower than in the Keep above, for it descended steeply. The cliff face and the wall at its top towered above us over our right shoulders. We could somewhat guess the early morning shadow of the wall, but no large yew trees could we see above us.

"The heather and heath be close in colour," Erhard offered, "though perchance deeper green this early of the season. Against the moss that clings to the walls it will not readily be seen."

"Could we see past this oak, we might view much more of the cliff face above us. It lacks a hundred years of being old enough to have blocked the view when those words were written," Mr. Gerhardt observed.

"Aye," Erhard agreed. "But still we be warned against cutting trees, though mayhap in the sacred grove only."

We built a cairn of stones beside the tiny burn, then worked our way farther down into the valley. The cliff gave way to a broad moor and peat bog where our horses walked with greater ease. Moving beyond bowshot of the cliff, we relaxed somewhat, but oak trees, smaller rowan and clumps of heath and heather still provided cover for a watcher.

We disturbed a herd of wild pigs and in another time would have given chase, for we all delighted in their savoury flesh. But we hunted for other than meat.

At the northern bend in the Greystone Burn, Mr. Gerhardt pointed to an ancient oak tree. He dismounted and handed the reins to Erhard. He scanned the surrounding area and checked that we were all alert with weapons ready, then numbered his steps to the oak tree.

"Seventy-one paces," he called. "How many trees can be mistook for this?" he asked. "What say the scrolls now?"

We rode to join him. Above his head, deep in the folded bark, carved letters still showed. "Seventy paces north *to* the oak tree," I acknowledged. "It would take some searching, but I believe all holdings south of *The Oak Tree,* and west of *Loch Graeg Clif* are titled to *Se Hus of Thorvæld.*"

"How reads that last? Hus of Thorvæld?" Mr. Gerhardt questioned me.

I dismounted and scratched it into the dirt where pigs had rooted beneath the ancient oak.

"Those words, or something close, are carved into the hearth stone in the great-room of my house," Mr. Gerhardt exclaimed. "The hearth stone itself was taken from older ruins. What mean the words?"

"House of Thorvæld is their meaning." I told him.

"So the Keep, and Woden's Circle are clearly within my holdings?" Mr. Gerhardt asked.

"That would appear beyond dispute, Surra," Erhard spoke quietly. "Still, it were well to have clear claim to the House of Thorvæld."

"Title to the House of Thorvæld?" Mr. Gerhardt snorted. "You throw words carelessly as the wind blows, and twist them like the thorn twists in the hedges." He turned toward me, though still questioning Erhard. "And this one?" he asked. "Be he a word twister?"

"The words he translates are frequently to his own hurt, Surra, not to his gain." Erhard paused, then chuckled a bit. "Strange ideas he clings to, Surra, though mayhap he'll outgrow them."

I stared at the words I had scratched beneath the oak tree. Mr. Gerhardt remounted his horse, so I did the same. "Sir," I spoke hesitantly. "The House of Thorvæld—I knew nothing of the hearth stone, else I would have spoken of this sooner."

"What is it, Thræl?"

"I cannot be sure of the words for they seemed of little importance. I did not know they might bear upon your house. If I remember them aright, they are, *He who warms his feet at Thorvæld's hearth stone—when the murthering horde sweeps from the north, will hold his life ransom to the shamed one and the stone to its rightful place will be returned."*

"And what is that supposed to mean?" Mr. Gerhardt demanded.

"It has the sound of prophecy, Surra," Erhard answered quietly. "I also did not know of the hearth stone and its writing."

"Well!" Mr. Gerhardt snorted. "When the murdering hoard comes they will find my arm strong and my sword sharp." He touched his heels to his horse. "Hold my life ransom?" I heard him mumble. "Bah! Tis not but an ignorant thræl twisting words."

He spat on the ground. "Except for the Keep, this be no place of great value, else the dispute would long ago have been settled—in blood if parchment and ink did not suffice. But who could find a thousand men, and who would that thousand hold it against? We are north of the wall. I think it little worth my while, except. . ." His voice died away to silence.

"Except for the ring," I completed the thought.

"Aye," he responded coldly. "The ring." He spurred his horse across the moor, heading west. Where the burn made a gentle turn to the southeast he reined in again.

I had almost passed the hoof prints before my mind acknowledged them. I started to draw my sword, then lifted my bow instead, notching an arrow. I swung in a slow turn, seeking to scan the entire valley. The watcher had done us no evil, but choosing to remain unseen in this wild place did not speak well of friendship. I tested the bowstring. I have skill with the bow, but would much rather face an enemy sword to sword than one who can kill from a hundred paces. Erskine rode slowly toward me, watching, a warrior on full alert.

"How long ago?" I asked as he stood his horse beside me and gazed on the tracks.

"Two hours perchance. Little more," he responded.

"So he is watching us now?" The middle of my back felt naked, yet tight, as if someone had painted a target on it.

"Aye, with his hand over his horse's nose so it does not nicker." His eyes searched every shadow and hollow as we spoke, very much the warrior. "He will have marked our presence at the boundary tree, but passed here before we forded the burn. Were you one against four, where would you take refuge?"

"The cliff under the Keep wall doubtless provides many places to become invisible," I answered.

"Aye, with clefts and caverns an army might pass without seeing."

Mr. Gerhardt and Erhard approached as we spoke. The tracks before us needed no explanation. Mr. Gerhardt clenched his jaw, staring slowly around.

"No threat have we received, Surra," Erhard murmured.

"You think it no threat that for days one watches, but remains unseen?" He snorted. "Does it only become a threat when an arrow finds the heart of one of us? I like it not."

"He knows not this be firmly your holding now, Surra."

"Is it?" Mr. Gerhardt challenged. "The thræl uses words like the poison in a serpent's bite. How shall anything be mine while such as he lives?"

Ten minutes later we found where the watcher had camped beside the Grene Loch. We searched his campsite, but learned only that he had skill in the wild.

As the shadows lengthened we stopped again beside the small cairn of stones we had built earlier in the day. We tethered our horses within a narrow cleft and made our camp in its entrance. If the watcher wished us ill, seizing or driving away our horses would cause us great distress. An outthrust of rock protected us on two sides and reflected back the glow of our peat-fire. Coarse, dry grass provided fodder for the horses.

I walked away from the camp for my presence added to the tension. Mr. Gerhardt fingered his sword and glared when I looked back. Some paces beyond where we had thought to search I marked broken trees above me. I climbed the treacherous slope, stiff muscles protesting. Screened by oaks and several yew trees below, a cluster of small trees leaned drunkenly from the ledge they clung to. Broken branches, tumbled boulders and loose rock cut a trail of destruction below them. The height of six tall men or more I had climbed through the loose rubble before I could see enough to confirm my suspicions.

I returned to the camp where the watches of the night passed without incident. Twice our horses nickered, and once it seemed there came an answer.

Chapter Eight
From Woden's Hall

It began to rain shortly before morning. The heavy overcast gave no sharp shadows, but we had found our objective. Leaving Erhard alone to guard the horses, we sought the ledge from which the tree had fallen, climbing the western slope directly above our campsite. Finding a trail barely adequate for a goat, we worked our way higher. Of necessity we abandoned our bows. Even our swords, thumping against our legs on the narrow ledge, gave more trouble than protection. I also carried a long coil of rope and a grappling hook. Draped over my shoulders it added greatly to my difficulty.

The weather changed from rain to mist and back to rain again before we stood at the base of the great tree. Roots thicker than a man's waist still clung and reached fingers into the tortured rock. The three of us could have rested side by side, leaning into the upturned root ball of the tree itself. Stone, rubble and smaller trees had fallen from above, leaving us standing in a tangle that overhung the cliff-face, unsure of our footing.

Rainwater poured upon us. Thunder growled and rumbled distantly. "How reads the prophecy, Thræl?" Mr. Gerhardt shouted over the storm. *"There in the shadow of the cleft find passage?"*

"Aye, Sir," I answered. "But is the cleft still here, or has it been closed by the fall?"

"It be here," Erskine called, drawing our attention to a narrow slash almost obscured by fallen rubble and trailing strands of moss. Fifteen minutes work cleared the opening and we moved into the entrance and out of the storm. A natural passage by its appearance, enlarged enough to let a man pass. The shadows deepened into blackness almost instantly.

"I like it not, Sir." Erskine gave voice to our fears. "A remorseless god Woden be, slaying jist for the peopling of his halls. Can other than the dead walk where his trump has sounded?"

"Not in this darkness will we walk." Mr. Gerhardt spoke decisively. "To seek a well while walking blind be to seek our deaths." His voice sounded strangely distorted for he stood in the lead and I closest to the light. "What think you? Can torches be made for a sustained light, or only those that will lure us deeper before abandoning us?"

"The world drips outside, Sir, yet can torches be made by one who has the skill." I heard a smug note in Erskine's broken voice in spite of his dislike of our location.

Within seconds the quick spark of a flint against steel brought a small yellow flame from a bundle of heather stuck on a stick. The foul smoke told me some form of tar filled a reservoir. The black stains on the ceiling of the passage, seen now in the dim light, showed that torches had been used here before.

"The keeper of the light earns privileges," Mr. Gerhardt said quietly. "I will compel no man to follow me deeper into this place. Wait here you may, Erskine. It were no shame and might be to the saving of our lives, for the watcher needs only stop the entrance and we are forever lost."

"Yet the watcher may seek the same prize," Erskine observed. "So closing the tunnel is to his own loss. Though loath am I to walk where the very vibrations of our feet might waken gods long undisturbed, I would yet bear sword before my lord."

"Tis well said, Erskine," Mr. Gerhardt acknowledged. "Hold the light as high as may be then, and keep your sword ready."

Walking behind the light blinded me. The passage twisted, rose sharply, then dropped in uneven steps. The sound of flowing water reached us just before our way led into a larger tunnel with a small stream flowing along its floor. The pebbled floor had none of the slime and moss normal to a stream exposed to sunlight. The murmur of the water itself, somehow amplified by the peculiar character of the tunnel, masked other sounds, though a low moan, like an endless sigh, seemed to flow with the water. The smoke from the torch drifted lazily in the direction the water flowed from.

When Erskine passed the torch to Mr. Gerhardt, bent and cupped water in his hands to drink, some compulsion stirred in me. I struck his hands, dashing the water from them. His hand went to his sword as his teeth bared. He glared at me.

"Sacrifices to Woden have been made in the well we seek." The words burst from me. "Drink not, till we know from where this water comes."

"Woden?" He stared at me, then spat. "The god you defy?" His voice cracked as he half drew his sword. "Speak no ill of him here, lest your blood make the first sacrifice."

"Fool you are, Thræl," Mr. Gerhardt broke in. "To strike a man-at-arms when a word would do, be to invite his sword in your heart. Nor could I have faulted him. Yet you are the one who defies Woden." Mr. Gerhardt snorted. "Fool and twice fool, and yet by the caprice of the gods I must now ask your advice." The distaste sounded clear in his tone. "What way, think you?"

"Blood was spilled into the well," I responded. "Whether Woden be a god or not, no desire have I to drink from such a source. If my reading be right, bodies of animals and men were often hurled into the waters as a sacrifice to the gods." I paused, gathering my thoughts. "Would you have stopped at my word, Sir? The word of a thræl? Fool I may be, but words oft come too late." I stared at him for a long moment, warring inwardly over my status.

"Left will take us under the Keep," I forced myself to speak quietly. "Right should lead to the well. But how shall we mark this tunnel, that our returning is to the same place?"

Erskine took back the torch, raised it high and marked a sooty black arrow on the ceiling, pointing into the tunnel we had just vacated.

"It is well, Erskine." Mr. Gerhardt paused a moment longer. "Choose you still to bear sword on my behalf?"

"Aye, Sir," Erskine answered. "But I'll have my sword behind this thræl, rather than the other way."

Mr. Gerhardt grunted and led the way.

The noise of our feet splashing in the stream, our voices and even our breathing, echoed strangely and repeatedly. It seemed we made a great noise, and could hear nothing else.

The passage rose in a slow, gentle slope, with an occasional small step over which the water tumbled. We thought ourselves moving westward, but each of us habitually took our directions from the sun or stars. The twists and turns could quickly baffle down here. It seemed an hour, but was probably much less when the passage swung southward, though still tending in a westerly direction. As it made a wide sweeping turn back to the north, it also began to rise more rapidly. We passed a shaft that reached up with steps cut into the floor, then came to an old door lying on the floor of the passage, water flowing across it. The remains of a leather hinge still showed above the water. The well overflowed beyond the door and fed the stream we had walked through. A faint glimmer of light reached us from above, with the sound, impossibly distant, of a storm. The moaning we had earlier heard came from this place, made somehow by the wind blowing across the top of the well.

The chamber widened here, with a raised floor surrounding the well. Benches of stone were cut from the walls themselves. A tiny stream overflowed into a huge stone basin directly under the opening from above. Off to the side of the shaft reaching up to light above, water welled up from black depths.

"Why this basin, and the well dug to one side?" Mr. Gerhardt questioned.

"Tis when people have been in their cups that they speak freely of Woden worship." Erskine muttered. "Tis a hlaut-bolla. For the catching of blood is it designed, as people are sacrificed. Any who drew from the surface would be drinking a blood sacrifice to Woden."

"Think you so, Thræl?" Mr. Gerhardt demanded.

"Aye, Sir. And in truth it is both evil and brilliant." We stood a moment longer in troubled silence.

"How seek we now, Thræl?" Mr. Gerhardt finally asked, an edge to his voice.

As Erskine shifted the torch, shadows cast by runes carved above the hlaut-bolla drew my gaze. In my months studying scrolls I had bolstered my meager ability with runes.

"*To quench the thirst of Woden,* this says." I heard a tremor in my voice. "And here, lower down—*To deceive the mighty and uplift the thræl—But both will be brought low.*"

I stood close to the well, trying to find courage to go another step. I had told Woden I would not follow him. The prophecies seemed to say I had some special role in all this. Mr. Gerhardt also owned me, like a man might own a horse or a dog, and he wanted the ring. But the prophecies said it would kill him. They hinted also that more shame would follow the thræl who found the ring, a less than happy thought in a place where happy thoughts belonged to another world.

"I do not know, Sir," I finally responded to Mr. Gerhardt's earlier question. "Yet it might be well to explore the stair we passed moments ago."

Mr. Gerhardt simply shrugged so we withdrew to the stairway. I heard Erskine draw a deep breath and let it out in a long sigh.

After ascending twenty steps we entered a narrow hallway off which a widening of the passage faced against a wall of roughly cut stone. Three bronze tubes thrust out from the wall. At about a man's height, the ends of two looked much like the blowing pipe for a trumpet. Part of the third lay broken on the floor. Having scanned the chamber and the faces of my companions, I leaned toward one, put my mouth against it and blew. Muffled by the stone wall and distorted by the resonating qualities of the well shaft and the tunnels, the sound reached us like the wail of lost souls. In the same instant the torch died. The embers glowed briefly, then guttered out, leaving us in intense darkness. Terrifying in its volume, the trumpet call, deep and mournful as if it had traveled so long and far that all lighter notes had failed, could well have come from the halls of the dead. The other complete trumpet, which I felt for in the darkness, sounded a different note, yet mournful as the first.

I heard a groan of terror, the rustle of clothing followed by a thump as Erskine dropped to his knees beside me. His voice, crying something about Woden, carried the sound of a face pressed into the stone floor.

"Here, Erskine, is the trumpet from Woden's hall." I found myself panting, almost gasping. "It is sounded by human breath, not by the dead. Light another torch. That one burned longer then I would have dared hope."

Scrambling sounds in the darkness in a chamber that amplifies and echoes cannot be adequately described. The brightness of a spark from flint and steel showed Erskine kneeling, sword on the floor, torch lying before him.

"Has a more fearful sound ever struck upon your hearing?" I stared at Erskine and Mr. Gerhardt as the new torch gave light.

"Aye," Mr. Gerhardt acknowledged. "Three people breathing by turns could make a sound as dreadful as living ears could bear, louder no doubt, when heard from around the opening of the well above us. Not knowing its source, they would ascribe it to Woden."

"And the priests would hold them captive to terror," I added.

"Sounding in the darkness," Erskine's voice trembled, "I was sure we had breathed our last."

Turning back from the widening in the tunnel, another stair led us higher. Here we found a network of chambers leading off a narrow passageway. Three chambers all housed the ruins of some strange piece of machinery. "It is a bellows," Erskine finally declared. "Like that of a blacksmith or armourer, it forces air 'neath the stone wall."

A stair beside the remains of the bellows led to doors of iron still hanging on rusted hinges. The first we opened collapsed with a clang and a cloud of dust.

"It has not been recent they were last opened," Mr. Gerhardt observed unnecessarily. Ashes lined the pit and a chimney of sorts angled upwards and into the well shaft.

We explored farther back from the well. Blocks of peat filled one large room. Large lumps of coal filled another room, while wine casks, cracked and long since empty, jars of baked clay, scrolls, ink jars and quills filled yet another, with recesses cut into the wall that looked like sleeping platforms.

Stone benches with shackles identified quarters for slaves, perhaps sacrificial victims. A body lay on one of the benches, little more than a skeleton, shackles still fastened at the ankles, face drawn into a leer.

Erskine spat and made the sign against the evil eye. Mr. Gerhardt cursed. I stared, both fascinated and repulsed. I had seen death twice through the winter, but something of this struck me different and immensely more horrible.

Checking the second fire-pit, we found bodies half consumed by the flames. The back of each skull had been bludgeoned. Lumps of half burned coal littered the floor. No one, apparently, had remained to pump the bellows. Dry and shriveled, skin still clung to bony frames, and bits of clothing still draped them. The third fire-pit showed only ashes.

"What would the watchers above see, with three fires burning hot, while the trumpets sounded their dreadful call?" Erskine asked.

"They would see a god of dreadful power. They would know nothing of the deception happening beneath their feet, that the god is only a mockery devised by the priests," I responded.

"Mock not, Thræl," Mr. Gerhardt's voice struck me with cold anger more than a bit tinged with fear. "How came you to be an expert on the gods? Here of all places, do not take Woden's name lightly."

"Then whip me or slay me, Sir," I responded, my own anger and the stubbornness that is the curse of my nature rising. "I will not bow to Woden, nor acknowledge as 'god' one who by trickery and deception holds his worshipers in bondage. Were he a real god, he would not need to kindle fires and pump bellows to make them burn. He would not need trumpets blown by human breath to sound his wrath."

I stared at the naked blade that pointed at my chest. "He would not need your hand to execute his judgment on a thræl. He would scorn your sacrifice, though he craves the spilling of blood, for you also were never a believer before today. You will doubt what you have seen so soon as natural daylight surrounds you again." I drew a long breath. "You stand dangerously close to the one who has earned his wrath, if real god he be. The blood of one thræl will not slake his thirst, who has received no sacrifices for generations past."

I struck the flat of the sword away, then strode past like I was lord and he was thræl. I heard the sound of his breath drawn through his teeth, then the sword sliding back into its scabbard. My feet began to feel their way down the steps in the darkness.

I counted the steps and soon reached the level of the trumpets, then felt along the wall until the next stairway led me deeper. I groped in the darkness towards the well, the faint light that penetrated from above aiding me. Where the door lay in the water flow, I stepped more carefully, moving to the brink of the shaft that descended below me.

My eyes had adjusted to the darkness now. I heard voices, but distorted and unintelligible. My companions had not joined me.

The hole so far above gave insufficient light to determine details. I slipped the rope off my shoulders, then searched for a place where I might tie an end. Iron rings and sockets that might once have held torches were fixed to the walls at intervals, but most showed rust beyond trusting their strength. The door itself however, underwater for all these years, seemed surprisingly sound. The portion that broke up the water flow had rotted away. However the bulk of the door, undisturbed beneath the cold stream, offered a solid anchor. I slipped an end of the rope through the hole the latch must have once filled, my hands aching in the cold of the water before I had made it secure. I began then to slowly and carefully lower the grappling hook.

With a length of 100 paces, the rope had proved a heavy burden to carry. Several loops still lay on the floor of the chamber when the feel of it changed, not sharply, but with the mushy feel of sediment.

Working it up and down a bit at a time, it seemed it scraped against something. I continued to kneel on the edge of the basin, eyes closed, bringing all my senses to the task of understanding what I felt, transmitted up the rope.

A sudden firm tug told me the hook had gripped something. With a slow, steady pull I kept a constant pressure. Muscles cramped and I fought the urge to jerk. I shifted myself awkwardly, for the ledge offered little room. I allowed rope to slide through my hands as I stood and took the pressure on my shoulder. A few moments more and the slow tugging released, though still with weight on the rope.

I raised the rope with its 'catch' coiling the loops behind me as I did so. A cloudy stain began to overflow the edge of the well, with bits that looked like coloured cloth. The faint light showed a grisly find when I had retrieved the full length of rope, for a portion of a human body hung from the hook. The cold water and mud had preserved it from complete decay.

I lay the body in the stream and lowered the hook again.

The conviction that my companions had abandoned me added to the horror of my surroundings as I raised two additional bodies, more decomposed than the first. Hardly could I force myself to lower the rope again. My numb fingers could feel little as the hook sank into the sediment. The roiled water that spilled out at my feet seemed the foulest stream ever to flow. Yet never had I been more a thræl than now, in bondage to some unseen force.

Woden did not compel me. The stubbornness of my nature would have chosen death rather than answer to Woden, even if here and now he proved himself a true god. Yet I had no name for who or what held me in bondage. I had no conviction that anything good would result, only that the task *must* be completed, though it cost all my strength and courage to do so.

The cold had numbed my fingers, dulled them to the tremors rising up the rope as the hook touched unseen things in the darkness below. Yet I sensed something different, a more solid scraping than decomposing flesh and bone. I heard the sobbing of my own breath as I stood and leaned against the rope.

The flicker of torchlight only vaguely registered. Muttered voices, exclamations, curses and whispered imprecations barely penetrated my consciousness. It seemed I heard the cries of a thousand victims, sacrificed to a god of blood and death, the moan of the trumpets, the roaring of the sacrificial fires. Yet strangely, I felt no surprise when my burden broke the surface and I opened my eyes to dancing orange light, far brighter than any of the past hour.

"What do you fishing among the dead, Thræl?" Erskine's troubled voice questioned me.

"This is what you would have drunk from, Erskine. Would you still take my life for preventing it?"

"You tamper with the dead? You lift them from Woden's very hall?" Mr. Gerhardt demanded.

"I do the task we came to do, Sir." I straightened slowly under my burden, turned and looked at the ghastly scene on the floor between me and Mr. Gerhardt and Erskine.

"Woden did not cut the throat of these, Sir. Priests—who held the people in bondage to fear spilled the blood and cast the bodies into the depths. I have yet to find evidence that Woden was ever here. I see only the results of those who used his name to hold people in a thrældom deeper than I have ever known."

I turned back to the object I had raised to the surface, too heavy for me to lift beyond the buoyancy of the water. My whole body trembled with something more than just exhaustion. "Help me then with this bucket. Perhaps we may bring our quest to an end."

Tipped at an angle and spilling mud from its brim, an ancient wooden water bucket hung from the grappling hook. Mr. Gerhardt cursed as he stepped past the bodies. Erskine seemed frozen in place. "Aye, Erskine. Wiser men than you would not walk past these grim remains, though brave they might be. Hold then the torch high and I will bend my back with this thræl, the sooner that we may leave this place."

Erskine also held his sword, the naked blade gleaming in the torchlight.

We tipped the bucket, spilling most of the mud and blocks of coal, then drew the bucket up and swung it clear of the well.

The water cut into the mud, trailing a roiled stream along the passageway. I knelt, almost in the midst of the bodies now, turned the bucket into the stream and scooping water with my hands, flushed more of the mud and sediment clear. Three rings that had withstood rust and corrosion still held the ropes that had once lowered and raised it. The ropes themselves held a stiff, ridged posture and felt more like rock than fiber.

A dull yellowish white gleamed through the mud and I lifted an object. A carved knife, pitted by years of decay, it showed skilled workmanship. The handle made the shape of a wild boar, uncomfortable to the hand. The blade held sufficient edge to still draw blood.

"Gungnir's blade it be," Erskine breathed. "The carved boar tusk by which sacrificial victims were bled, so named after Woden's spear."

"Gungnir's?" Mr. Gerhardt questioned. "Why say you that?"

"The stories from the taverns, Sir," Erskine responded. "The blade was usually longer in the tales than the tusk of the greatest boar that ever lived, but the description fits."

For long moments Mr. Gerhardt turned the blade over and over in his hands, staring at it with a kind of fearful fascination. "You are slow, Thræl, while bodies rot around us and the ring lies undiscovered," he finally said. He dropped the knife and stared at his hands as if he expected to find them stained with the blood shed by that very blade. He shouldered me aside and tipped the bucket further, exposing its bottom. Once again nothing of significance showed.

His lips curled back in a snarl. "You make a mockery of me, Thræl." His riding whip came forward, cutting across my face and chest. "Mock Woden if you will, but mock me at your peril."

Blood dripped from my face and mingled with the foul water at my feet, before flowing away down the passage. "I have in no way mocked you, Sir. But you mock the prophecies even while you fulfill them." I fought to control my breathing, to resist the impulse to draw my sword and end the arrogance of this one who *owned* me. Erskine held his sword, watching me, waiting.

"A word of warning, Sir." I fought to keep my voice low, to let the tension dissipate.

"What is it, Thræl?" Mr. Gerhardt's harsh voice demanded.

"I know not what power prophesy holds, but the scroll says a thræl *only*, must first lift the ring from its hiding place, lest he die."

"So you would put yourself ahead of me?" He drew his sword and stared at me in the light of the flickering torch. "Come, Thræl. We will see who dies."

I glanced from the sword to the face of the man who held it, then turned to where Erskine watched silently. I had the skill to take it from my owner's hand, strong and utterly fearless though he was. But lifting my hand against him would earn me the sentence of death. Erskine would take his side as he must. Against the two of them I stood small chance, though the narrowness of the chamber would limit them also.

"Well?" Mr. Gerhardt held his sword before him and faced me. I stood with my back to the darkness of the well.

"The prophecy speaks of death for any but the nine fingered one with the name of infamy, Sir," I responded, choosing my words with care. "Much that the prophecy speaks has come to pass. I cannot know if I am the thræl spoken of. I know only that if the prophecy speaks truth, death awaits those who wrongly handle the ring."

Mr. Gerhardt snorted and sheathed his sword. "A hanging be your reward for any treachery," he said in a cold voice. "But a flogging first, Thræl, so that you beg for the hanging ere it comes."

Further searching found nothing. With anger barely controlled we responded slowly to Erskine's pleading to quit the chamber before his final torch burned out.

Chapter Nine
ABANDONED

"I WOULD REMOVE THE BODIES to the fire pit above us, Sir, rather than leave them here in the water flow," I urged when it became plain that we would continue our search no longer.

"No more will I hear from you, Thræl. You have failed in the quest, mocked the gods and kept us too long in this place of death. The very smell of death is on you." He snorted his disgust, as a hog snorts at an empty trough. "You carry flint and steel. Carry the bodies up then. Put peat and coal about them and give them a fitting funeral fire. Burn your own clothes as well, for the stain of death be upon them."

Mr. Gerhardt and Erskine drew back as I stooped to lift the first body, shuddering at my grim load.

"A light, Erskine," I requested as I started up the stairs.

"Without light you came down those steps. Without light you can return." Mr. Gerhardt's voice carried a rage beyond anything I had known in him before.

I think I knew, even before I had felt my way to the top of the second stair, that they would be gone before I descended. Ever so faintly, light penetrated the fire-pit. I lowered the first body and gathered the other remains close together. Feeling my way in the darkness, I found the storage room with coal. Carrying two blocks I walked back toward the dark fire pit.

My fears were confirmed when I descended to the lower level again. Not even a distant flicker of the torch showed, nor could I hear sound of my companions. Something close to a sob escaped me. Still, the task before me gave some focus that held panic off for a while longer.

In the dim light at the bottom of the well shaft I found that they had taken the bucket. A heavy load, it would slow them down. With a faint hope rising within me once again, I hurried with the second, and then the third body, both surprisingly heavy. It is beyond speaking to describe stripping my sark and scooping the pieces into its folds, for these bodies would not hold together.

The storm sounds came louder, distorted by the well shaft. A tremor passed through the very rock, followed by a strange pulse of air and a muffled boom.

The intense dryness in the fire chamber allowed me to ignite the peat quickly, although the coal took longer to catch. I carried more coal and raked the fire closer around the bodies. The smoke choked me and showed little inclination to pass up the well and out. With no bellows feeding air from below, the fire burned but poorly.

In the weak fire-glow I stared down at my own clothes. No reluctance did I feel at leaving the sark behind, still wrapped about corrupt human remains.

Strange things happen to one who has been a thræl for any length of time. Orders, even orders given in unthinking, heated anger, carry with them a sense of absolute requirement. I had little skill in cursing, but fixed that little on the name of Mr. Gerhardt. My trousers and even my boots went into the fire. I hesitated with my undergarments, but the orders had offered no exceptions. Naked, I stood there, hatred sour in my gut.

The ashes and grit stung my bare feet. The cold air seemed instantly more intense, the fire offering only a mockery of heat. I shuffled back to the storage rooms, glad for the darkness.

A bit of peat ignited under the spark from my iron and flint. I took a couple of peat blocks back to the priest's quarters. They made a poor light, but sufficient for me to search for anything I might cover myself with. I found nothing useful for clothing.

With no clothing, no purse or even a sheath for a sword, the need to feel my way in the darkness meant I could carry almost nothing. At the bottom of the stairway I retrieved the rowan staff I had seldom put down since first cutting. I abandoned the sword to carry the staff, calling myself a fool for doing so.

The corruption of cruel death stained this water, while the cold against my nakedness bid to take my life too.

Minutes or hours became impossible to distinguish. My feet grew numb as I groped blindly down-stream, stumbling at each small lip the water tumbled over, feeling constantly for the opening of the side passage. When I finally reached it a dank, churned-mud smell came from air without a breath of movement. I knew before taking a half dozen paces into its dark length that they had closed the outer end.

Again I cursed Mr. Gerhardt with passion.

My naked body knew the direction of air flow when I returned to the main passage. It gave some small hope of another entrance. The chill deepened. I found myself hardly shivering anymore. I fought the urge to sit and rest, even here, where cold water covered the floor.

When the rowan staff clunked against the wall, then splashed into the water beside me, I roused from a half sleep. Whether I had continued to walk or had stood here for hours I could not know. My hands held nothing, the flint and steel lost.

Kneeling in the water, feeling the cold bite even deeper, I felt for the staff and picked it up again. The passage seemed to end here, while a stair reached up before me.

For long moments I stood. I would have prayed to the unknown god, but did not know how. I would have cursed Woden and Mr. Gerhardt, but had no strength for either task. Feeling before me with the staff, I began to ascend the stairs. It took me up a short distance, then I again walked a level path for a few paces before coming on a stair that led both up and down.

In long slow spirals, the stair took me upward. I lost count at about eighty steps, nor did I know how much the stream had descended, so could make no guess how high I must go to the Keep itself. My foggy brain had decided that must be my destination and again I moved with some bit of hope, not just the stubbornness to put off dying for another hour.

Hunger plagued me and my feet felt heavy and slow when I heard the grunting of pigs. A rowan staff is no weapon to face a wild boar with, or a sow with young. Well able to kill a horse by raking its belly with their tusks, either one would be more than a match for a naked youth. Yet here was both food and clothing.

The remains of a door hung drunkenly from a rubble-strewn opening. Starlight, painful in its brilliance after long hours in absolute darkness, showed a small herd of pigs close to the doorway. A young boar already showing battle scars sniffed the air suspiciously as it roused and approached the doorway. I cursed myself for trading the sword for the staff.

Measuring my swing through the narrow opening, I brought the staff down with all my strength. An uproar ripped through the small herd as squealing their rage, pigs charged in all directions, tusks gleaming, ripping even at each other. The herd disappeared in seconds, while the one I had stunned struggled to regain its feet.

I leaped through the doorway, struck it again, then deliberately aimed for one of the tusks, breaking it off. The broken piece proved too short for a good weapon, but a quick, hard stab with it opened the throat of the animal.

Eleven stone of young wild boar sporting a bad headache and feeling its lifeblood draining—against a naked youth armed with only a staff, makes for a dance the gods would laugh at. I suspect I survived only because of the shortness of the conflict. I had thrust true with the creature's own tusk. The bleeding took its strength within moments. A long and dreadful squeal died into a strangled gasp as it made a last attempt to slash me, then fell.

I dragged the animal onto clean grass where I gutted it. With the tusk as my only knife, and possessing little skill, the eastern sky had begun to glow before I completed it.

Leaving the carcass, I searched among a group of storage rooms close to the stairs I had ascended, hoping to find a flint and steel, or perhaps a proper knife. My hopes proved unfounded. However a bit of glass came to hand. I knew little of glass, but had read of its strange ability to make fire from sunlight. I had found peat blocks, dry and old.

Some ten minutes after the sun had lifted above the eastern wall of the Keep, I nursed a tiny flame to life. I added peat until a good bed of coals glowed in the morning sunlight, then hacked a piece of flesh off the muscular shoulder and set it into the coals. As the meat began to sizzle, I set myself the task of skinning the boar. My lack of skill showed clearly, but an hour later I had succeeded in removing the hide.

My hunger pressed, and I rooted the meat out of the coals. I burned my hands and mouth as I tried to gnaw a piece off. It tore away, but still showed raw in the middle. I chewed the tough flesh, but put the remainder back into the fire.

A raven circled above me, soon joined by a second as I began to scrape the fat from the hide. The sun indicated mid-morning before I lifted the heavy hide with its stiff, bristly hair and wrapped myself with it. The hair stuck against me like so many needles, so I let the hide fall from me.

I added more peat blocks to the fire, then dragged the hide to the small burn that passed under the wall not far from where I stood. Bathing myself first in the chill stream, I then dragged the skin into the water.

Nakedness has a way of forcing questions. *Who am I? Is Theodoric even my name? Would Dierdre mock if I paid suit to her?* I stared down at myself and felt bitter laughter rise within me. *All I need now is some woad,* I thought. *As a Pict warrior I should suit her well.*

I stomped back to the fire, dug the piece of meat out of the coals and allowed it to cool. Scraping away the charred portion, I found the flesh tough and dry. I tore pieces away with my teeth and gulped them like a starving man, then sank back against a mound in the grass to rest.

Warm sun upon me and food in my belly after a long and exhausting night lulled me. The croak of a raven sounded from some far distance. Then all became still. *Dierdre walked beside a burn, carrying Ilsa. I called to her, but she did not hear. I ran then, my feet bare against the stone, hurting, bleeding. I called again and she stopped and turned. Her face showed astonishment, then contempt. Her mouth opened, but the sound of grunting, squealing pigs reached me.*

I woke, confused. My hand reached for my sword, finding the rowan staff instead. The herd of pigs sniffed at the butchered animal. Two ravens sat on the carcass itself, tearing at the flesh with their strong beaks. When I sat up the ravens heaved themselves into the air and swept away westward on strong wing-beats. The pigs tore eastward in a squealing mass.

I glanced at my naked body, astonished, embarrassed and humiliated all at once, then covered myself with my hands. I half stood, crouching, wanting to hide, then spat and forced myself to stand like a man.

I spent the rest of the afternoon scraping the hide, taking most of the stiff hairs off it. Before nightfall I had wrapped myself with the skin, clammy and cold.

I cut another large hunk of meat and set it into the coals, ate a big meal from the piece that had cooked through the day, then set myself to explore more of the Keep before nightfall. No longer naked, I did not feel so vulnerable, though my blistered feet found the way hard and the wet hide clung heavy and slick.

Near the gatehouse an old door gave way into a room with the roof fallen in. There among the clutter I found swords and spears. Most had rusted beyond use, but a few, protected from the years of weather, still offered comfort to a hand that longed for a real weapon. Knucklebones and crude dice I also found, deeply pitted from the years. Better armed, but still barefoot, I returned to my fire.

The pigskin stunk when I woke well before morning. I again scrubbed and scraped it, and bathed myself as well. It seemed I could not take the stink from me.

Wrapping the clammy hide about myself once again, I dug my piece of meat from the ashes and strapped on the sword I had found. I had made myself a purse of sorts from a piece of the pigskin. In it I carried the bit of glass I had used to light the fire, some dry peat, and as big a piece of meat as would fit. Gripping my rowan staff, I passed through the gateway of the Keep at sunrise.

I covered little distance before my tortured feet forced me to stop. I finished the meat, though I would have been wiser to have rationed it.

I had no knowledge of making shoes, but managed to wrap my feet with pieces of the pigskin and tie it in place with rawhide thongs. Still, I had done such damage that I walked with difficulty.

I brought a squirrel down with a sling-stone once, and later scooped a small fish out of a shallow pool. But the weather had clouded up again. My bit of glass could ignite no fire. I ate the rank flesh raw, choking and gagging, but forced myself to hold it down. I ate the bitter berries dry and shriveled from beneath a rowan tree, and a few fruits still clinging to a hawthorn. My belly cramped, my head pounded and a fever began to plague me.

I thought I heard the nicker of a horse once, and feared the closeness of the watcher. I worked to refine the crude sling I had fashioned and practiced by the hour when my injured feet forced me to stop. I had never fully mastered the needed skill, but necessity is a demanding teacher. Without fire the incentive for fresh meat pulls weakly, yet hunger is a powerful force of its own, and the need of a weapon almost as demanding.

Three times more I scrubbed and scraped the pigskin till little odour remained. More soft and pliable it became each time. I scrubbed myself each time as well, for the pig smell clung from the skin.

I slashed the "T" brand off my shoulder with the pig tusk, sickened by the pain, yet surprised that it was not greater.

Five days after leaving the Keep, I approached the gate to Mr. Gerhardt's inner holdings. A movement caught my attention. The watcher sat his horse in a small clearing and raised a hand in salute. I stared long at the unknown man, till he turned his horse and disappeared among the trees. Puzzled, I turned to face the gate-keeper. He rubbed his right arm and muttered curses, never raising his gaze to look about him.

"Æthëlrd! You stand watch? Is Mr. Gerhardt so desperate then?"

Æthëlrd's head jerked up and he stared about him. "Name yourself, stranger." His voice rumbled when he saw me. "You bring to mind someone who earns nothing but a flogging and the dark hole from this house, though you dress as a savage."

"You know me well enough, Æthëlrd. But take your pick of

names, the Nine Fingered One, Horse Killer, Theodoric." I lifted the rowan staff. "Let me pass, for I am still Mr. Gerhardt's thræl, though he would sooner meet Woden himself now."

"Pass then to the flogging that waits you." He flexed his right arm, grimacing, then grinned at me. "I'll be glad to do my part." He opened the heavy oak door. The inner doors stood open.

Bertrm stared in astonishment when he returned from some task and found me washing in the stable. In the pigskin I must have looked a true savage. I straightened and faced him, leaving the spear lay, but picked up the rowan staff.

"I never thought to see you alive again," he whispered. "Erskine won't say what happened, 'cept that lightning hit the tree. Even the master thought t'was Woden, and gave you up for dead."

"So they didn't close the tunnel?" I asked.

"They wasn't waiting to see. Erhard says they was scared stupid." Bertrm answered. He reached a hand toward the bloody scab on my right shoulder. "The brand?" he questioned.

"Is no more," I answered simply.

"What of the bucket?" I questioned. "Did they return with it?"

"I cared for the horses. I know nothing more, 'cept that our owner has since been savage and cruel as I ever seen him."

"I would speak to Erhard before the evening meal."

"You can't think of going to board dressed like that?" Bertrm protested.

"I am dressed as I am because I obeyed the last orders I received, yet was left to die." I bent and picked up the spear. "Mr. Gerhardt should be told that his orders have been carried out." I opened the stable door and stepped outside.

On a warm mid-afternoon most workers laboured in the fields. I saw no one as I walked to Erhard's cottage and rapped on the door.

"The god's be praised. I had not quite given up hope, but with every day that passed . . ." His voice fell silent as he pulled me into the small house. "Thunder 'n damnation! What treachery did they play? And how come you dressed so, and looking like you have not eaten for a month?"

When Erhard's gaze fixed on the scar on my face where Mr. Gerhardt's whip had cut me, I reached up and touched it. "It ages you," he said. "As does the beard. You have grown much in these days."

"A scraggly thing, no doubt." I responded.

He drew down a wooden box of ointment and lifted the lid off it. A sharp odour penetrated his small cottage. "For your shoulder," he said simply. "Few I know with courage to remove a brand."

Dipping my fingers in the ointment, I rubbed it onto the raw wound on my left shoulder, sucking my breath at the pain. We talked more, yet said little of significance until I asked of the bucket.

"The bucket?" Erhard questioned.

"The water bucket from the well. They carried it with them when they left me."

"It got a right hard tumble when lightning hit the tree. Broke the handle off it. They was scared spitless, but still went back for it. It had rolled down beside the burn." Erhard snorted. "For all of a hour, Master believed in Woden, was sure he'd sent the lightning. We were on our way then, and it was worth my life to try to go back, see if you was still alive. Master threatened to cut out my tongue when I argued."

He stared at me a moment longer, then turned and pulled a cup from the shelf. "Here, sit yourself. Ale?"

"No ale. I would speak with no courage not my own this day." I drew a slow breath. "What of the bucket?" I asked again.

"Master threw it on the fire, but the waterlogged wood refused to burn. When he found no ring he cursed it and you. We dragged it home and he searched it again, but there be nothing there. He threw it behind the stable, vowing to burn it when it be dry enough."

"It is near a sen'night since we raised it. The wood will be starting to dry and shrink. Show me," I requested.

Erhard shrugged and we stepped out of his cottage, entering the smallest of the three animal pens between it and the stable. A rubbish heap had grown almost too high to remain hidden from the house. Kitchen scraps lay on top of the ancient bucket, but I pulled it free of the pile.

Cracks had opened between the upright staves. The bottom seemed still to hold its form more tightly, but one piece lifted slightly two-thirds of the way across.

I had used the boar's tusk for so many days that I thought nothing of pulling it from the crude purse that hung from my waist and prying the piece up. It came with difficulty.

Water sat in the bottom of the small cavity exposed. I leaned back and motioned for Erhard to look. He said nothing for a long moment, but backed away from the bucket, looking fearfully at his hands where he had touched it. "Thunder 'n damnation!" I heard him whisper.

I leaned forward again and rested my left hand across the cavity that sheltered the ring. I stared at the stump of a finger. Length enough remained to wear a ring on that finger, and for such a ring I had searched. This, though, would fit my arm.

"The time had to come when I must risk all to know if I am the thræl spoken of in the prophecies. Is it the fever, Erhard? Am I thinking clearly?"

Erhard chose not to speak and the silence stretched long.

"Woden I will not serve," I whispered. "If this be his talisman, not to his honour will I wear it." My fingers reached for the gold band, yet still I hesitated.

I leaned back, sighing heavily, then stood and reached up to the limbs of a young oak tree that overhung the fence. I broke a small branch with a fork near the end. Using the boar tusk once again, I trimmed young leaves and new spring growth away, leaving me with a piece of wood that separated into two branches clear of the handhold.

Using the boar tusk, I carefully raised the ring from its place, lifting one edge sufficiently to slip the end of my branch through the circle. Careful not to touch it, I raised it from the ancient water bucket, then gazed in silent wonder. Inlaid in gold, the carving of a boar showed in some yellowed white stuff. Four tusks of gold thrust out from the corners of the carving. I held the branch bearing the ring in my left hand and brought the boar tusk I had used for so many tasks up beside it. The carving seemed to be of the same material.

Leaning over the bucket again, I pressed the wood into place to cover the cavity, then stood. I returned the boar tusk to the purse, then gently lay the branch holding the ring onto the ground. Turning to Erhard I asked in a voice that trembled slightly, "Where lead the prophecies now?" He gave no answer other than shaking his head.

I lifted the bucket, astonished at its weight. "It gives no magic strength, anyway," I gasped the words as I carried it a few steps back to the ancient fortress wall. I left it lying against the wall.

I picked up my rowan staff and for a long moment gazed at the two slight bulges above the handgrip on it. "Hmm," I grunted, then lifted the branch bearing the ring. "I would read the prophecies again, Erhard. How can a thræl carry such a device?" In the cottage we looked again at the old prophecy. The more recent works I knew from memory.

Feared the nine fingers that wield weapons of war yet give no quarter when weapons be broken all. Restored will be the ring. Renewed will be the kingdom.

Of old has it been told. By the ancients has it been prophesied. Yet will it be said in his day, Of no importance is it. Neither of any consequence.

ᚾᚢᚾ ᚴᛁᚾᚷᚱᛞ ᛣᛁᛚᚱ ᚫᚴ
ᚺᚫᚱᛋᚴ ᛗᛁᛏᚢ ᛁᚾ ᛒᚫᛏᛚ

"The Runes," I said. "I can read them. *Nine fingered killer of horses. Mighty in battle.*" I stared at Erhard. "Why mighty in battle if it speaks of me?" I received no answer, so turned back to the writing.

> *He of the nine fingers. With many stripes his back is crossed. Clouded his memory.*
>
> *Many the blows of his beating. He the accused. Yet of old is the prophecy. The ring by him found shall give proof of his office. He is a warrior born. His destiny from of old is sealed. Yet few will his title recognize or give the honour due him.*
>
> *Trials and much wrong will first ensue. Then will be restored to him the ring who alone may rightfully wear it.*
>
> *Of nine fingers is he. Mighty in battle. Called of old Killer of horses.*
>
> *His son perchance will better fare with seemly honour and the tribute of men. For fierce will be the battle in that day. Many the dead. Loud the weeping. The raven and the vulture feed. Black the smoke of funeral piers.*

"Is it a true translation? Dare I believe it and the words of Riordan the Wise speak of me?"

Chapter Ten
The Ring

"THE EVENING MEAL APPROACHES, Surra," Erhard spoke as if to a lord. "What will you do?"

"I am still his thræl." I stood and stared at Erhard. "I will inform him that his orders have been carried out."

"A great evil has he done you," Erhard said. "A greater evil has he done himself. He has ever felt shame for not going back for you." As he spoke he examined the rowan staff closely, then lifted the branch bearing the ring from where it lay on his table. He fell silent, turning the staff several times, gazing especially at two humps below the handgrip. A faint smile played on his face as he worked the ring from the bottom of the staff with the branch. Taking great care not to touch the ring itself, he maneuvered it between the two bulges till it set firmly in place. Turning the staff, spinning it and even thumping it solidly on the floor, the ring remained fast.

"Better answer than I can give be the very staff you carry, with this ring upon it." Taking a knife from a shelf, he cut a section from the pigskin. He wrapped it around the rowan staff, covering the ring from sight and also from accidental touching, then tied it in place with a rawhide strip.

"You barely knew your own name when you came to this house," Erhard spoke quietly. "You still have few memories of where or how you was educated, or why your hands welcome the grip of a sword. If the prophecies speak falsely, it is not from your misuse of them. It could only be that the prophets themselves was false." He pushed me toward the door. "Go now. Expect no smooth road before you, but already you have proved yourself where many a man with twice your years would have failed."

I drew several deep breaths and headed to the big house. Conversation fell silent as I walked to an empty place at board, close to the salt. The rowan staff thumped loudly as I lay it on the table. The pigskin swayed with my walking. I stood and rested both hands on the table, my fingers spread that any might count and find nine only. My gaze slowly swept the company. A strange joy filled me at sight of Dierdre. I then turned to Mr. Gerhardt. "I have fulfilled your orders, Sir."

"You? How?" Mr. Gerhardt's face showed ashen as he stared at me, then he made a visible effort to reclaim his authority. "You dare come to board dressed so?"

"I dare, Sir, because it is the fulfilling of your orders that has necessitated my dress. Burned are the clothes I wore, with the bodies we found. Naked—by your orders—Sir, I found myself abandoned in the darkness." I lifted the rowan staff from the table. "With this staff I stunned the boar whose skin I wear. With this staff I broke one of his tusks, and with his own tusk I cut his throat. With that tusk I gutted him. With that tusk I skinned him. With that tusk I cut meat and scraped the hide and made clothing for myself and protection for my feet. That is why I am so dressed—Sir."

"You seek a flogging, to speak so to me?"

"Who of your people will flog me, Sir?" I jerked the rawhide thong free around the piece of pigskin on the rowan staff. As the pigskin fell, I raised the staff, exposing the ring. I turned it slowly, that all might see. "I carry the ring, the emblem of the boar. If the prophecies speak true, you, Sir, would be dead had you found it. You abandoned me underground and left me to die. Yet you carried it home—this very ring. You sought to burn it, then threw it behind the stable. The prophecies declare, *of nine fingers is he, called of old, Killer of Horses.* It is not a name I sought. Will anyone therefore challenge my right to bear the ring?"

I sat heavily, suddenly exhausted. "I have been long on the road with few choices in my food. I would have bread and meat. I look on the face of a man who has slept less than I and enjoyed his meat less. Evil exacts its own revenge. I need add nothing to it."

Dierdre set food before me and I fought the impulse to catch her hand and hold it against my face.

I glanced longingly at the saltcellar, but left it untouched. While still a thræl I would not claim that privilege, though I had sat in a place of honour. I ate swiftly, then spoke again into the lengthening silence. "I am still your thræl, Sir, though the very people of your house will recognize the bearer of this emblem as your master—a difficult position for both of us." I raised my gaze and stared long and hard at Mr. Gerhardt.

"My freedom, Sir." I paused a moment, choosing my words with care. "I once was called fool for not purchasing my freedom."

I tore off another piece of meat, then continued. "You, who do not believe in Woden, yet sacrificed me to Woden. You abandoned me among his dead. You, who lusted for the Ring of Thorvæld, carried it home after I lifted it from the depths of the well, yet even then you cursed and abandoned it and sought to burn it. At the well you name after Woden, you cut me with your whip. At the well you name after Woden you left me to die. At the well you name after Woden you ordered me to burn the dead and to burn my own clothes. Naked I came from that well. Naked I fought and killed the boar in Muninn's Keep. Naked I scraped the hide and made clothing for myself. Will you then, Sir, or any here challenge my claim that I have purchased my freedom?"

"Think you that I called the lightning forth?" Mr. Gerhardt's voice rose to an angry growl. "You defied Woden," he spat the words. "We paid for your folly."

"Then you did not close the tunnel?" I questioned.

"I would not stoop so low, even for a thræl such as you." Mr. Gerhardt stared at me coldly. "My sword, or the gallows would better serve."

For a long moment I remained silent, applying myself to the venison before me, then spoke again. "I have misjudged you then, Sir. I have thought ill of you these last days." I stared about me, then blurted, "I will take for a name Theodoric Thorvæld, unless someone can prove another name is mine."

Mr. Gerhardt started violently at my choice of names, though I knew of no reason why.

"Though I could press claim for much more," I continued, "I will ask title to Muninn's Keep, the Ring of Stones with the Well, and all the lands for one league west and south of those two places, and north to the old boundary in the valley where the ancient oak tree stands. The ring, if I understand my reading aright, belongs to the rightful heir of all these lands, including this farm on which I am thræl. I will not so far press my claim." I paused a moment and then continued. "I will ask though, for three horses: the filly, Lorellefue, Lena, the old mare of the blood of Radburn, and Ogden, the young stallion of the blood of Rolf, with saddles and tack for each. If they will go with me, I ask the company of Erhard, Bertrm, and Dierdre, with her bairn. They must first be given papers of freedom, for I will not be the owner of thræls. Some will dispute my title and I would have them free whatever the outcome."

"Fool you are, Thræl," Mr. Gerhardt scoffed. "The wench? You declare your own shame neath that stinking pig skin. Tis an admission the whelp be yours."

"Were I a man grown and she willing, I would own the bairn as my own and take Dierdre to wife. But even I can count. The six months I have been thræl in this house were long months to have accomplished such a feat."

"Fool still," Mr. Gerhardt continued to mock. "You know nothing of the name you claim for your own. It be a name too rich for a penniless fool. The ring you have stolen. Why should I hear your claim when I can order you whipped and thrown in the dark lockup?"

"Who of your people would carry out such an order against the emblem I bear with the added evidence of nine fingers and the name of *Horse Killer*? Offer your finger to the knife, Sir, your back to the whip, and slay the horses in your stable. Some might then support your claim. Is it worth so much to you?"

Mr. Gerhardt paced the floor, his boots punctuating his anger.

"I gain nothing and lose much," I said to Mr. Gerhardt, "if I leave you penniless. You know better than I how to manage the farm. I would begin to build my own holdings at Muninn's Keep." Again I cast my glance around the room.

"An army grows to the north. A wall stands to our south. Little aid will the south give. I had rather stand beside you facing the enemy than treat you as the enemy also. As Muninn's Keep begins to grow, the trade will cross your holdings. That trade will increase your wealth before many years have passed, though that wealth may not be sufficient to face the army who will surely come."

"You know not of what you speak, Thræl," Mr. Gerhardt's bitter voice interrupted. "Tis more like to leave me a beggar." He spat on the floor.

"Erhard can draw up the documents," I said after a brief silence. "I will remove myself. I would have an answer by tomorrow noon." I covered the ring again with the small piece of pigskin and tied it in place. I walked close beside Dierdre to make my exit and it seemed her eyes brimmed with tears.

I camped outside the inner holdings of Mr. Gerhardt's farm, for while still a thræl in name for a few hours more, I no longer saw myself as thræl or guest to the owner or his people.

I killed a rabbit with a sling-stone. I had availed myself of flint and steel, so quickly kindled a fire and cooked this meat, though night had fallen before it could be eaten.

I did not present myself in the house until after the noon meal.

Erhard had drawn up the documents and Mr. Gerhardt had signed them. They needed only my name to make them binding. I quickly finished the task, adding Thorvæld to my name. Strangely, my hand formed the word without hesitation.

Bertrm, Erhard and Dierdre, holding Ilsa, her young daughter, stood uncertainly before me. "You are free," I said to them. "No law binds you to me. It will be long before I can pay wages. I too was thræl until just moments ago. And though I now own lands and horses, I have less money than a common beggar. The fields have not been worked for generations. No crops have been planted. No house stands on my holdings. A long and weary season lies ahead with a long and hungry winter to follow." I grinned now. "I carry the emblem of the boar, but it will not fill your belly or my own. Will you join me?"

"Not for the others will I speak, Sir," Bertrm responded, stumbling a bit at the unaccustomed 'sir'. "But I would follow willingly as thræl. Newly freed, I am more in your debt than I could be as thræl. I will follow, for so long as this twisted body can put one foot afore another."

"And I also," Erhard added.

Dierdre, holding her daughter at her hip, stared at the floor. "Hard words are my usual fare, Sir. I have nothing here and hope for nothing." She raised her gaze for a second, then blushed crimson and stared again at the floor. "The gold coins you gave were a kindness beyond imagining. I never thought to be free, or treated as having worth. If you will have me and my bairn in your household, we will go with gladness."

Turning away from me, she drew a small pouch from her bodice and offered four gold coins. "You will need to buy seed," she said timidly. "And tis your own earnings in any case."

I held the offered coins, warmed by her body, then turned to Erhard. "Please make a record that I owe two gold pieces to Dierdre, with the hundredth part added. It will be used to purchase seed, though the season be late for planting."

Turning back to Dierdre, I handed back the two remaining coins. "Thank you Dierdre. You do me honour. I will not take more for we risk much to make a beginning."

"A risk that will not fail, Sir," Bertrm spoke firmly. "Though a twisted stable hand, an elderly teacher and a young wench with babe at breast are unlikely stones on which to build a house."

"Aye, Bertrm. Unlikely it is, led by a penniless youth of questionable reputation." I mused quietly for a moment.

"Erhard, please to make the necessary purchases." I handed him both gold pieces. "I would have wheat, barley and oats—as much of each as the money can be made to purchase, and a milking goat with kids. Also obtain half a dozen squabs, that we might begin our own pigeon cote so soon as possible. Spittin' Sheffield dislikes the grey with yellow bars on its wings. It has two fledglings almost ready to fly. Take those and what others he will give. Bertrm, prepare the horses. Saddle each, but packs will be the burden two will carry. Bring you each one any personal belongings you possess, what provisions you can rightfully carry and what weapons are yours. Two damaged skeps lie in the rubbish heap. It will soon be the season of bees swarming. Bring them and we will hope for honey in years to come. Will an hour be sufficient?"

An unlikely company, we took leave with three of us on foot, Erhard riding for the moment and leading two heavily laden horses. I carried the bairn, while clutching the rowan staff in my left hand. The horses carried large sacks of provisions. A milking goat on a short lead followed the horses, while two kids gamboled free beside her.

The weight of the bairn seemed nothing at first, but she soon proved a heavy burden who squirmed and wiggled in my arms. I gazed often at the small round face that looked up at me, the big dark eyes and tight black curls. Ilsa, Dierdre had named her, *Nobel.* Not given to poetic impulses, the beauty in her face struck me. I had reason to marvel at Dierdre's strength before we finished the day, for she bore the child much of the time.

We made slow progress, but the summer evening lingered long and we pushed on till we reached an old campsite. We built a fire and prepared a meager meal. We ate eagerly, having earned sharp appetites by our hours on the road. A hunk of hard cheese for each of us, and water drawn from the small burn we rested beside completed our meal.

Ilsa, not yet crawling, squirmed happily on the blanket Dierdre spread on the ground, delighting in her freedom.

The meat of two squirrels cooked on our small fire. Our campsite overlooked a steep gully down which the burn raced and tumbled. Leaving Erhard on watch, I picked my way down a treacherous pathway and found a sheltered cove at the bottom. Rushing now, for little daylight remained, I returned to the camp above and hurried everyone down the path, leading the horses and taking all provisions with them. Again I carried Ilsa, whose tiny hands patted my face and clutched at my beard. Her small weight and grasping fingers brought a thrill to me almost painful in its depths.

Returning again to the original campsite, I built up the fire and scraped moss and small branches together to create three mounds near it. In the fading light it looked like sleeping forms. I had barely completed the task when the nicker of one of our horses sounded. I slipped away from the fire and watched.

The moon gave little light through the cloud cover, but I positioned myself where the fire itself did not trouble my vision. My eyes quickly adjusted to the night conditions.

Three riders approached at a slow walk, then dismounted. Leaving one to guard the horses, two began to creep toward the fire.

Moving furtively in the darkness, I approached the keeper of the horses. He muttered and cursed while one of the horses moved restively. I recognized the voice of Æthëlrd and felt no remorse as I fit a stone to my sling.

The darkness hampered my aim and the first stone missed completely. He fell without a word when the second struck him in the side of the head. I murmured to the horses as I approached. They quieted at my voice, for they knew me.

I removed each saddle. I took the bow from Mr. Gerhardt's saddle and slung it over my shoulder, removed the horse's bridles, then gave each a soft slap on the rump and sent them toward home. Using a strap cut from one of the saddles, I bound Æthëlrd. I stuffed a rag in his mouth and left him lying on the ground, still senseless.

Finding no other weapons, hampered by the darkness in my search, I pulled his boots off, then moved in a circle around the fire.

I saw Erskine step into the fire-glow, his naked sword gleaming faintly. Mr. Gerhardt approached a step behind. A sling stone took Mr. Gerhardt in the forehead, dropping him. Erskine stepped back into the shadows and disappeared. However, I counted on his loyalty to Mr. Gerhardt. I had moved into a better position when I saw the shadow of Mr. Gerhardt seem to lengthen. A sling-stone brought a dull thump, a groan and a curse from the shadow. I leaped from my place and stood over Erskine with my sword drawn before he could catch breath. I had hurled a heavier stone this time, deadly if it struck in the head. I had risked much to disable him.

"I have not forgotten that you abandoned me beneath the circle of stones, Erskine." I said to the groaning man before me. "Yet I hold that to Mr. Gerhardt's account. You are a better man than he deserves it would seem. I hope I did you no permanent hurt." I tied him where he lay, took his sword, his longbow and sheaf of arrows, then turned to Mr. Gerhardt.

His sword I took and thrust into the fire. I would not carry it away with me, for the sword of the leader of a house is seen by many as a powerful talisman. I would not however, leave it unblemished by this night's work. I stripped him of all other weapons, then took his and Erskine's boots and threw them in the fire along with Æthëlrd's. Leaving the three of them barefoot, stripped of weapons and without horses, I took the squirrel meat and slipped away before Mr. Gerhardt had fully regained consciousness.

From the shadows I spoke to Erskine, whose gasping breath made me fear I had injured him more than intended. "Inform your master when he is able to hear, that next time he enters my camp with drawn sword, I will consider his horses and men as fair booty for war, and his own life also. If he makes himself my enemy I will treat him as he has chosen to be treated."

"Bah, Thræl! Be that your voice I hear? The documents have already been burned." Mr. Gerhardt groaned as he struggled to his feet. "Show yourself like a man, 'stead of skulking in the shadows like the coward you are. Get on your feet, Erskine. We will make an end to this. By the gods, my head hurts. For that you will pay, Thræl."

"You call me coward, Mr. Gerhardt?" I challenged him. "Yet you creep into my camp with sword drawn—you, who abandoned me to die." I fit a small stone to the sling. "Talk not of cowardice till you next look in a glass. Your life is forfeit today, yet do I give it back to you, but not without cost." I slung the stone, striking him in the side of the head. He fell backwards across Erskine and all became silent for a time.

I felt my way down the steep path to the bottom of the gully, found Erhard on watch and Dierdre murmuring to the baby as it nursed. Her gaze searched mine in the faint light. "All is well," I said softly as Erhard approached. "They will go home humbler than they came, but none badly injured." I lay the weapons I had acquired on the ground, then stood. I could not prevent my gaze from lingering longer than necessary on the swelling pale flesh that showed above the baby's mouth.

"Glad I am that you chose to come, Dierdre." I cleared my throat, searching for words. "Glad I am for each of you. I trust that freedom will not prove a bigger hardship than slavery."

"Tis beyond belief, Surra," Erhard responded.

"Aye," Bertram agreed. "Long I have dreamed of this day. Dreamed with small hope."

"And I too," Dierdre joined in. "Born into slavery. Sold to a joyless house. Bringing a bairn into a world without hope."

"Just once, I heard you laugh, Dierdre." I knelt beside the fire and reached for the baby as Dierdre adjusted her clothing. "Laughter has been a rare sound in Mr. Gerhardt's house." I blew into the baby's neck and she giggled. "I trust it will prove more common at Muninn's Keep."

"Aye," Erhard affirmed. "The sound of laughter would be a fine thing."

We shared the meager ration of meat, then I took the first watch.

I pushed our tiny company hard the next day, but no one complained. We crossed the multiple ditches that formed the outer battlements of Muninn's Keep as twilight began to deepen, for I determined to camp within the Keep itself. We were a weary company who lay upon the ground around our fire. I almost persuaded myself that we need keep no watch. I fought to remain alert on my shift, for I had slept but poorly the night before.

A makeshift pigeon cote occupied half a morning to construct, then we turned to the urgent need of planting crops. Where wild pigs had rooted for acorns under oak trees, we found the soil sufficiently prepared that we put grain into the ground. Taking the southern exposure of each tree, we sought the greatest benefit of the sun, though the trees themselves provided much shade.

All of us, even Dierdre when the babe could be laid on a blanket for a time, put our shoulders to the work. The will with which Bertrm and Erhard laboured forced me to doubled effort, just as a matter of pride. Every muscle ached by sundown.

Dierdre placed some bits of coloured cloth, tiny barley cakes with a few drops of honey and two treasured Freya's Tears in the low crook of an oak tree. An Alf-blot, she informed me, an offering to the elves and faerie folk that they might do us no mischief. Never having seen any of the faerie folk myself, I teased her about it, though warmly.

The next morning we herded the wild pigs out of the Keep, killing a couple and feasting well on our third night there. We set ourselves then to building a gate.

Often when my time at the watch came I would catch up little Ilsa and carry her, blowing on her neck till she giggled, or swinging her high till she gasped with delight. I remained vigilant in my watch for all that, but her presence fed some inner hunger for which I had no words. Still she would stretch out eager arms for Dierdre when I brought her back and I felt something akin to jealousy.

Dierdre stirred baffling emotions in me, and ill-defined hungers. I longed for her presence, yet felt a strange discomfort when close to her. I had heard enough talk among the men to not be completely ignorant of the way of a man with a woman. Yet some distinction held a wife apart from much of the talk. Questions had only brought mocking laughter.

I thought often of the deception practiced by the priests of Woden, and wondered if there was not somewhere, a god worthy of honour.

On the first morning of the second sen'night since our departure from Mr. Gerhardt's house, the last watch saw the flicker of fire-glow. The night had been misty, but the temperature had dropped and the air cleared shortly before daybreak, else it would have shown earlier. We doubled our watch through the next hours, though we each attempted to complete our work in the off hours.

At mid-morning Dierdre called me to the wall to see a wagon

stopped at the outer ditch, the driver apparently baffled by the obstacle before him. A horse stood in placid idleness in the harness. Two additional riders sat their horses beside the wagon.

I saddled Lorellefue. With the longbow I had taken from Erskine over the front of the saddle, I rode the slow and torturous trail across the first ditch.

"What do you at the gate of Muninn's Keep?" I called out. "If you come in peace you are welcome, though poorly equipped are we yet to receive guests. If you come with threat you will find us few in number yet resolute in will."

"We come to join your company if you will have us," a man shouted back.

"If you will swear fealty to me and work for your daily bread this twelve-month ahead, you are welcome. Are you free or are you a thræl?"

"Free I am, though two who join me are thræls, disenchanted with their masters."

"Will you swear fealty?"

"Aye, Sir. That I will."

"Come then and welcome with what your horses can carry. The wagon cannot be brought across at this time."

All three I stopped outside the gate. "I would know your names and where your allegiance lies," I said. "I will not be owner of thræls, but to send you back is to ensure a flogging or worse. You will be treated as freedmen while you are here. So soon as I can pay wages, which will probably not be for a twelve-month, you will work first to purchase your own freedom, then may apply your wages as you choose."

"I am a tinker, a tinsmith and merchant," the first man informed me. "I go by the name of Chester Tnsmith. Till last season I wandered the trails and peddled pots and pans, repairing ofttimes. But my knees like the trail little. I owe allegiance to no one, but seek a place where I can grow old in peace."

"South of the wall you should go then, for ere many years pass, peace will be an almost forgotten dream, else I am much mistaken. Welcome, Chester Tnsmith. We will seek to bring your wagon across as soon as can be." I gripped his forearm as one warrior greets another. He had a hard, muscular arm. A broad grin broke across his face.

I addressed the other two men directly now. "To whose household do you belong? What say you of your masters and yourselves?"

"I be a blacksmith and farrier, as skilled as my teacher, which earns me only his hatred and jealously. We belong to the house of Marshall Carroll, a proud, cruel man born to wealth and prestige. My companion is a simple man with a poet's heart. He has not the strength for unending labour and his verses are not of war and heroes, so he earned the lash oft. His name is Harlan and I be Pollard."

"And what seek you here?" I questioned. "I have no gold to buy your freedom."

"Yet your first act as lord was the freedom of your thræls," the 'poet' exclaimed.

"Nay. For I was not yet myself free," I responded. "Their papers were signed ahead of my own. I was thræl myself not two sen'nights ago. Though how that news has traveled beyond Mr. Gerhardt's farm I do not know. Come. Of an evening I would hear your verse, but while daylight lasts what little bread this house affords must be earned by labour. There is that which requires more of the mind than of the strong arm. Wish you still to enter?"

"Aye, Sire. That we do." Pollard answered me again.

"Enter then, and make you first a forge. Old iron with rust beyond salvage can be found. Some little might still be made useful. We have need of many tools. Harlan, can you pump a bellows?"

"Aye, Sir," he replied simply.

"Work then with Pollard, for he brings a skill we are sorely in need of. I know not how we will provide your daily bread, but a way will be found. Welcome, Sirs."

Chapter Eleven
The Brand

I LABOURED LONG, HARD HOURS, preparing more soil for seed, though the season had grown late. I dug beneath rubble to recover iron that had survived the generations and might be made useful by Pollard. At times I would saddle Lorellefue and explore some of the higher reaches of the Keep. I found a narrow entrance into the rock itself. It proved to be a burial sight, a catacomb.

The pigeons had fledged and each day I carried one or two with me to release at some point within the Keep, that their training might begin. They returned directly to their companions in the crude cote we had built.

The next month brought numbers up to nearly a hundred, not all of whom were a credit to my household. Camp followers, women of ill repute, charlatans and gamblers made up a small portion. Honest labourers made up the bulk, with the simple skills of farmers, husbandmen, and shepherds. They came with all their meager possessions. Some few of noble birth came with arrogance and pride, despising honest labour and anyone who did such.

The Feast of Litha, the summer solstice had passed, little celebrated for we had nothing to spare. A solid gate now stood at the entrance to the Keep and working drawbridges spanned the inner two ditches. I wished for them to carry an army riding eight abreast, but these were too lightly built and narrow beside. We spanned the outer two ditches with fixed bridges, though these too I wished to replace so soon as possible.

Though little could I spare the men, guards manned the gatehouse and kept watch on the walls at all times. Several times they reported a distant horseman, but he chose to avoid contact.

A small village grew on the meadow west of the Keep. I forbade the ring of stones to them, unwilling to have worship offered to Woden.

A wagon, ladened with barrels of ale and beer stirred much excitement when it arrived. The bridges would have born it into the Keep itself, but the driver had his own ideas and remained in the village. For the price of a jug of ale, he hired labourers to build a tavern. He had chosen well. What little wealth could be found among the people quickly beat a trail to his door. Within weeks his wife, a harsh woman of great size, had established a brothel. The trail became a highway. It distressed me somehow. We had no chapel or shrine other than the ring of stones, no priest or bard, but men could buy drink and the pleasures of a harlot.

Four houses of solid stone now stood within the Keep. We roofed only one with thatch, so little could we find that could be spared from animal fodder. The stone roofs on the others, heavy and hard to build, seemed a pauper's trademark. They shamed me, though they shed water and sheltered few vermin.

One room became a library for the scrolls discovered in the ancient priest's quarters. I found little time to examine the writings and camped still on the ground like most of my people.

We dug great cellars, built a smoke house for meat and shelves to hold grains, pulse and earthen jars of pickled stuffs in vinegar and salt. The shelves stood almost empty, though a potter had begun to experiment with some of the clays found within the Keep.

We had great need for winter fodder for animals, but little could be found on my holdings. The broad meadows that spread south and west of the Keep provided the best, but much of that land lay under Mr. Gerhardt's control. I had no resources to buy from him.

With early summer duties well underway, I explored even while the sun shone brightly. Thus I found a narrow stair that led into a natural cleft in the rock. Sometimes tunneling into the rock and often exposed to the surface, it took me to the peak itself. A low ridge bordered a flat platform seven paces broad from which the whole of the Keep could be seen. A watcher from here could command an army worthy of the fortress. A skillful enemy it would take to creep up unseen. Two ravens circled, *below me,* I realized with a sense of wonder.

I saw a strange pattern carved into the floor. The weathering of the years blurred it and I could not be sure of what I saw. I spoke to none but Erhard and took him up the stair the next day. He gazed on the figure, breathless after the long climb. "It be a wyvern, a winged serpent," he said at last. "Tales, some not so very old, tell of three here-about."

I had of course read tales, for legends spoke of such creatures ravaging towns and villages. Even Mr. Gerhardt's house made claim to hide the lair of one.

"Will the men be fearful to set a watch here?" I asked.

"Aye," he agreed. "Yet they follow a leader who fulfills ancient prophecies." He swept the far horizon with his gaze. He pointed to a ledge on a crag farther south, where a jumble of twigs and branches formed an unruly heap. "The raven's nest, or a eagle's, Surra." He paused a brief moment. "They will fear, but they will follow you, Milord."

"The brow of the tor to the west. Another fifteen cubits would see beyond it, would it not?" I finally asked.

"Aye, Surra. Fifteen cubits I think would be sufficient," Erhard replied.

"If men were to stand here at all times in all weathers, how would you gain that extra height and still give some protection?"

"A platform on poles might answer, Surra, though the wind at times will be fierce, so it would need be anchored well."

I wasted no time in establishing a watch. Two weeks did a dozen men labour on the tower, for I built it to stand more than a man's lifetime. The added height gained a view beyond the tor to the west and showed the great wall to the south, dim and purpling in the distance. I hung trumpets and shields polished to mirror brightness on pegs on each of the six poles and kept two men on watch at all times. The lone horseman was now seen more often, the height of the tower making him visible where trees sheltered him from the Keep walls.

"He means us no ill, though his purpose is beyond my understanding," I stressed when men desired to surround and take him. "He will choose his time and come to us." Muttered curses sounded that I pretended not to hear.

I established trumpet calls and mirror signals and made them clear to all my people. While that work progressed we found two swarms of bees. The damaged skeps brought from Mr. Gerhardt's farm held the smell of bees and honey and quickly lured one of the swarms. I knew little of bee-keeping and the second swarm stung me badly. They had chosen a cavity in the wall of the Keep and showed a resolute unwillingness to leave it.

Good-natured taunts greeted my swollen face and blotched arms at board that night, yet the taste of honey on their morning porridge would be welcomed by all.

I dreamed that night, as I often did, during those brief moments before sleep fully claimed me. Memories of a great house, training with swords by a man whose face I could not see. I fought to hold the dream, to examine it, but sleep dulled the images and I awoke the next morning with a sense of loss. Bits of memory mocked me, but would not make a whole.

Those who chose idleness I sent outside the Keep to join the growing village. Still they came under my command. Thus I had the misfortune to deal with the abuse of a woman of the night. Badly beaten she was, her face swollen and bleeding, bruising on her throat and other parts of her body. Two men deep in their cups had run her through the village, naked, pelting her with rubbish and horse dung.

"Beware, Surra," Erhard counseled me. "One of them be a lord's son."

I stared long at Erhard. "There will be one law only," I finally said.

"It will be the same for the lord and his son as for the thræl. Bring them before me, and the woman also."

When the two men were brought into my presence I asked, "Why come you before me one bound and one loose?"

"Because they know better than to bind Filmore, son of Medwin," the loose man gloated.

"Bring me shackles," I ordered. "There will be one law. Thræl or lord alike will be bound by it."

"Think what you do, Surra," Erhard whispered to me.

I turned and gazed at the woman who stood in the room, head bowed, bloody scabs showing on her head and neck. The smell of horse dung clung to her, with some other sickly odour. The anger in me deepened.

"Not even one so young and stupid dares such a thing," Filmore boasted when one of my men brought the shackles.

My left hand grabbed his chin and neck, thrusting his head back. His knee came up, seeking my groin, but the manacles in my right fist drove down. It was a short punch delivered from the wrong angle, but he met iron with his knee. He would have fallen without my hand at his throat.

Five spears now ringed him, in the hands of people just beginning to forge a loyalty to me. I could depend on only one of them. Grabbing a fistful of Filmore's hair, I forced him down in the dirt. Kneeling on his back I shackled him while he cursed me, then jerked him to his knees.

"One law only there will be," I repeated "What crime of the woman earned her such treatment? How justify you your actions?"

"She is a whore," Filmore snorted. "She is diseased. Pure filth!

She should be burned, that she spread it not farther."

"Then the man last with her should also be burned," I observed coldly. "Let no man blame her for the disease men pay gold to risk. Let no man speak of her as lower than those who seek her kind!"

"Bah! You're not even a man yet. Probably have no parts. What do you know of it?"

"You!" I addressed the companion of Filmore. "What say you to your guilt in this matter? Who are you and why treated you this woman so?"

"He is my freedman. Get these shackles off both of us now and perhaps I can persuade my father to kill you quickly, rather than the lengthy death you deserve."

I stared at Filmore as a smirk began to play at the corners of his mouth, then drove my fist into his belly. He doubled over, gasping.

I turned back to his companion. "Perhaps for a while Filmore, son of Medwin will find it possible to keep his mouth shut. What say you of this matter? Why did you so treat this woman?"

Grown men are pathetic when caught in a truth they cannot lie their way out of. Turning to the woman I asked, "Are you diseased?" She did not speak, simply nodding.

"Is there a cure? I am unlearned on this subject."

"I know of no cure, Milord."

"How will you live if you cannot . . .?" I felt the heat rise in my face. She shook her head, again silently.

"I know of no way to help you, woman," I confessed. "I have nothing to spare. I cannot offer shelter from the shame even if I could put a roof over your head. For reasons I cannot understand the shame attaches to the woman, while the man boasts in the taverns." I drew a long breath. "I want not this disease among my men. I wish you to leave, though it were another injustice to demand that of you."

"Aye, Sir," she answered with bowed head, then shuffled from my presence.

I sighed heavily, then turned to Erhard. "Send for Pollard, the blacksmith." To the guards I said, "Do not release these men on pain of death."

When Pollard came I took him aside and commanded him to fashion a brand that would fit a man's cheek with the letter "F". I picked at my evening meal, struggling to force myself to eat. Pollard sent word that he had completed the brand.

"Heat it," I said wearily. "I will come shortly."

A sickness raged in me as I forced my feet to approach the blacksmith shop. The forge glowed in the deepening twilight, though I knew Pollard had banked it for the night before my last orders. He had missed his evening portion also. "My apologies, Pollard. Get you to the kitchens while something remains of the evening bread and cup. I can manage here."

"Aye, Sir." He left quickly. I doubted not that he had understood the reason for the brand.

When my men brought Filmore and his companion before me, I held the rowan staff with the Ring of Thorvæld exposed. "A short time only have I been other than a thræl. Young I am and leading a house is a great task."

"You are still only a thræl and a fool as well," Filmore spat the words at me.

I grabbed the brand from the forge and held it a half inch from his mouth. "Wish you to repeat what you just said, son of Medwin?" I questioned.

He shrank away from the glowing brand, the colour draining from his face.

"No love have I for this day's work." I returned the brand to the forge and pumped the bellows a couple of times. "Yet will I ask no one among my people to do that which I fear to do myself." I fixed Filmore with my gaze. He glanced at the forge. A sickly pallor marked his face.

"Every thræl on my lands ranks as high as you do, son of Medwin. Only in this do you differ. The privileges of your birth and training expect a higher level of manhood from you—an expectation in which you disappoint." I turned my gaze to his companion. "You who make Filmore your companion and share in his crimes, will share also in his punishment." I pumped the bellows again.

"Naked, you ran the woman through the village. Naked, you will leave this Keep." I spoke the words harshly. "Remove your garments or I will remove them. Shall I have my men undo your shackles?"

Filmore spat at me. I leaned the rowan staff against the wall, then drew my sword. Starting at the neck of his cloak, I split it down its length, then cut the pieces away. Filmore writhed in the hands of the guards, but they feared my wrath more than his at the moment. Turning to the forge, I pumped the bellows twice more, then lifted the brand, glowing a deep red. "The *F* stands for *Fool*. A fitting tribute to your actions. Hold him," I commanded, then drove the brand into his chest.

The stink of burning flesh and Filmore's scream combined in a moment from Hades. I fought the urge to vomit, then quickly pressed the brand against his cheek on the right side of his face. Returning it to the forge I forced the bellows down again while my knees tried to buckle.

I repeated the branding on the companion, then thrust the brand into the cooling tank to the hiss of hot iron. "Let them go," I commanded in a weak voice.

I took the small bucket that stood near the forge, dipped water from the cooling trough and dashed it across the two of them. "Get out," I ordered, "else I will kill you here and now."

They staggered toward the door. "Great is your punishment, but not greater than your crime. The brand will mark you for death if ever you are seen within the boundaries of my holdings." I dismissed them and a guard escorted them to the gate of the Keep and turned them out, naked.

My shoulders slumped as I turned to Erhard. "I have watched punishments and the lord seemed to gain strength from them. Why do I not?"

I instructed that the remains of their clothing be taken to the trees a half mile from the Keep entrance, along with a bow and four arrows each. I told the guards to set a watch at the edge of the village, and to find the woman and instruct her to not leave for a sen'night.

Dierdre nursed her baby near the peat fire. She had brought cheese and bread and a dipper full of water. The fire glow on the pale flesh of her breast awakened a storm within me. I drank from the dipper, then dashed the rest into my face.

I sank to the ground and reached a hand toward the baby, but the breast pulled like loadstone pulls a compass. "Two men I just branded for treating a woman with contempt." I barely whispered the words, then rose abruptly, grabbed the bread and cheese, thrusting them into my bag and strode away. I stopped once, thinking to thank Dierdre, but did not trust my voice.

When I looked across the village two days later tents had been folded and numbers had dwindled. Some from within the Keep also crossed the bridges and did not return. I wondered what gruesome tale they carried with them, but the brand had been used. I could not undo my actions, and though I sickened at the memory, I did not wish to.

I dealt stern justice for other minor crimes, but sought always to fit the penalty to the wrong done. I saw a growing awareness among my people that to the least of them, they mattered. The energy and creativity of their work increased.

The branding had another outcome also. The tide of idle people flowing toward the Keep turned. The justice I meted alike to thræl or lord's son made it clear that a haven for mountebanks this would not be.

Craftsman came in increasing numbers, bringing with them tools and skills. Starving families came also, though I despaired to give them a roof and put sufficient bread before them to sustain life.

Twice on nights when the fog settled deep and heavy, the watch reported a faint glow coming from the Circle of Stones. Fear and superstition sounded in their halting words. Each time when I rode the next day I could see evidence of trammeling feet, but no sign of fire. That somehow fueled the superstition. I, like many of my people, ached for a god worthy of worship. But Woden, though deserving fear, had failed to earn my worship.

I had no answers for the happenings in the Circle of Stones. Of necessity, I continued to look to the needs of the Keep. We gathered acorns and beechnuts by the bushel. We brought in the fruit of every hawthorn for miles around, plus the berries of rowan trees and the few rose hips that could be found. None gathered on Mr. Gerhardt's land, but parties daily took the hard trail between the Stone Circle and the Keep and gathered farther eastward and to the north.

We cut peat blocks and stacked them to dry. Forage, little as could be found, fell before the scythe. We brought in a scanty crop of barley, followed by oats and then wheat. Gathered into a storage barn scarcely completed in time to receive it, it would finish drying there. The barn itself drew wagging heads and barely hidden sneers from many, for below the floor I instructed that a fire pit be built at one end. Covered with stone, it fed the hot smoke under the length of the building to a chimney at the far end. Still, I heard exclamations of satisfaction when bundles of wheat brought in from a quick shower steamed from the warmth of the floor the first day we lit a fire.

Chapter Twelve
Of Priests and Fools

Rumours reached me of one who fancied himself a priest of Odin. He had begun to draw a gathering in the village. Odin I understood to be kin to Woden, though the stories at times seemed to make them one and the same. I spoke to the 'priest,' but he refused to answer my questions. I gave stern warning that the Circle of Stones remained forbidden.

The next heavy fog, I left the Keep at dusk in company with Durward Morton, a young warrior of unusual skill. The fog quickly swallowed us and we circled back to a growth of oak near the northwest curve of the Circle. Tying our horses, we proceeded on foot into the Circle itself. Lighting no fire, the damp air made our watching miserable.

The hours stretched long before we heard footsteps and voices, strangely disembodied. Five shadows did we count, three of whom moved clumsily, as if they carried some heavy burden. The shadows merged for a time, then a fire cast its strange glow through the fog. A sixth figure now approached.

Two fowl, held above the flames, beat their wings frantically. The figure that stood apart approached, swaying and moaning, a strange headdress covering his head.

Motioning Durward forward, we approached the group of worshipers. We each notched an arrow.

As the 'priest' swayed and gyrated, a blade gleaming in the fire-glow, the man holding the first bird approached the well. A faint crackle sounded from peat blocks that burned—on a broad flat stone I noted. I drew my bow partially and released an arrow as the priest swung the knife.

A grunt of surprise mingled with the quick gulping sound that escaped the now headless bird. The knife fell, clattering against the rocks at the edge of the well, then tipped into the dark opening and disappeared. The gushing blood from the bird followed the knife.

The priest's incantations fell silent. The shaking and moaning of worshipers ceased and all stared dumbly at the arrow protruding from the priest's upper arm. I had launched it with little strength, else it would have penetrated even through bone and continued its flight.

The man who held the bird whirled to search for me in the fog. His foot encountering empty space he flung out his arms, hurling the bird from him as he fell.

While one man drew sword, two of the six turned and fled into the fog. I had no time to draw sword, but had already notched another arrow. As the sword-man hurled himself at me I sidestepped and drew back on the string. The arrow took him high in the gut as he spun back to face me. He staggered and the sword dropped from spreading fingers. His mouth opened upon a curse, but sufficient breath he could not find. His eyes widened in recognition before he fell.

Durward dropped both of the running men with an arrow each. I was astonished that he got two arrows off in the time needed.

The one man left, uninjured, stood in dumb amazement, then knelt before me, laying his own knife on the ground before him. "Blood sacrifices I will not offer." I spat the words angrily as I kicked the knife away.

Five men I bound, then sent Durward to bring our horses. The sixth would fight no more battles unless Woden chose him for his halls.

Durward had brought his targets down with an arrow through their upper legs, crippling, but not killing. My arrow had struck too low to enter the heart, but the man was dying moment by moment. Sickness settled in my gut. The dying man had shown the most courage.

I ordered the men with leg wounds thrown onto one of our horses. To the "priest" I spoke harshly, "Tis not a sen'night since I spoke to you, Sir, and you refused to answer my questions." I bent and picked up the headdress. "Tis more than foolishness that you do here. A man is dying because of your actions. A man more worthy than you." I threw the headdress on the fire.

The priest and the man who had bruised himself at the mouth of the well, I forced to walk. "Hold them in bonds, but have the leech tend their wounds," I commanded Durward. I sent him then to take the prisoners into the Keep. "I will come when this is done."

For more than two hours I remained beside the dying man. His breathing grew more laboured as the night passed. The arguments in my mind could not quell the guilt. I had done what I must. But the man had not attacked out of malicious motives.

I glanced at the dead bird, a pigeon, I now saw. There had been a second one as well. Hopefully it had escaped. I dozed a bit during those hours troubled by disturbing dreams. *I laboured in combat training with sword and spear. I also heard a voice demanding that I apply myself to the books. A great library spread before me. One scroll lay open on a table, lamps burning brightly. A sword cut through the parchment and split the table beneath it. The lamps spilled their oil and flames spread. I fought the flames like I would fight a deadly enemy. They caught on my blade, spread to the hilt and finally engulfed my hands.*

Thunder rumbled. Rain descended in a torrent. Flames guttered out. The walls of the library faded. Clay jars crumbled to dust, then thin grey mud. I stood in a field, trampled grass rising through ashes and blood. A man lay before me. He gasped a final breath, then his face went slack.

I woke to the rumble of thunder. The man before me had breathed his last. I walked with slow and weary steps to my horse, then led her back to the body.

The sun had risen and people had broken fast before I dealt with the prisoners. I stood wearily near the forge with the rowan staff bearing the Ring of Thorvæld and gazed with distaste at the men before me. The leech had removed the arrow from the priest's arm and bound the wound with a rag. "The Circle of Stones has been forbidden," I said quietly. "Why must someone die before that message is understood?"

"Aye. Forbidden," the priest mocked. "And while ye murder innocent men, ye bring folly and invite the wrath of Odin."

"Thunder 'n damnation, man. You invite a flogging to so speak to your lord," Erhard burst out.

"He's not my lord. He's a horse-killing thræl. Too stupid to know that Odin won't sit back and be ignored. And now he's taken to killing his own people."

I lifted the brand from its hook, held it a moment and then thrust it into the hot coals of the forge. The priest's gaze followed the brand. His mouth continued to work, but no words escaped.

"Woden, or Odin as you choose to call him, will never be satisfied with the blood of a couple of pigeons. If he is a real god at all, that will only stimulate his thirst." I pulled the brand from the forge and held it before the man. It had not yet begun to glow, but he shrank away from me.

"I despise the whip and the brand both," I muttered. Then I raised my voice. "Twenty lashes," I said. "Get you gone from my holdings then. You refuse to accept me as lord of this place. I refuse to accept you as one of my people. Do not return on pain of death. Be gone before the first watch of the night."

I used the whip rarely for I despised it, but it fell hard. As the man fled from the blacksmith shop, I called after him. "Guard your tongue in the hours before you leave. The brand hangs over you every moment you remain on my holdings and well you have earned it. You call me murderer, but the blood of the one who died is on your head, dead because of your choices. Do not give me greater reason to build a gallows."

To the other four I gave a choice. "Ten lashes or lifetime banishment. It is your choice, but the time for decision is now." I paused, then continued. "And never do you enter the Circle of Stones again, except for the defense of the Keep, on pain of death."

Three of them chose the lashes. The fourth had departed by nightfall.

We burned the body of the man I had killed. Durward had given a true account of the conflict and my counselors affirmed I had acted honourably, yet my sickness over his death would not lift. Again, I ached for a god worthy of the name of god.

Little had I seen of Dierdre, both to my relief and disappointment. My beard, when I chanced to see my reflection, had grown thick and dark. The scar from Mr. Gerhardt's whip disappeared into it. No hair grew from the old wound on my head, but long and heavy growth covered it. None had laboured harder than I. Strong and determined, I still felt too young for my task.

Of livestock we had little, but of fodder we had even less. Besides the three horses and the goat with her two kids we had brought with us, newly arrived people had brought five horses with them. A pair of oxen from a farmer otherwise without resources had worked hard before a plow. Four sows and twenty young pigs foraged for nuts. Three cows, six calves, one bull, eight sheep, three more goats and two small flocks of chickens made up our total inventory of animals.

I sent parties to net quail and snare pigeons. Rabbits risked great danger anywhere on my holdings. As winter approached every animal that could be spared come spring felt the knife of the butcher, though we spread the killings that the meat might feed us and not spoil.

The first snow fell and we dug the turnips. They alone of our crops exceeded expectations. The rye that grew in the same fields suffered considerable damage, but we horded what remaining seed we had for spring.

"A fire burns in Woden's Circle," Erhard informed me during the second watch one night. Weary muscles protested as I rose from my bed. I pulled my robe about me, strode outside and climbed the stairs to the Keep wall. We could see a man on horseback while several other figures moved about a fire. The fire threw high flames and sparks into the air—a wood fire, not peat.

"Have my horse saddled," I instructed Erhard quietly. A tight knot formed in my gut. Three warriors rode with me, followed by ten footmen carrying spears. Two sat their horses on the wall, awaiting commands while twenty more footmen stood in readiness.

"Raise the bridges again so soon as we be passed. Hold the Keep at all costs," I instructed as we passed through the gates

The iron shoes of our horses clipped sharply on the bridge, followed by the thump of marching feet. I heard the solid crunch of the gates closing and the rattle of chains as the bridges lifted after our crossing.

In the Stone Circle I found one mighty oak deeply wounded as three men swung axes at it. An arrow from my longbow bit into the tough wood above the head of one who hurled away his ax and leaped back. "What do you here—and under whose orders?" I demanded. Nothing of boyish cracking sounded in my voice today. It sounded, even to my ears, the voice of a lord.

"We pull down the strongholds of false gods, and their idols destroy." A pompous voice sounded from the rider who sat his horse near the fire, but did none of the work. "Stand aside, for in the name of Christus we come."

"Christus I have heard of," I said. "Mostly tales that have the sound of the cup being passed too many times. Who are you? Who gave you leave to cut and burn in this place?"

The man I spoke to dressed somewhat like a holy hermit, yet a hermit whose cell was gold lined. He wore more gold on the fingers of both hands and the chain about his neck than would have made the Ring of Thorvæld twice over. He also carried a purse that hung heavy from his belt. A tall, conical hat of foolish design sat on tightly curled hair.

"I need leave from no man, for the Christus I serve."

"Then the Christus had better turn aside my arrows, for the next one seeks your heart." As I spoke I released an arrow that took the hat off his head. With a startled grunt he jerked back and toppled from the saddle.

"Bind him and bring him to the Keep," I ordered.

"God will not be mocked, Thr*æ*l, nor will his servant." The fallen figure had leaped to his feet and drawn a sword.

"If this god is mocked, it is by his own servant who has acted the fool." I hurled the words like stones from a catapult. "Put down your sword or I will kill you where you stand." Lorellefue stood unmoving beneath me. My bowstring, fully drawn, aimed an arrow at the middle of the arrogant chest.

"You know not who you tamper with, young fool," the man spat the words at me as he dropped his sword.

I shouted to the cleric's followers. "Draw no weapon on pain of death. You are here in violation of my express orders. I have no reason to respect your presence or the presence of the rich man who plays at serving a god about whom I know nothing." I drew a deep breath, then continued. "How many are you?"

"We were six, Sir, plus our master, but the earth swallowed one just beyond the fire." The man's terror sounded clear in his tone.

"The earth will vomit him up again, whether dead or alive I cannot tell." I uttered the words in a cold, harsh voice. "But if you value your life you will be far removed before that happens."

I raised my voice again. "Five minutes you have before I give my men orders to kill any of your party still on my holdings. If your god prevents that happening perhaps I will hear more of him, even from the arrogant fool who curses me in Latin since he thinks me too ignorant to understand."

The muttered imprecations fell silent.

"Get you gone," I shouted. "Return not to the village. If you have belongings there, they are forfeit. Your time has shrunk to four minutes and several of my men are mounted."

With cries of terror and prayers in which the Christus seemed only one of several gods called upon, they fled, running blindly in a southwesterly direction.

"Wait the allotted time, then spur them with arrows as close as you can come short of killing them." I gave orders to five of my footmen. "But if any of them tarry, their blood be on their own heads." I glanced at the priest then and quietly instructed, "Bring the prisoner."

"His hat, Sire?" one of the guards questioned.

"Throw it on the fire," I commanded. "If he gives you trouble, add the rest of his clothes. The gold will survive and be the purer for having his touch burned from it."

As I reentered the Keep I told the gatekeeper, "They bring a prisoner. Five guards escort others off my holdings. Receive them and let me know if any do not return within the next watch."

I called Morse and Peyton to join me. "Fear you to go beneath the Stone Circle to approach the well where sacrifices to Woden once were made?"

They looked uncertainly at each other. "We—will go, Sir," Peyton said hesitantly.

"Good," I responded. "Prepare torches and meet me at the coal shaft in five minutes. The earth has swallowed one who followed orders from a fool tonight. Some small hope I have that he might be alive still."

We took the steps two at a time till I turned aside at a crack in the wall. My companions hesitated a moment, then plunged in after me. Three steps only I took before another stair took us deeper. I had last walked this path in absolute darkness, carrying only the rowan staff. We could hear the murmur of running water. Our feet left the final step to splash in the small stream.

"If we should become separated or our lights go out, walking into the direction of this water flow takes you to the well itself. Walking with its flow brings you back to this stair with passage to the Keep above. Tis a grim place to be without light."

"Aye, stories we have heard," Peyton acknowledged.

"Exaggerated no doubt," I said. The noise of our passage made conversation difficult, but we pressed on with urgent haste. Shortly beyond the side passage we heard a groan, amplified by the tunnel into a kind of wail.

"He lives still," I said with a sigh. "Think what his terror is to have fallen into this place. His belief in the Christus of his master may be little developed, but doubtless he has heard of Woden and was fortified for his task by how much greater the Christus is than Woden. How then will he accept falling into Woden's halls?"

We passed the stair to the trumpet chamber. A sword lay on the bottom step. We stopped to see a man, bloody and bruised, cowering against the back wall at the edge of the stone basin. His eyes stared fearfully, reflecting our torchlight back.

"Be at peace, Sir," I said in a quiet voice. "I am Theodoric Thorvæld, not Woden or one of his thræls. Glad I am to see you still alive for tis a mean fall from above." I reached my hand toward him. "Come. You sit in a hlaut-bolla, a sacrificial basin, so designed to catch the blood of those sacrificed to Woden. Tis a poor place to bathe."

The man fearfully accepted my hand and staggered as he stepped clear of the basin. Bruising and scrapes marked his face. Blood blackened the back of one hand, yet no broken bones seemed evident.

We walked slowly back to the stairs. Unseen injuries made mounting the stairs a great difficulty, so when we reached the coal shaft I sent my two companions to the surface. They quickly lowered the coal bucket, and raised us in it. With instructions to give the rescued man ale for the pain and a blanket to cover him while he slept, I turned my steps to the blacksmith shop.

Chapter Thirteen
A Fool's Mission

BERTRM, ERHARD, AND SEVERAL GUARDS awaited me, our prisoner in their midst still bound by ropes. Bertrm handed the rowan staff to me. I unbound the piece of pigskin that covered the Ring of Thorvæld.

"An idol, to a most despicable creature," the captive's quavering voice spoke.

I ignored him and turned to my advisors. "Erhard, know you aught of the device on this man's clothing?" I asked.

"Tis a lion, Surra, and a cross—an instrument of the most cruel death. Tis also the symbol of the Christus, for on it he died."

"Hung, like Woden's victims are hung?" I questioned.

"Aye, Surra. But t'was the god himself who so hung."

"Again like Woden," I observed dryly. "He does not sound like the one I seek. Did he too hang for nine days and gain wisdom?"

"Nay, Surra. Not like Woden, for he had wisdom before the cross, yet died and was laid in a cold crypt. Yet a powerful god he was, for half a sen'night later he broke open the tomb—if the tales be believed," Erhard added.

"A long 'if' that one be," I said dismissively.

"Prisoner!" I shifted my focus abruptly. He jumped and stared like a rabbit cornered by a wolf.

"I hold no love for Woden. The Circle of Stones has been forbidden to my people that none might worship him there." I paced the room near the forge, then turned and pumped the bellows a number of times. "I have been beneath that circle and know the deception practiced by the priests." I returned to my pacing. "Why, in the name of whatever god is real, have you turned the attention of my people back to Woden?"

"Had you not so recklessly intervened, and threatened the servant of the living God with bloodshed, the name of Woden would be no more. The grove would be felled. The name of Christus would be elevated."

"You elevate this god by cutting trees old before your grandfather drew first breath? You elevate this god by losing men of your party into the very well where blood was spilled in worship to Woden?" I held the rowan staff before his face, the tusks of the Ring of Thorvæld almost against his throat. He leaned away as far as his bonds would allow, face blanching.

"In the name of the Christus, you have revived interest in Woden. In the name of the Christus, you have given reason to take no further interest in this Christus, unless it were to dismiss him as a weak god with foolish followers."

I turned to Erhard. "Whippings I despise." I muttered. "But fools who wound me and my people by their foolishness I despise even more. How then shall such a fool be rewarded?"

"Blasphemy!" the man sputtered. "You will be banished. It is blasphemy of the worst kind to speak so to me."

"I was not speaking to you—Sir. I sought the wisdom of my advisors. How will I be banished from something about which I know nothing? And how can I blaspheme a god I do not know? Is your god also a fool, or only his servant?"

The man thrust his hands at me, shaking his fingers as though snakes might come from them to swallow me and put an end to my affront to his god. Hampered by the rope that bound him, and with a several spears leveled, he became still once again.

"Give me reason you should not be flogged and branded for a fool. Strongly do I believe in justice, but no love for the whip do I hold."

"You dare not," the man burst out. "I am bishop of Drahæm. The wrath of the church would pursue you. The wrath of God would condemn your soul to Hades." Sweat dripped from his nose.

"So you tell me," I observed. I fixed him with my stare, holding the rowan staff before me. "You dared enter my holdings, cut trees and light a fire where I had forbidden people to enter. You spoke not to me about the requirements of your god, though I am deeply interested in finding a god more worthy than Woden. You came not to seek audience with me before you began destroying. Even your god must recognize that as a crime."

I paced for a few moments, then stopped abruptly before the man, holding the rowan staff with the boar figure close before his face. "Take that unspeakable idol away from me," he gasped. "Defame not the name of Christus by bringing it into my presence."

"Is not your god bigger than this emblem of a boar? More gold than this you wear, with the likeness of lions and an instrument of death displayed. Speak not then to me of idols, lest you ascribe powers to this ring greater than I do myself."

I turned to my guards. "Know any of you aught of this god?" I asked "Is he worthy of worship despite his unlucky choice of servant?"

"I know that which earns respect, Sir," one man said hesitantly. "But I know not enough about him to merit worship."

"It is well," I said quietly. "A bitter task I ask of you, for I would not have it done by one who disrespects this god." I paused long, for deeply I hated whippings.

"Ten lashes is as light sentence as I have seen, yet there is some measure of true belief in the man before us. Foolishly has he acted on that belief, to the hurt of the name of his god. Strip him to the waist and have an end to this. Send him on his way then, for I would not have him longer within my walls. Leave him his rings and all the wealth on his person. Sorely as we need such, his crime is not one that can be paid for with gold. Anything found of his or his followers shall be divided among the guards. Only scrolls and parchments, if any be found, shall be brought to me. The horse with its fittings is forfeit to this house, for he rode it here to our hurt."

Much I longed to leave the room prior to the whipping. The pitiable cries from the man who claimed the Christus of the cross as his god sickened me, for he bore the stripes with less courage than a lad of nine might.

I ordered ointment for his back, blistered but uncut, for the man who swung the whip leaned not into it. I also provided him with a skin of water, a piece of bread and a wedge of cheese. "Get you south of the great wall," I told him. "Winter approaches and poorly prepared are you."

As the guards ushered him from my presence I shouted, "Hold!" I stood before the priest who trembled, stripped of his arrogance, though he wore again the rich garments he had come with. I loosed my robe and dropped it, standing before him. I turned, that the stripes on my back could be seen, and I spoke my contempt. "It should never be said that one of my age who knows no god worthy of worship has greater courage than one who follows a god who chose the cross." I stared at him and spoke my longing. "I would have welcomed learning more of this Christus, did the learning come from a teacher I could respect. You have done foolishly, Sir, and shamed the name of your god."

In the morning I questioned the man who had fallen down the well. He knew little about the Christus, having but small imagination for superstition, nor was he a reader. "I have heard the bishop declare in the words of the Christus himself, that the greatest should be the least," he told me. "Like the veriest slave, the Christus washed the feet of his closest followers. I have not seen the bishop live that teaching."

The man suffered considerable pain still, but walked easier than the night before. I gave him freedom to stay, but he chose to return to Drahæm. I allowed him to carry his ax and gave him a portion of bread and cheese, as well as a flint and steel. I thought long on his words and wished to know more about this Christus.

Two days later a trumpet sounded from the watchtower. Three piercing blasts signaled, *'Danger! Get inside the Walls.'* The village population poured in disorderly fashion across the bridges and into the Keep. The bridges rose and the gate closed firmly behind the last stragglers. The watch at the gatehouse sounded their trumpet as I galloped Lorellefue to join them. Twenty mounted warriors emerged from the trees a half mile distant.

A single trumpet blast from the watchtower and the flash of signal mirrors indicated a party of five hunters who had left the Keep early that morning. They crouched at the edge of a clump of rowan to the southwest, beyond the border of the village. I signaled them to make their way to the trenches. They must pass under the guards on the wall so any treachery must be at great risk, but we had oft trained for such an event. Two men I sent through the southern tunnel to give assistance as necessary, then looked to the defense of those of us already inside.

I quietly praised the gatekeeper and the watch for their swift response, then called advisors to me as we stood atop the wall of the Keep. "Do my eyes see aright? Does the way that man with the helm sits the saddle bring to mind Filmore son of Medwin?"

"Aye, Surra, and the helmet would hide the brand," Erhard agreed.

"Bring every archer," I instructed. "Let every able-bodied man take up his weapons. How many skilled with the longbow have we?"

"Jist four, Surra, and yourself," Erhard responded.

"Five warriors I wish to take the tunnel to the ditches. Much you risk against horse and rider, yet only that one, so heavily armored, would I have you target. He wears mail, yet his arrogance has him with nose in the air, losing therefore the protection at his throat. Not but a longbow or a spear will penetrate his mail. Every arrow then, should seek his throat. Have I five willing?"

More than twenty stepped forward, some pale, some with childish eagerness, a few knowing well the risks. I named off four of the most skillful, two of them with longbows. Durward Morton, who handled the spear and the longbow with unerring skill, but better, showed a natural facility to inspire men under difficult circumstances I named also.

"Wait for my signal, for if it be another man under that helmet I would take no life unnecessarily. With so many arrows aimed the horse is like to be killed. That cannot be helped."

As my men hurried to take up their positions, two horses crossed the outer bridge and pranced onto the second, bringing them to the limit of accurate bowshots from the wall. A shout came from a voice I recognized and despised.

"Filmore son of Medwin, heir to an Earldom—demands justice on him who styles himself Theodoric Thorvæld, lord of this ruin. Send me out his head and I will consider withdrawing my men."

"It is indeed him is it not?" I asked those around me. Nods and shrugs answered me. "And will you send my head or will you fight for me?"

Bowstrings drew taught, aimed across the wall at the one who shouted. "Never was a brand better deserved than that one got, Sir," one of them responded. A number of muttered *Ayes* sounded from all around, while eyes and weapons focused on the one.

I waited, forcing Filmore to voice his demands a second time, giving my men time to position themselves, then shouted back to him.

"Justice shall you receive son of Medwin, for you were forbade to return on pain of death. Get you now from my holdings, for the bowstrings are tight with your arrogant neck as their target." I raised my left arm, holding the rowan staff with the Ring of Thorvæld.

His chin dropped slightly, but his hatred for me sounded in his next words. "Ha! You think that trinket scares me. See you the armed men behind me. Even you cannot be so stup. . ."

My arm dropped and forty archers on the wall loosed their arrows, as did two in the trenches. One longbow arrow struck his helmet a ringing blow, but catching on the curve, bounced away. The second hit his right shoulder and stung him deeply, though the extent of the wound could not be known.

A shout came from the horsemen beyond the outer bridge as they put spurs to their horses and charged toward the Keep.

Filmore held his sword high, a shout of defiance and mockery ringing from him. Weak sunlight penetrating an overcast sky flashed against steel to his left. The spear pierced him. Almost I could see the denting as the point drove against the armour on his right side, for Durward had thrown it with great strength from close by. Filmore lifted from the saddle and seemed to hang, impaled on the spear, then plunged into the ditch, followed by his horse.

The second horse that had accompanied him reared and lunged, falling into the steep sided ditch and taking its rider with it.

The flight of arrows stopped. The riders charging across the bridges reigned in their horses. An uneasy silence settled, cut by the screaming of injured animals. I had not known horses could make such a dreadful noise.

"Take your dead and go," I called. "Justice the son of Medwin demanded. Justice he has received." I gestured toward my men on the wall. "Why choose death today when against five times your number we could easily hold the Keep. I seek no quarrel, but will not suffer fools to abuse my people, be they thræl or lord's son."

"Withdraw then from the walls and we will remove our dead," one of Filmore's men called.

"Nay, for t'was you brought the fight to my gates. Bear your dead from under our bows or leave them to sicken the vultures. My word is all you have to trust in, and the loyalty of my people who have been with me but a short time."

The horses milled at the limit of bowshot till one man dismounted. He drew his sword and cast it on the ground. Several paces he walked toward me. "Your word will I trust, Theodoric Thorvæld. In happier times I would pay you honour with a good will. Hold not the actions of Filmore against his father, for he is a worthy man and gave no blessing to this venture."

"On my life none will hurt you, Sir," I called to the courageous man. "Take care that you stumble not though, for the arrows are still notched and the battle blood pumps hot."

"The hunters be inside the Keep, Surra," Erhard murmured to me. I nodded.

Unseen by any of his own company the warrior jerked the helmet from Filmore's head and gazed for a moment at the eyes staring blankly from a scarred face. He turned and spat, then grabbed the body under the arms and struggled up the steep embankment. Returning to the bottom of the ditch he knelt over his companion. "He breathes still, Sire," he called up to me. "But is twisted like his back is broken."

"Aye," I responded. "Tis a long fall with the horse upon him. What will you with him?"

"He cannot live, Sire. But he has a wife. I would take him to her."

I turned from the wall, fighting the grief that rose in me. When finally I turned back the man had struggled again to the top of the ditch dragging his heavy burden. "I would know his name," I said softly to Erhard.

"Aye. He be a man with courage much like yourself, Surra."

I stared at Erhard, fighting tears that threatened. "I have made a widow today, Erhard. That sits like a sickness in my gut."

"Nay, Surra. The fault with Filmore lies, who commanded his men on a fool's mission to restore a fool's honour, when t'was honour already damaged beyond repair. You did what you was forced to do—with a heart free from evil." He gazed out to where men struggled to throw bodies over the backs of horses. "No weapons was fired at any but the one, yet twenty mounted warriors you turned back with no loss of life to your people."

Eighteen horses moved back from the outer bridge. Erhard turned also and scanned the warriors of Muninn's Keep who stood their places at the wall, bowstrings slack, but arrows still notched. "Tis not like to be the subject of song, Surra, for tis only when the burns flow red that men sing of it. Yet your men have seen honour in measure few men see in a lifetime."

We gazed down to where one horse struggled to rise. "I will send men to butcher the horses, Surra," Erhard said, "that the meat be not wasted, and they suffer no longer."

I nodded, then walked slowly along the wall, thanking the men for their steadfastness. I descended the stair and greeted the five who had gone outside the safety of the wall. "Would that I had gold by the bushel to divide among you," I said as they stood around me. "No lord ever commanded knights to make a heart prouder. Twenty warriors on horseback you turned away with no loss of life to my people. What storied warrior of old has done more?"

I gave orders to sound the trumpet at the threshing floor. "There can we gather the biggest number. Stand still to your watch men, you whose time it is. Take the full circuit of the Keep and remain alert. Others of you gather to me."

The trumpet call brought a quick gathering. I stood and gazed upon the crowd, numbering close to 150 with those of the village added. "We have become one people," I told them. "Courage have I seen in abundance, and honour—among warriors with little experience and a short time only to learn if my leadership is trustworthy."

I raised my voice to a shout. "Honour the men who today have risked their lives for you. Cheapen not the victory because little blood was spilled. Look you each one to those you love. Had it gone otherwise, though we would have endured for the Keep is of incredible strength—some among us would be in mourning. No victory gives back the husband to the widow, the son to the mother."

A great shout rose, echoed and re-echoed when I became silent and simply lifted the rowan staff with the Ring of Thorvæld upon it. I heard my own name among the accolades.

Dierdre brought me a cup of ale. My fingers touched her hand as I took it from her. I ached to pull her to me, to hold her close. "Ah, Dierdre," I breathed the words, almost bursting with things I did not know how to express.

The way of a man with a woman, I mused while I climbed the stair to the watchtower. *Are there words? Is the stuff of tavern boasting all there is to it? Should I just take her, do what men do?*

The questions and the raging hunger for Dierdre had quieted somewhat by the time I reached the watchtower. I praised the men for their alertness. I stood an hour with them, watching the party of horsemen who had dwindled to mere specks in the distance. I searched in all other directions as well, wishing I had the eyes of an eagle.

Chapter Fourteen
The Great Hall

A SMALL, FLAT TABLELAND showed to the right of the stair below the rock peak, broken by piles of boulders. Little grew on it, but like the dry patch northeast of the Keep, this seemed to show the hand of man as I gazed on it today. When I descended I found Erhard waiting for me, mounted and leading Lorellefue.

"You know me well, Erhard," I complimented him.

"You are not a deceitful man. Knowing you be easy and rewarding, Surra," he responded. "You have won a great victory today. Still you grieve over those who have died. I thought you would choose to be alone. I will leave you now."

"No, Erhard. Ride with me. I would have your company."

I turned my horse toward the tableland. At its widest it reached eighteen paces, and perhaps thirty long. The sound of our horse's hooves seemed to confirm my suspicions, but I reigned in and dismounted. Erhard started to do the same, but I intervened. "Ride in an easy canter around me, Erhard," I instructed. "I would hear the ring of your horse's hooves on this ground."

With my ear pressed to the ground I clearly heard the hollow echo. I rose to my feet with deep satisfaction. "Let us find the door, Erhard, for we ride on the roof of a hall."

He stared at me, then turned his gaze to sweep the flat surface we stood upon. "Thunder 'n damnation, Surra. None but you would dare believe such a thing." His grin matched my own, "or make me dare believe with you."

I strode to the nearest pile of boulders. A stale odour of old dust came from them. "Here are ventilation shafts with the smell of dust undisturbed for an age."

A ridge of natural rock with a few weather-blasted trees fronted most of the tableland. A gap showed along its northwest portion. A narrow ravine reached back from the lower level of the Keep.

A bulge of rock hid the entrance until we had ridden within a few paces of it. A few steps more and our horses hesitated in the doorway. The twisting entrance blocked the sunlight. Faint light filtered from each ventilation shaft and showed us that two rows of pillars supported the roof six cubits above our heads. Since we sat on horseback, that made it nearly fifteen cubits high. Water leakage showed between courses of stone, but the roof had stood for generations. It showed the touch of a master stone-worker.

Half way back the sound of our horse's feet changed once again. "Cellars lie beneath us," I observed.

A small colony of bats dropped from their roost and shrieked around us. Lorellefue shied, almost unseating me. My hand had reached for my sword at the unaccustomed noise.

We found a stair cut into the rock itself at the back of the hall, reaching both up and down. The faint light gave barely sufficient illumination to see the natural surface of the back slope climbing steeply before us. We could explore no more without torches.

"It has been an eventful day, Erhard." My voice broke as I spoke. "Thank you for your friendship."

"I'm free, Surra, thanks to you," Erhard said softly. "I'm not under compulsion to stay, and I'm proud of what you have done as if you was my own son."

The next several days we explored more, finding a large kitchen, a number of forges, rusty armour and weapons. The kitchen and forges backed each other, built into a great stone wall.

An ancient liquor filled three jars found in a storage room. As lord of the house they brought the first cup to me. I could barely quell the urge to spit the burning stuff out. "Are you sure it is meant for drinking, and not for fueling lamps?" I asked, to the mirth of all.

Laughter sounded around the threshing floor that night. Still, my people had worked hard and won a victory. I could not begrudge them a good time.

A low stone wall bordered a narrow channel in the deepest storage room. Water had filled that room to half the height of the wall, then spilled through gaps into the channel beside it. The water ran into a narrow crack. Widened so that a man could walk with minimal discomfort, it descended in a northeasterly direction until it disappeared into a broken mass of tumbled stone.

Pollard moved his blacksmith shop inside. Dierdre took command of the ovens. Great enclosed hearths with an ash pit beneath formed ovens so large that I found her crawling out of one, covered with soot and half-dried clay. Not given to poetic impulses, I found her soiled figure and face somehow delightful. I reached up and brushed wet clay from her nose. For a second she caught and held my hand. She held my gaze also.

"Ma. . ." Ilsa's laughter bubbled up. At eight months only a mother could recognize words in her babble.

I knelt down to the bairn. "I'm afraid she's cooking the mud. Is that what we have to eat now?"

"Drrr," Ilsa giggled and grabbed a fistful of my hair. Warmth swept over me. I turned to her mother and felt again that nameless emotion.

Dierdre's face showed the hard years, though she could scarcely have passed 16. Clay and soot stains, calloused hands and old, patched clothes somehow did not take from her appeal. Bits of hair escaped the cloth bound over her head and hung damply against her forehead.

I stood and pulled her to me, held her close. For a second she leaned into me, then stiffened and twisted away. I was 'lord' of the place. My hands continued to grip her arms, but something in her expression changed. I stopped, bewildered by my own feelings, ashamed, yet not quite knowing why. "Ah, Dierdre . . ." I uttered the words in a long sigh. I stood a moment longer, then released her. She backed a step away and stared up at me.

"Theodoric. . . I. . . you." She stumbled over words.

I bent and picked up Ilsa. "Seems we both have things we don't know how to say." I whispered to the little girl. "You've got lots to say. How about you help us out."

"Drrr." She squirmed in my arms and reached for Dierdre.

Winter pressed and hunger overshadowed us. Two heavy snowstorms stopped the roads and turned back all but the most persistent hunters who took bow or spear and sought meat. The scant supply of wool from our few sheep kept a few hands busy. Rabbit skins, when someone managed to shoot or snare one, found their way into a garment somewhere. Coal continued to rise from the depths below the Keep, for I sought to have a year's supply ahead.

I turned often to the scrolls. I had deliberately ignored the one taken from the saddle of the priest of the Christus. Somehow his shame seemed to attach to it. Yet finally I spread it on a small table. Against my will it gripped me, stirred my deepest longings. Written under the name *Isaiae filii Amos,* it seemed a holy book. *Dominus locutus,*[ii] the Words of the Lord—it read unlike anything I had seen before. Could this "Dominus" be kin to the Christus, sorry choice though his priest had been? I read long that first night, till the candle guttered out. The scroll talked of a vision, a rebellious nation, dumb farm creatures who knew their owners, but a people who had turned their backs on their own god, a sick people, like a city under siege. Their god hated their sacrifices and festivals. The blood and burning wearied him. He wanted them to quit killing each other, to care for the fatherless and the widow. I had never heard of such a god.

It sounded too, like the author had seen the dark holes at Mr. Gerhardt's house. "*Why should you be beaten more, you who insist on revolt? Your whole head is sick. Your whole heart is bowed. No soundness can be found. From the sole of the foot to the top of the head you are sick. Wounds and bruises have not been bound, nor dressed, nor soothed with oil.*"[iii]

As the leader of a people however, with a long, lean winter underway, I found little time for reading.

The threshing floor did double duty. With sheaves of grain broken upon it, I trained men-at-arms. Shuffling feet, as we practiced with blunted swords, separated the grain from the straw. The room proved overly warm for our exertions, and we broke the straw finer than I liked, but my people gained much skill with weapons while threshing wheat, barley, oats and rye.

My reading showed the women and children as likely to die in battle as men, often after being shamefully used. So I thought it well that they should be able to defend themselves and allowed any who would to participate. The women did not have the strength to fare well with swords, but three of them, Dierdre among them, matched skill with any of the men with lance or bow.

The spiteful comments I heard from some of the men amused me until Dierdre became one of the targets. I offered then to teach the women how to truly humble a man. The comments stopped—at least in my hearing.

Most days we swept the threshing floor in the late evening. With a heated floor, it became a favoured gathering place. Harlan would share verse. His work was not actually effeminate, but lacked in the robustness that appealed to me. I suspect my own total inability to produce verse influenced my judgment. I had found though, in the scroll of *Isaiae filii Amos,* poetic writings more stirring than the work of any bard I had read. It became my habit to read portions to my people, though the labour of translating it made my reading slow and tiresome.

Who was this god? Did he have a name? What did he require?

Terrible in many ways, a god of judgment and condemnation, he seemed to cry for justice, to plead for his people to come back so he would not have to destroy. I had never imagined such a god.

As winter progressed the larger gatherings began to move into the *Great Hall.* It lent itself wonderfully to the purposes, though the air quickly became stale. Sufficient torches to make the hall bright burned the eyes with smoke.

I had read much of Woden by now, for he figured in many stories and songs, some few of which scribes had put to parchment. The tales never told of deception among the priests, yet I read with a harsh and judgmental view and deception seemed a common practice. Still, I could not convince myself a corrupt priesthood proved the falseness of the gods themselves. I wanted to disbelieve in Woden and every other god I could name, yet longed for one worthy of belief and honour. It made me harsh in my judgment of priests, perhaps unfairly so. Still I hesitated to speak against the gods themselves, even Woden, about whom I knew the most and believed the least. I ached to believe in the god from the scroll of the priest of the Christus.

I put my stone workers to the task of fashioning a door that looked like a natural part of the tunnel wall where the passage from the Circle of Stones met the stair under the Keep. One of the obvious weaknesses of Muninn's Keep, I sought to close it quickly. Pollard fashioned an iron gate also. A rope led from the gate to a bell on the Keep wall. The gate could not be opened without alerting the guards.

I searched for other weaknesses in the fortress. I gave my men-at-arms the challenge of finding any and all ways of entering the Keep unseen by the guards. Many times men would go outside the gates and search for a way past the guards. Those on watch determined it should not be their length of the wall breached, so diligence remained high as they too searched for weaknesses one might exploit.

Tunnels on either side of the main gate gave passage of warriors to each of the ditches. The last defender could drop a gate of timber and iron by slashing a rope as he retreated. It made each ditch and the low wall that topped it a highly defensible barrier long before an enemy approached the main Keep wall.

A small number of my people celebrated Imbolc, the Feast of the goddess Brighid, on the second of February. Two days later I was called to the village to deal with the death of an infant. Although I made it my habit to ride in the village most days, I had not seen the mother. She showed a pale, pinched face, as if she had eaten too little. Her husband carried the gut of a hard drinker. I knew only that he evidenced no inclination to any task. I had not known he had a wife.

The smoke from a peat fire blackened the interior of a hovel. A mean bed of straw with a single thin blanket filled a quarter of the space.

The infant lay on a piece of sacking. Not plump and pink like a newborn should be, this one looked pinched and starved, with a ghastly white pallor.

No bread or meat did I see, nor other foodstuffs. A pottery jar stood beside the bed. When I moved it, the smell of liquor confirmed that drink consumed what little they had.

"What name gave you to the child?" I asked.

"Name a whelp what gots no hope of living?" The man spoke his contempt. "This useless wench can't keep a fit house nor cook a decent meal." He snorted, shoved me aside and jerked the wrapping from the baby, leaving it lying naked in the cold room. "She couldna even give me a son."

I took the piece of sacking from him, wrapped the baby again and lifted it, astonished at the lightness of my burden. I turned to the mother. "Do you wish to hold her again?" I asked softly.

Her eyes brimmed with tears, but she seemed too numb to respond.

I turned back to the husband. "While I hold authority on this land," I spoke slowly, searching for the right words, "no man will with my knowledge leave his wife to starve—except starvation becomes our common lot." I turned to the woman then and addressed her directly, "Woman, you are ordered to the Keep. Food is in short supply but is not traded for ale. There are tasks by which your husband can earn his daily bread. But I will not leave you to starve while he seeks his death with drink."

The man leaned toward me with big fists raised, mouth tasting curses as he searched for the right one. "Git outta my house, horse-killing thræl. Git your hands off my bairn and don't even think you can interfere with my wife."

"Already you have disowned the baby and shamed your wife in my presence," I responded. "She starves while you drink." I passed the baby into the arms of the mother, who wept aloud for the first time in my presence.

"Shut up woman!" the man roared at her. He raised a hand to strike her, but found my sword at his throat. He backed into the wall, the colour draining from his face. I pressed the blade against sagging flesh. He began to gasp.

"You like not my authority." I measured my words and spoke harshly. "I have intervened little in the village. Yet once before a woman was shamed."

"Nooooo," the man groaned. His strength failed him and he sank to the floor.

"She was a harlot, despised by most people. How then, should I treat the shaming of a wife?"

"Mercy, Sire. I will'na strike her again."

"I'm Sire now, though I was horse-killer thræl moments ago." I sniffed. "Just as firmly as those two fit together, does your promise fit with who and what you are."

I ushered the woman with her dead infant from the house, then turned back to the guards. "Ten lashes for him, Chapman. Increase it by one for every time he curses me, or any of my people, but do not exceed 20. Then let him return to his ale jug. He is more in chains to it than any thræl to his master."

Back in the Keep I sent for Dierdre. "Give this woman what aid you can," I instructed quietly. "You will know better than I how to help her. Her milk is probably in. I have seen cows in pain after losing a calf."

"She is starving. She has no milk." Dierdre stared at me a moment. "What of the bairn?"

"I don't know if she will want a funeral fire or a burial."

"And her husband?" she asked.

"He is facing the lash as we speak. While she starves, he drinks."

"So you have made her a widow the same day she lost her bairn?"

Dierdre's gaze searched my face.

"A widow?" I questioned. "I'm not hanging him. I have several times offered him work, little though we can afford more mouths to feed." I stared at her helplessly for a moment, then burst out. "Would you consider marriage, Dierdre—to one so young, who knows so little about women?"

"What?" she sputtered. "You throw that at me now. You scarcely speak to me for months. Then, with a dead baby and a starving mother . . ." She burst into tears.

I stared at her, searched for words, but found none. Totally baffled, feeling like a failure and a fool, I fled the room.

I shunned company and spent the afternoon and evening clearing the entrance to the catacombs. Whatever decision the woman made there would be future burials. Dressed stone closed in few of the shelves. Most waited for the final sleep of people who never returned to this prepared place. Ramps led up two levels and down three. Built for many bodies, it housed less than a dozen.

The morning dawned bleak and cold, a raw northwest wind blowing. Lacking the stimulus of a real storm, it simply sucked the warmth from anyone out in it. We made a slow and solemn procession to the crypt, though we little knew the woman and none but her had held the bairn alive. The burial of infants was common to my people, but my memory had nothing to put beside this experience. As master of the house I carried the infant. It seemed with every step my grief grew heavier, though the bundle itself seemed weightless.

Alone, I entered the crypt and laid the tiny body in the place prepared for it. Torches gave a weird and ghostly light to this place of the dead. I heard the sound of wailing outside, first one voice, then several, and it seemed the cry of my heart. I left the torches burning, turned and shifted the stone across the opening.

Chapter Fifteen
Mighty in Battle

A MARRIAGE TOOK PLACE two weeks later. I blessed the couple and strained our meager rations to give as good a feast as could be provided. They left the celebration amidst laughter and snickering advice. My gaze caught and held Dierdre's. I ached with a nameless longing. "I am a fool, Dierdre." I muttered the words as I stepped up beside her.

"Aye, Theodoric. That you are." Dierdre responded with a smile that took the sting from her words. She passed Ilsa into my arms and turned to face me. "You also care for your people, even this fatherless bairn." Her hand reached out to her daughter, touching my arm and lingering there for a moment. Ilsa patted my face and babbled excitedly. "Aye," she continued. "And young enough for a leader, but not unable for all that. You've done much good and stood strong against the evil."

I gazed across the crowd who continued to celebrate. "Who will prepare the feast if you wed? I fear to ask again, for we might all starve."

"Ha!" she responded. "Like most men. Thinking of your belly."

The moment passed and again I had left so much unsaid. Dierdre took Ilsa back and returned to supervising the feast.

I went often to the crypt and held vigil for I was master of the house and the first of my people had been laid there. I would wordlessly cry to the unknown god. I had by now read all of the *Isaiae filii Amos* scroll and longed to know more of this god. A passage that drew me even stronger to him came far into the scroll. Written in a poetic style completely beyond my skill, my translation still caught some hint of the wonder:

Thus sayeth that high and excellent one,
him that liveth where eternity dwells,
whose name is holy,
I dwell in the high and holy place
with him that is contrite and of humble spirit
to revive the spirit of the humble,
and to give life to them that have sorrow for the ill of their actions.[iv]

The baby's death left me with deep questions about life and death. The tales of Valhalla, where Woden's heroes fought epic battles, did not stir my desires. Endless war and bloodshed did not make such a future attractive. None of the old gods seemed to offer anything worthy of pursuit. Perhaps our deaths meant nothing, but the ache in my gut would not ease.

Erhard and Bertrm knew more of the old gods than I, for they had heard many stories over the years. They evidenced no burning need to know what the future held, yet the best the old gods seemed to offer dissatisfied them also at some level.

Glenine, the baby's mother lost her sickly, pinched look within a couple of weeks, but her eyes showed little life. I had not seen her enter the crypt to grieve there, but felt little surprise the day I found the door open.

What can someone like me know of a mother's sorrow? I slipped inside the crypt and knelt beside her, a deep ache welling up within me. I don't know when my own tears started or when she became aware of my presence.

"Thank you, Milord," she whispered when I stood to leave. I noticed a bundle of rags tied into a rope beside her. I felt a new wave of grief over her pain. For a long moment I did not trust myself to speak, though I did not know where she could have attached the rope.

"You won't need that now, will you?" I finally asked. I kept my voice as gentle as possible.

The pain washed across her face once more. Her lip trembled and tears again flowed down her cheeks. She shook her head, then grabbed the bundle and thrust it toward me.

"I would have laid you beside your daughter," I said softly. "But I think—I hope you'll soon find life worth living again. Does your bairn have a name?"

"Guinevére," Glenine breathed the word in a voice I scarcely heard.

"Guinevére," I responded. "The white wave." I gazed on the box for a moment, then turned back to her. "I will leave you in peace now." I wiped my eyes with the bundle of rags. "If I knew a god of comfort, one I dared trust, I would pray to him for you." I paused a moment, then continued. "The nameless one from the *Isaiae filii Amos* scroll—him I would call on if I only knew how."

Life had beaten Glenine down, though she could have been at most a few years older than me. She began to smile occasionally as the days passed, and to receive and give friendship. But the worn and weathered look of a wearied grandmother did not leave her.

I tried to find moments with Dierdre, but she found ready excuses to evade me. The vision of creamy white flesh as the baby nursed had stuck with me, burned into my mind like a brand.

Fractured memories are a curse. I could not make even a good guess at my age. Spittin' Sheffield had just turned fifteen, with a new scraggly beard when I left Mr. Gerhardt's farm. He had seemed painfully immature to me, yet my beard had not begun to grow until less than a year ago. I had talked of *marriage* to Dierdre. No wonder she had cried.

Leadership had matured me, as had each crisis we had weathered. I wondered if the Ring might have an effect also. I sometimes checked my reflection, fearing to find grey in my beard. Some days I felt older than the grandfathers who leaned on staffs and could no longer see their cups before them at the board.

I had never actually touched the Ring. It sat on the rowan staff, covered most of the time with the skin of the wild boar. Over and over I had read the prophecies. I often held the staff and gazed at the boar carved into the piece of tusk inlaid in gold. I called myself a superstitious fool, but still hesitated to touch it.

Two families showed up in early March after a thaw. They came with all their possessions on a pair of wagons pulled by a yoke of oxen each. Between them they also brought a milk cow, an old horse and true treasure, a barrel filled with wheat seed. Two plodding men and their worn wives, two sturdy boys in their early teens, a pretty girl, not yet nubile, and four younger children made up the families.

The fields we had planted with fall crops of wheat and rye showed first through dwindling snow, but we put the plow to other land even before the snow had departed the hollows and shaded places. Two more yoke of oxen and men who knew their nature proved of great assistance.

The sun finally emerged after several days of cold rain in early April. We began preparing garden plots within the Keep and also in the village. I set men the task of digging a well in the village. I also marked out fields, that the villagers might begin to do something for themselves. The lone horseman appeared also, and twice, some of my men found themselves within shouting distance. Again, he chose not to respond and quickly fled when pursued.

Guests continued to arrive, many bringing gifts from the lords of other houses. The gifts included seed, livestock and bolts of cloth, kegs of wine and ale, barrels of pickled pork and beef, and a flock of chickens with a feisty rooster. I could not repay in kind, but welcomed the guests and showed them about the Keep.

April drew to a close. Crops showed early green in a number of fields. On two fields I had ignored the advice of all, scattering seed in double measure before the oxen dragged a harrow across to cover it.

A new mood prevailed in the village. As more people arrived I did not discourage some of the industrious ones from settling there and plying their trades. They had planted fields and built a low stone wall around the burial place.

Beltane, the first of May approached. I had risen before sunrise to walk the wall. Heavy fog drifted from the west. Two-thirds of the circuit had I made when the trumpet sounded. Blood-curdling yells and a wild, undulating trumpet sound reached me seconds later, screams and the sounding of several of our own trumpets. I broke into a run, shouting to each guard as I passed to remain at his post.

I descended to the floor of the Keep, then sprinted for the stable. Bertrm had my horse saddled and weapons ready. I nodded grimly and swung into the saddle.

I rushed my horse to the top of the wall near the gatehouse as the eastern sky began to show pink. Fire already poured from several buildings in the village, glowing eerily through the fog. A scattered few ran toward the nearest bridge, but dark bodies swinging savage blades cut them down. Screams and cries and the wild war cry of the Pict tore the early morning apart. The strange warbling trumpet call continued to sound, a dreadful din such as I had never heard.

"How many of them?" I shouted to the watchman as I descended from the wall.

"Not more'n twenty, Sir, 'less the fog hides more. Tis a raiding party of those blue painted devils, not a army."

"Then it's a raiding party that will not be going home," I spat the words. Armed warriors came from all directions, flowing toward the gate. Only five of us had horses.

I chose thirty warriors, simply drawing them to me with the sweep of my hand. "Four at every post, for the rest of you. Twenty in the ditches. Hold the walls even if we perish. Bridges up behind us." I shouted my orders, then galloped toward the gate. It swung open as I approached. Four horsemen spurred madly to join me while the foot-men came at a run behind. My horse's hooves rang on the surface of the first bridge before it had fully descended. I wore no spurs, not having had time to put them on, but my horse, Lorellefue—Little Fool—gave the lie to her name.

I had left the other riders several lengths behind when the screaming mouth of the first Pict I had seen leered at me, aiming a spear at my chest. I leaned aside at the last second, even as my sword swung at the obscene body. Before he hit the ground I had turned to the next, intending to simply run him down. I had read of horses trained for battle, but Lorellefue was not so trained. She tried to miss the man even as I leaned, trying to turn her into him. She almost un-seated me as she struck his shoulder. The full length of my sword edge, swinging low, came across belly and chest. A sickness welled inside me even as my eyes searched for the next enemy.

An arrow struck my lower leg and the horse screamed, for it pierced through and pinned me to her. I shouted then, a battle cry of my own. Leaning to the left, I forced my leg to slide along the shaft of the arrow, then slashed the bloody exposed length with my sword. My horse screamed again and jerked to the right, for the arrow had torn her.

We had entered the burning village now. Lorellefue leaped over bodies, twisted and turned to the pressure of my knees. We fought and bled as one.

I did not see the spear that took her down. She buckled beneath me at full gallop. I hurtled past her and struck chest first on the ground, beside a boulder. My sword struck the boulder as I fell, breaking the blade.

With the breath knocked from me and my head ringing, I turned to see a warrior charging with a wicked looking battleaxe. I ripped the broken shaft of the arrow from my leg, jerked myself sideways then drove my arm upward, the splintered end of the arrow finding his belly.

His mouth hung open in a scream as I grabbed his long braid and jerked him backwards. His head hit the boulder with a solid crunch. Blood trickled from his mouth and one ear, but I barely saw, grabbing up his battleaxe and swinging toward a scream that drew close. While a spear ripped at my cloak, the axe cut down my attacker.

I stood then, chest heaving, searching among the wreckage. Cries of pain and terror still sounded, but the Pict trumpets no longer added their horrific noise and no Pict screamed their war cries. Flames crackled and timbers fell, but battle cries had stopped. I called my own battle cry again, a long and high pitched savage call, and knew myself in that moment as much a savage as the Pict who lay dead around me, naked bodies tattooed with woad.

I stared at the man before me, entrails spilled on the ground, staring eyes already starting to glaze. The sickness hit then and I vomited, all my great battle skills forgotten.

The sun had fully risen and melted the remnants of fog. I sent out scouts, searching for other war parties. Two of the groups carried a caged pigeon. The others had none who could write. We gathered the Pict together. Two still lived, though badly wounded. Two of my men-at-arms and many from the village had died. Taking a spear from one of my footmen, I drove it through the living Pict, rage battling the sickness that washed over me in waves.

Ravens circled as we gathered wood and prepared to burn the bodies. At mid-morning a runner brought the scroll from a pigeon's leg. It reported a camp guarded by ten Pict three miles north, beside a small burn.

I left 30 men to guard the Keep, dragged myself painfully onto another horse, and with the footmen breaking into three groups started them at a swift march. I took the horsemen, now just three in number, for we had lost two horses. Two more caged pigeons the footmen carried with them.

We made a long loop. I dismounted when we approached close and crept up on the Pict camp. The wound in my leg throbbed, but the battle-blood pumped hot. I recognized two horses stolen from Mr. Gerhardt's farm. A cow hung from a tree, gutted and partly cut away. A huge roast turned on a spit over a fire.

A guard picked his teeth with a knife as I crept up on him. He cursed in a language I did not know, swept his hand at the gathered booty in a gesture of dismissal and shouted to someone close to the fire. My left hand cupped his mouth while a short, sharp blade cut his throat. Beyond a slight gurgle, he never made another sound.

Two more guards, over-lax in their watching, died under my hand. My belly had nothing more to vomit, but still it tried. I had the skill, it seemed, for a warrior, but not the stomach.

Birds bursting from the trees drew the attention of the five Pict close to the fire. Two more guards watched from the other side of the clearing. I held their skill in contempt, for it seemed I had made a clumsy circuit to take down the three who had already fallen, but they had not seen me.

With their focus drawn toward the east, I slipped among the horses stolen from Mr. Gerhardt. They seemed to still know me, so made no disturbance at my approach. I caught up a spear from the ground, cut the rope that held Mr. Gerhardt's prize gelding, then swung myself low on his back. I caught the gaze of my companion peering through the trees and signaled him to return to the horses and prepare to charge. He disappeared from my sight.

Three long minutes I waited while the horse stamped impatiently beneath me. I could feel that now familiar tightening of my gut, then I drew a deep breath, drove my heels into the horse's sides and shouted my battle cry as I burst upon the startled Pict from the midst of their camp.

The spear impaled two of them as the horse ran down a third. I wheeled around, though the horse, without a bridal, responded slowly. An arrow whistled past my head, then I flung myself aside as a spear flashed. A single dreadful trumpet sounded, then fell silent as an arrow tore through the trumpeter's throat. A Pict arrow, it had missed me by inches.

My other two mounted warriors exploded into the campsite, shouting and swinging swords. The two Pict close to the fire fell. The shout of the footmen sounded with the crash of breaking branches as they drove directly toward the sound of my battle cry. I shouted it again, then turned my horse toward the two remaining guards. An arrow took the horse from beneath me. He reared, screaming. I rolled to the side and hit the ground hard. I dropped, then heaved myself up again, climbing the short, steep incline to the guard's post. An arrow struck a tree beside my head, then a form emerged, charging me with screaming mouth and sword swinging. I met the charge with my feet planted, parried his blade and drove my shoulder into his greater bulk, flinging him sideways.

He came at me again, scrabbling on the steep slope. We both had need to use one hand for balance, fighting awkwardly with the other. Fighting on my left, he put me at a disadvantage, for I must twist to bring my sword into play. He also showed great strength and skill. An arrow grazed my throat, bringing a shout from the footmen who had arrived and witnessed our battle with bows drawn. A volley of arrows brought a gurgling scream that died into silence from some ten paces to my right.

My enemy used his sword like a battle-axe and it seemed as hard and heavy. When mine broke, leaving me only the stump of a blade, a leering grin made his face even more hideous.

I threw myself backwards and rolled down the hill. He followed me. My men-at-arms held their weapons ready, but left the two of us to fight it out.

A small rowan sapling tore from the ground as I tried to stop my plunge to the bottom of the short hill. With the small tree and the broken sword, I faced the biggest man I had ever fought. He stood a head taller than me, with massive shoulders and a deep, muscular chest. The woad added to the image of incredible strength, while tattoos of slavering jaws on his chest brought even more to the horror of his appearance.

His gaze took in the warriors who surrounded us. He faced certain death, but it seemed I did too. He screamed his war cry again as he charged me.

The rowan sapling slapped at him, snagging his sword. My own broken weapon caught him in the belly. He laughed, a drunken, insane sound, rubbed his left hand in the blood and smeared it across his face, making himself even more hideous than before, then brought his sword up and swung it in a two handed blow. It sunk into the wood and I released the sapling. As he tried to stamp on the small tree and jerk his blade free, howling his rage, I hurled myself at him and again my short piece of sword cut him, this time in the chest. He closed on me with bare arms, a contest I could not survive. I dropped backwards and drove the heel of my boot into his knee. He screamed as he fell toward me. My sword caught him and his own weight drove it into his chest the full depth of the broken blade. His hands strained for my throat. The grasping fingers clawed at me, but I thrust back against his great weight, lifting him, holding him above me, then rolling to the side, leaving him impaled on my sword as he fell clear.

My men raised a shout that rose and swelled across the forest. The footmen formed a ring, slapping shields with their swords. Blood covered me. Still my men stood about me shouting and cheering.

They brought the horse I had ridden from the village. I pulled myself up and managed to drag myself into the saddle while everything spun around me. The men shouted again, a great and triumphant cry.

Blackness played at the corners of my mind. I told the men to set a watch, but to take their rest and eat of the meat already cooking. One company of footmen I ordered to Mr. Gerhardt's farm under Durward's leadership to see if we could offer assistance. I ordered signal flashes sent back to the watchtower.

Voices faded as the brightest shield in our company caught the sunlight. My hand no longer held the sword. The ground came up to meet me.

Chapter Sixteen

A Power Not Understood

Dierdre sang to her child just out of sight. I walked toward her, but never drew closer. I called, but she did not answer. I tried to run, but my legs would move no faster. A man with woad-stained face held Ilsa, holding a great sword also. Dierdre cried to me to save her, but the hand that tried to grasp my sword had no fingers and the blade clattered to the ground.

A warm cloth touched my face. I awoke in my own bed. The broken sword, still bloodstained, leaned against the wall. A strange trumpet leaned there as well. Memories flooded in. I still wore the robe I had fought in. A savage headache answered my first attempt to move, but I slowly swung my feet to the side, then forced myself to stand.

"You should stay abed, Milord," Dierdre whispered.

"Aye," I agreed, "but even more, I should tell these people how proud I am of them." I stood and swayed, waiting till the room stopped spinning.

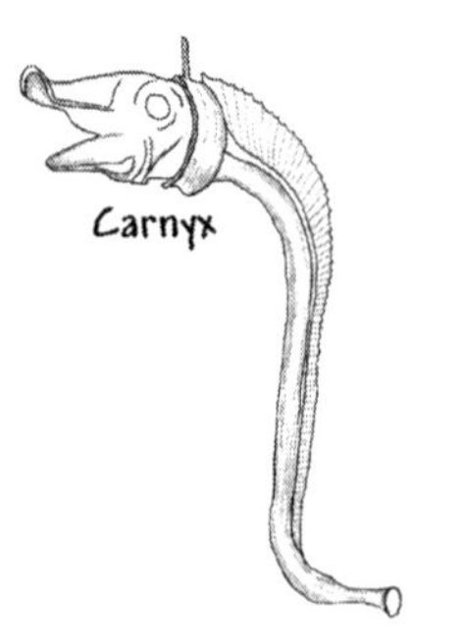

"What is that thing?" I questioned, nodding at the trumpet somewhat resembling a boar's head on a serpent's body.

"Erhard called it a carnyx," Dierdre informed me. "It be the Pict war-trumpet. And a fearful sound it makes."

"So that was what I heard among the screams. The halls of the dead could scarcely sound a more dreadful noise."

I leaned heavily on Dierdre as I walked from the room, my left leg barely holding me. I smelled at once the sweetness of her flesh and the stink of my sweat.

The shout, when I emerged, struck my pounding head like the blacksmith swinging his biggest hammer at it. For a long time I gazed at my people. The headache seemed to recede and my pride in them swelled. I raised my hands. The shouting stilled.

"No one knows, I think, until the midst of a battle, how they will act. I have seen a people under a young, untried leader—act as a disciplined army in the face of a ruthless enemy. I have no words for my thanks. I have no words for my pride in you."

They shouted again. Erhard approached and stood on one side of me, while Bertrm came to my other side. Bertrm held the broken sword. Erhard held the rowan staff and a piece of parchment.

The crowd became quiet. Erhard shouted to them. "Thirty-two men have we counted among the slain enemy." They shouted again. He waited for them to quiet. "Four died under our young leader's hand in the first battle, seven under his hand in the second." The shout again swelled and echoed.

"In both battles he broke his sword," Erhard continued when he could make his voice heard again. "In both battles his horse was killed under him. In both battles with weapons broken he fought on, and in both battles he prevailed. Two men he took down with one spear thrust. And with a broken sword he faced a huge man who fought like a fiend. Let me read you an old, old prophecy, and if there be any doubt lingering that this man is the true heir to the Ring of Thorvæld, may this put it to rest."

"Some of you know the first thing he done at Mr. Gerhardt's farm," Bertrm interrupted Erhard, "was to water a horse when it was hot, foundering it. The horse was a stallion, Master Gerhardt's favorite, and it had to be destroyed. He knowed no better, for he was totally ignorant of horses."

Erhard read from the scroll fragment I had first translated in his presence.

Feared the nine fingers that wield weapons of war, yet give no quarter when weapons be broken all.

Bertrm grabbed my left arm and lifted it. I spread my hand, showing the gap. In his other hand, Bertrm raised the broken sword. The shout drowned Erhard's reading. He paused, then continued.

Many the blows of his beating. He the accused. Yet of old is the prophecy. The ring by him found shall give proof of his office. He is a warrior born. His destiny from of old is sealed. Yet few will his title recognize or give the honour due him.

Trials and much wrong will first ensue. Then will be restored to him the ring who alone may rightfully wear it.

Of nine fingers is he. Mighty in battle. Called of old Killer of horses.

His son perchance will better fare with seemly honour and the tribute of men.

For fierce will be the battle in that day. Many the dead. Loud the weeping. The raven and the vulture feed. Black the smoke of funeral piers.

The crowd continued to shout. Then more and more voices took up one call. "The ring! Let him wear the ring!"

The call could not be denied. I could not explain my reluctance at a time like this. I doubted even Erhard and Bertrm knew I had never touched the ring, though I had carried it often on the rowan staff.

The voices seemed to recede. My wounded left leg threatened to topple me. I found myself turning the ring, sliding it down, off the staff. My vision seemed dim and cloudy as I slid it onto my right arm. The shout grew louder, but came from farther away. I seemed to see two worlds, misty and distant. I turned to question Erhard. Bertrm still held the broken sword, and Erhard the scroll, but the back of the hall had disappeared.

A great hall roofed with stone and lit by many torches resounded to the shout of an army. Men wore heavy armour and carried swords and spears. Exhaustion marked the faces of many.

"The Ring of Thorvæld will not be taken, whether we live or die. My kinsman will see to it." The speaker sat a white stallion in the midst of the hall, lathered from the conflict and stained with blood. The sword he held aloft showed the nicks of hard blows. His own blood added red streaks on his warhorse.

"We ride to glory, in victory or defeat." He turned and fixed his gaze on me. "My son, not yet a man, will live to bear the sword again. Muninn's Keep will echo to the sounds of an army."

"For Muninn's Keep and for the House of Thorvæld! Glory! Valour!" the shouts rose. "For the champion of Muninn's Keep! For the nine fingered one!"

The man who had called me, 'son' rode to the big double doors that stood open to a narrow gorge and a cloudy sky. His left hand, resting on the saddle, was short one finger.

An old man stood near the great double doors, holding a wooden box high with a large ring resting in it.

"Guard well the Ring, Uncle, for his son and all his seed who follow." He rode from the hall and the army poured out behind him.

Above the door a carved stone displayed the words, "Se Hus of Thorvæld."

Panting, I smelled the sweat of battle, heard the shouting from some far distance, felt the exhausted muscles, the wounds. The dream slowly faded. The shouting drew nearer. Erhard and Bertrm steadied me. The rowan staff Erhard carried did not hold the ring, a strange and troubling absence. The parchment lay on the floor.

An unusual weight drew my gaze to my right arm. I slid the ring off my wrist and placed it again on the rowan staff. A shaky laugh escaped as I gazed across the crowd, then back at my close friends.

"The ring should not oft be worn," I said as I tried to steady my trembling body. "There is a power about it I do not understand."

"Rest now, Milord," Erhard shouted over the crowd's noise. "You have led your people in battle and given them praise. You be wounded and exhausted. You have eaten nothing."

"Aye, rest Milord. All be in good hands." Bertrm added. "Your people have seen a true lord in action."

Someone held a cup to my lips and I drank. In a strange dream the nine-fingered man who had called me 'son' held the ring and shouted as he fell—endlessly—down the well, with the boar-tusk knife plunging down behind him.

I awoke to the confusion of men-at-arms returning from Mr. Gerhardt's farm. The smell of blood and sweat still clung to me. My clothing, newly washed and still damp, draped a chair. A tub of warm water stood in the room.

I found my left leg reluctant to bear my weight. I wrapped the blanket about my body and threw back the door to the tramping of many feet.

"Half we left to help rebuild Master Gerhardt's stable," Durward answered my unspoken question as my gaze searched for the rest of the group. "Three men and one wench did Master Gerhardt lose. But they sold their lives dear, for twelve did we count of Pict dead," Durward continued. "Erskine, of whom I have heard you speak well, must have fought much like you, Sir, for five of the dead lay around him. No living enemy did we see."

"Eat of the best the house can provide." I told the group. "Rest yourselves and bathe, but listen still for the trumpet call. One battle does not win a war." As if on cue the trumpet sounded a warning that strangers approached. "Rest while you may, warriors of Muninn's Keep," I called. "But lay your weapons not far aside."

As a messenger rushed into the room the men shouted again, then began to file out, their weariness forgotten for a few moments. "Mounted warriors approach from the south, Sire," the messenger informed me. "Their number lacks a few of twenty. Heavy armour they and their horses wear. No footmen follow and nothing can be seen in any other direction save smoke from Master Gerhardt's farm. They come at a trot, Sire, making haste while saving their horses. A half hour will have them at our gate."

"Bear they any standard?" I questioned.

"Aye, Sire, but the wind holds it behind and it cannot be clearly seen. The Wyvern of Stigelburne, one of the watch swears—the banner of the lord of Drahæm—but I know not how he sees enough to tell."

I turned to Erhard who had approached. "It is probably not to our help if it is them," I observed quietly. "The priest whose followers cut the trees in the Circle of Stones was Bishop of Drahæm. Little friendship will he hold toward me."

The bath water still beckoned my sweaty body, but I shrugged. "Sound the alarm. Have everything of value brought from the village, little as there is. Leave no person behind, even if you must bring some in chains. I would have the Keep secure and warriors in the trenches. Send forty of the young and swift to the village—not those newly arrived from Mr. Gerhardt's farm, willing though some would be. Prepare a horse for me."

"They be a powerful people who might be your allies that you set yourself against, Milord," Erhard said softly to me, even as the trumpets blasted the alarm.

"I set myself against none, Erhard. But a powerful people who serve their own interests only, yet demand tribute, will be as welcome to my hearth-fire as the Pict. Still, if they come in true friendship I will welcome them. But twenty mounted warriors I will not invite inside the walls till I know their allegiance."

The wounded already lay within the Keep. No second alarm did it take to bring a stampede across the bridges.

I strode back into my room, biting my lip against the pain in my left leg. Dropping the blanket I stepped into the tub, now cool. I scrubbed myself with a rag and a lump of harsh soap, ripping scabs off. With the water blood-stained I stepped out. Not taking time to dry, I pulled my robe on, attached my scabbard and checked the blade now nested in it. The stink of the forge clung to a new sword so I knew Pollard had worked through the night as I slept. Again the industry of my people astonished me.

A horse approached the house at a trot as I limped out the door. Hardly had the groom dismounted before I swung into the saddle, again struggling with the weakness of my left leg. "Thank you, Sir," I shouted as I spurred the horse toward the Keep wall.

Three young men struggled to bring a balky ewe and twin lambs into the Keep. Otherwise all stood empty around the village. A rope caught the animal and with one pulling and two pushing, they dragged her across the first two bridges. The lambs then, bleating in panic, raced after her. As riders emerged from the trees a half mile distant, the bridges rose.

"What is that on the wall—beside my standard?" I questioned, hoping my supposition was wrong.

"I suspected you would not be pleased Surra," Erhard responded. "It is meant to honour you. It be heads of men you slew."

"I would have them down before the riders reach the wall," I said softly, holding my anger in check.

"It will be done," Erhard affirmed. He turned to a messenger and gave swift, terse instructions, then turned back to gaze at the approaching riders. "Tis the Wyvern of Stigelburne on the standard, Surra," Erhard confirmed. "It will be men from the lord of Drahæm who approach. And you have read aright, Surra. They make but poor friends."

"Come they to our aid or our hurt, then?" I asked.

"Tis too small a number to give threat to the Keep, except they was invited inside. Their words, I think, will be words of friendship, yet a self-serving group have they ever proved in my years with Mr. Gerhardt."

My own standard, a wild boar, blew on a banner over the gate and also from the watchtower. The pikes with Pict heads were just now being lowered. I turned and gazed up to the watchtower. "The watch has reported no others approaching?"

"Nay, Surra," Erhard confirmed. "And no fog today hinders their vision." He paused a moment, then continued. "The tavern keeper, Surra. He was loath to leave his barrels unguarded. Two men he struck down with his fists before a spear convinced him of your orders."

"Then he chose poorly when he built outside the Keep," I responded. "Are the men injured?"

"Only in their pride, Surra."

"Then we will let the matter rest. I may have words with the man after this is over. Then again, it seems a small thing in light of the last days."

Twenty men had already taken up position in the trenches, crouching behind the low walls with arrows notched and their spears beside them.

"They are a good people, Erhard," I observed with swelling pride.

"They follow a good leader, Surra, wise beyond his years who cares for the least of them."

The approaching warriors walked their horses slowly past the village where smoke still drifted from destroyed buildings. They stopped and gazed at the pile of burning Pict dead. Erhard and Bertrm had begun the burning while I slept. The warriors put heels to their horses again and slowly approached the outer bridge.

"Come you to our aid or to our hurt?" I called from the Keep wall.

"Why are we met as an enemy with closed gates and raised bridges? Better had we heard of the nine-fingered thræl who styles himself lord of this place," a helmed rider shouted.

"You see clearly the answer behind you," I responded. "The burning that drew you was kindled many hours ago. Aid so slowly offered has the look of something other than aid."

I glanced at Erhard, then continued. "Three adult souls and one infant accompanied the nine-fingered *thræl* to this place, free, each one of them and able to make their own choice. All others have come also by their own choosing. Yet thræl is he not for his freedom did he purchase and high the price he paid. State then your business. Armed warriors who stand outside the walls and cast slurs on the leader of this house choose a strange way to show friendship if that is their intent."

After several minutes one man moved forward a few paces. He drew his sword and passed it back to another. He thrust his spear into the ground, then pulled his helmet off. Thus vulnerable he walked his horse forward and crossed to the second bridge. "Poorly have we begun this interview, Milord," he called up to me. "Nor can you be faulted for taking precautions. It might amuse you to know three of us have lost costly wagers, for we thought to ride directly into the Keep under the banner we fly."

"Your banner earns little love north of the wall, Sir. In the twenty years past, nine times have riders approached the farm of Mr. Gerhardt under that banner, each time following a battle with the Pict. They have ridden through his crops, eaten meat of animals they have butchered and demanded tribute before they hurried back to the safety south of the wall. Tis a history clearly set in the writings."

"I can little comment on that, Sir. Two years only have I been with the lord of Drahæm. I have not before today ridden north of the wall."

"And was exacting tribute not part of your purpose in coming?" I challenged him.

"Aye, Sir, for we were assured the strength of our sword gave you much safety and t'was a tribute readily earned. That, and word of the bishop who came this way and did not return."

"You see the bodies of the enemy burning behind you and the destruction in the village," I responded. "Four hours from the smoke first rising could have brought you here while yet there were enemy alive. It wants but a few hours to be 48 since the battle began. Tell then the dead for me, the safety your sword has won for my people."

"Tis both a bold and a rash statement," the man said, then paused for a long moment. "The Pict begin early this season," he finally said. "Though you threw them back your losses have been high. Do not so quickly reject our help. And the bishop?"

"The bishop left before the first snow with all the wealth on his person, alone and in shame," I declared. "He proved a sorry and foolish servant of the god he followed."

"Aye. That may be. But to flog a man of the church?" He shook his head as if it was beyond belief. "He was a powerful man. One with more years and wisdom would not have made an enemy of him or the church behind him."

"If the church wants respect it has need to earn respect," I replied bluntly. "The Bishop failed at that. More, he brought shame to the god he claimed to serve."

The man looked past me, searching for someone else. "Who leads this people?" he asked. "I would speak with Theodoric Thorvæld, the one who bears the ring."

"Have a care, Surra," Erhard spoke from beside me. "Theodoric Thorvæld it be who has spoke to you."

"Nay. It is a war leader I seek, not a man-child. No bairn overcame this enemy."

An angry mutter swept among my men. "You endanger your life to speak so before the men who have watched him fight," Erhard's voice rang out hard and cold. "Thirty-two men have we counted among the Pict dead. Eleven of them by this man was slain in battle and two more by him executed. Two horses was slain under him.

Two swords he broke, yet fought on. Tis no laddie you speak to, Surra."

"Peace, Erhard," I said firmly.

One of the young lads ran up to me with the rowan staff. I nodded my thanks as I took it from him. I untied the piece of pigskin that covered the ring and lifted the staff. "Here, Sir, is the Ring of Thorvæld, held by the nine-fingered one. If too savage I am, or too young, then you have come in vain."

"Is it possible then?" the man questioned.

"Ask my men, many of whom are still battle-weary and some wounded."

"Yet you will welcome us not? Seek you to make an enemy of us then?"

"I seek no enmity, nor turn down any friendship. Yet hard pressed am I to call it friendship when you come at this hour, expecting to go home with tribute."

I thought long before I continued. "Hard pressed am I to find reason to put trust in the strength of your sword, when in twenty years that sword has shown more likeness to the beak of the vulture than to the tusks of the boar, oft picking among the dead, but not engaging the enemy in battle."

"No more can I say then," the man responded. "Poorly will your words be received by my lord. Poorer indeed, if there be truth in them. Where shall I look for the body of the bishop?"

"In his shame he may have fled south. He had wealth to sustain him, or make him target of every thief for a hundred leagues."

I rewrapped the Ring of Thorvæld, then walked my horse from the wall, deaf to the voices around me. The unresponsive mount I sat made me ache for Lorellefue, killed beneath me so recently.

"You are a good friend and advisor, Erhard," I said quietly. "If you know who placed the heads on pikes, inform them I thank them for the honour, but do not find such decoration to my taste." I drew a long, slow breath. "I must speak to the issue soon, but would choose another day if I might." I reluctantly turned my attention to tending the dead.

Chapter Seventeen
Wounded Warrior

I FOUND MYSELF UNABLE TO CLIMB the stairs to the watchtower. My leg wound would barely let me walk level ground.

"We have another problem, Sir," Bertrm informed me. "The father of the bairn what died, Burleigh, he barters gold for wine. Tis a ring of the priest of the Christus, else I am much mistook."

"So leaving the priest with his wealth was sentence of death upon him," I responded. "His crime was not so great as to deserve that." I limped slowly to the blacksmith shop. "Have the man brought to me at the old forge," I commanded softly.

I unbound the pigskin that covered the Ring of Thorvæld, then leaned towards Burleigh. The flesh of his cheeks sagged and his body seemed more than his legs could bear. "A priest of the Christus, a foolish and arrogant man, wore rings of gold and carried a heavy purse when sent from my presence," I said. "The rings were seen by many of my people for gold is in short supply. How came you into possession of one of those rings?" I asked.

"I could buy the whole Keep," the man boasted, yet his voice broke. "A drink to steady my nerves, Sir."

I dipped the cup that hung beside a water jug and held it out toward him. He eagerly grabbed and lifted it, then cursed and hurled it down, breaking it and spilling the water.

"You mock me, Thræl. A man's drink I would have." His face twisted into a sneer. "You wouldna know what a man's drink was—newly weaned calf."

"Your own greed mocks you. Tell me how you came by this gold, for it has the smell of murder about it."

Turning to Bertrm I asked, "How long to prepare a gallows?"

"A hour, Sir. Less if two able bodied laddies give help."

"Nay, Sire! T'was no murder." The man gasped the words in terror. "Torn by wild pigs he was, and eaten by vultures. Within sight of the great wall. I found him jist after the first snow."

"And while you hoarded this wealth and drank the winter away, your wife starved," I observed bluntly.

"I dared not spend it freely. I wouldda gone south, but winter was too far advanced. I feared to use it here, but the purse is buried in the village. I hadna but the ring sewed into my clothes when the Pict attacked. A drink, Sire. A small drink only. So much have I risked for one, and now you know all."

"I know what you have chosen to make known, whether true or not." I pointed to the broken clay cup at my feet. "A drink I have already offered. Suck from the mud what you will. Till another day dawns you will receive no more."

I turned to Erhard. "Hold him in chains. When we break fast in the morning, see that he is offered food and water. No one shall give him ale or strong drink. After several days, when he is able, he will guide searchers to the remains of the body. If those remains verify his story he might be set free. If they indicate murder, he will hang."

To the rest I said, "You who love strong drink, look well to this man. He calls me thræl, but never was I in such bondage as this man to the jug. Tis a sickness beyond his strength to break. It has totally unmanned him, though he calls it a man's drink. He is reduced to begging for the cup like an infant cries for a breast. Mark it well and turn not oft to the jug."

I wrapped the pigskin around the Ring of Thorvæld once again, then walked from the blacksmith shop, leaning on the rowan staff.

"I had a strange dream during my sickness, Erhard," I confided, the memory clear in my mind. "One who called me 'Son' rode to war. From the great hall he rode, an army with him. Bleeding and exhausted, he left the Ring in the keeping of one he called 'Uncle' and left a boy in the uncle's care." I mused for a moment. "The dream was painfully real, yet it could not have been my father—riding from this hall. It had to have been from many generations past."

"Would that I had skill to interpret dreams, Surra." Erhard responded slowly. "It sounds more a memory than a dream. Do you doubt—still—that you be the true heir of the House of Thorvæld?"

"Only rarely do I doubt it—and fear the Ring in those moments. In all the time I had carried it, I had never touched it until my people called for it after the battle." I sighed. "I am perhaps more superstitious than I care to admit. It was while I wore the ring that I dreamed.

I was not asleep."

Unseasonably warm weather kept the fog clear most days. It brought swift and encouraging growth in our fields. The green of young grain gave promise of a rich harvest. Where I had sewn double measure of seed, the growth looked richer, with fewer weeds. It would be the harvest, however, that would tell the tale.

A number from the village moved into the Keep for the security of its great walls. The low stone wall that surrounded the village itself rose in intermittent bursts of industry, but still gave little protection.

Fog lay heavy on the valley below the Keep walls when the watch reported a large Pict war-party passing well to our west. I doubled the watch on the walls and alerted the village, posting a number of armed men. As fog broke into smaller patches a group of half a score showed themselves close to the Keep beneath the southern wall.

I led a party of forty men armed with spears and bows. I rode, for I could scarcely walk, but dismounted and had my horse led away. Crouched behind the low, unfinished wall, we met the enemy before they entered the village. I slew one only. It had more the feel of murder than battle, for he charged naked except for his tattoos, while I crouched behind a wall with a longbow. Arrows and spears cut all but one down with no loss among my own men, for the Pict had made an ill conceived attack.

The one did not make good his escape. The rugged land confronted him with a cliff face before and eight of my men behind. He leaped, and shattered his body on the rocks below.

Smoke from the southwest indicated a battle, but the great wall there provided a mighty barrier. We had insufficient men-at-arms to take the battle to the open field.

Numbers had risen to more than 300 souls within the village and the Keep itself. Increasing industry could be seen among the villagers. The second Pict attack spurred them in the construction of the wall. It rose quickly in height and they closed the gaps. My small land-holdings could not support such a number with trade but poorly established. So even in this season of peak growth, we hungered.

The summer solstice approached. Forage lay drying in heaps in many fields. Careful weeding among the growing grain occupied many people as did countless other small tasks. Continued building and maintaining a diligent watch kept others employed. With spring planting behind and harvest ahead, for a short time no urgent tasks pressed. I turned my attention to justice.

"You begin to look a man again," I said to Burleigh when he stood before me. "I will not leave you in chains if you can show you are without blood-guilt in this matter."

We rode out a strong party of nine mounted horsemen, eight of us heavily armed, one lightly bound. I limped less now, but the wound in my leg still troubled me.

Three hours ride brought us within sight of the wall. There, near a great oak tree, we found the remains of a human body. A few tattered remnants of cloth gave a scanty identification. Nothing indicated the use of a human weapon. Two broken lengths of gold chain, large oversights for a murdering thief, we also found.

"Release him," I said simply, then spoke directly to Burleigh. "Whether I like it or not, you fall under my authority. You perhaps cannot change what you are. I, though I lead a great house, cannot do some things I wish. Return if you will, a free man—or leave, a free man. BUT, if you return," I paused and measured my words, speaking them slow and hard. "The first time you are involved in a disruption, if the smell of liquor be on you, you will be banished from my holdings. Do you understand, Sir?"

"Yessuh," Burleigh mumbled.

"Tis no weak enemy you do battle with," I spoke in a gentler voice. "A hard task I set before you, and costly choices."

We dug a shallow grave and lay the Bishop's remains in it, then remounted our horses. We continued to the wall where we left a message with the guard on watch that we had found and buried the remains of the Bishop of Drahæm. Then we turned our horses toward home.

One day later Burleigh stood before me, trembling, holding a leather wineskin and a badly soiled purse. "Take them both, Sir. For my life, take them." The sweat ran down his face. "I have tasted no drop, but havena the strength to resist. Take them now, ere I change my mind."

I took what he offered, finding no ready words to respond.

"I was sure the gold would be gone." His shaky voice continued. "I dug only to prove it so, for you had to know where to find it." He stared at me. "You wouldda done me good to have stoled it. Take it then, for t'will damn me if I keep it."

The heavy purse would prove of great assistance. In truth I *had* known where to dig and more than once had fought the temptation. I gazed now at the man before me. "You have fought a hard fight, Burleigh. I did not leave the gold to add to your torment. I left it to prevent my own. What you give I can accept, knowing it will aid this house and you also. Had I taken it, I would have looked a thief in my own eyes and the eyes of my people. Thank you, Sir. You do honour to this house and raise your own stature as well."

I knew nothing to aid in breaking the grip strong drink held on the man. He stood taller, however, as he walked away from me.

Litha, the summer Solstice passed. We had brought the little forage we could gain under roof. The barley showed a blend of green and rusty gold, wanting but a short time till harvest. Hunting parties probed northward with my reluctant approval. The watch frequently saw bands of Pict, though they chose usually to steer a wide detour around Muninn's Keep. Some of my people spoke of cowardice among them, but that faulty assumption I ruthlessly quelled. Many things they could be accused of, but not cowardice.

Burleigh took up an unspoken apprenticeship with Pollard, the blacksmith. The heavy gut that overhung his belt firmed, but refused to shrink. His florid face took on a look of health. His chest deepened and his arms bulged with muscles.

He swiftly gained in skill for he had a natural bent for the task and an eye for the exact shade of glowing metal at which it could best be worked and tempered. Much of the growing defense work of the Keep took shape under the hammer blows that shaped a man from a wreck. He was my senior by not less than ten years, yet I felt the pride of a father as he began to make something of himself.

I found a moment to speak to Glenine, Burleigh's wife. "There is a new man working with Pollard, the blacksmith, a man you will find familiar, yet unknown. When I took you from his house I thought him beyond hope. Happily, he has proved me wrong."

"I have heard talk, Milord," Glenine acknowledged. "I fear to believe it." She stared up at me, seeming to ask for direction.

"None knows less than me about marriage," I confessed. "The only words I have spoken on the subject have proved a disaster. That I dare speak should make the gods laugh." I stared at the floor. "You are wise to fear. The pull of the jug is strong. But he is a man I am proud to have among my people."

On the day I first took scythe to the standing barley, a young man breached our defenses. "Durward, you look like you just found the wyvern sleeping and escaped with all its hoard of gold," I told him.

"Not so rich as that, Sire," he grinned back at me. "But I have crossed the wall under the guards' very noses. I thought you would wish to know."

My full attention he had then. I dropped the scythe and stared at him.

"Just now?" I questioned. "In daylight, with no fog?"

"T'was just before dawn I crossed the wall, Sire. Minutes after you passed on your circuit."

"So under my nose too," I complimented him. "Do any know? There is much desire to be first."

"None know, Sire." Durward responded. "With my face blacked I made my way to the gatehouse. There was the usual bluster and taunts."

I bent and picked up my scythe, cutting a few more sweeps through the barley before I spoke again. Finally I straightened and faced him. "I would have you repeat the feat if you are sufficiently rested. I will put the guards on alert, but will give you several hours with none but the gate-keepers knowing your identity, that you not slip back through the very gate and proclaim yourself successful."

Durward drew himself up before me as a flush rose in his neck and cheeks. "You would give the lie to me, Sir?" He spat the words bitterly.

"Nay, Durward Morton," I assured him. "Tis no lie that has you straining your sark like the father of a new son." I grinned at him. "But if you succeed a second time they will take much convincing that you did not come in by the gate. I will not leave that option open, though it be my own watch you cross."

I glanced at the afternoon sun. "Go then," I commanded him. "Take provisions for three days. At dusk I will give the alarm. If you succeed you will prove yourself an outstanding warrior and expose a great weakness in our defense. Both are goals of value to this house."

The announcement that someone had successfully crossed the wall created a great stir after the gates closed that evening. Few of my people had believed it could be done, though many had made the attempt. Not a man bore a willingness to have his watch crossed, so challenged the very shadows repeatedly.

Early morning saw the excitement still strong as a team of four hunters headed north. A horde of Pict emerged from the shadows of a gorge as the hunters approached it. Two miles of rugged ground lay between them and safety.

Even before my horse was saddled, the signal from the watch-tower told the grim news. The morning excitement disappeared as swiftly as a summer storm sweeps in from the ocean. With no command, armed warriors milled in clusters near the gate while every post on the wall boasted a double guard. Twenty men had taken positions in the trenches.

"Many will die to no good purpose if we charge without forethought to the battle," I shouted to the angry men who surrounded me. "They come now at harvest. They will bring the battle to us. Yet I would have them weakened before they approach our walls. Twenty of you with me—who know every rock and crevice of the Greystone Burn where it cuts deep through the cliffs one mile north. No horses do we take. Bows, spears and longbows our weapons."

More than 60 men stepped forward. I numbered off the first 20, dismounted my horse and started at a swift trot toward the gate. "Swiftly now, for we have a hard mile to run if we would be in place."

I turned back as the men rushed past me, down into the second trench and heading north to the treacherous climb to the valley floor. "Hold the Keep at all cost," I shouted. "Erhard is in command till I return."

My leg wound began to throb, but the battle blood pumped hot. As we spread out in our swift trot across the valley, I shouted more instructions. "We hide in silence till the Pict are fully within the valley. We sound no battle cry till the first flight of arrows is released. Let every arrow find a heart. Tis them who bring the battle to us. There is no nobility in unnecessary death." I gasped for breath, the pain in my leg increasing, hard pressed to keep pace with my men.

"Those of you who wish to be heroes, we will bury tomorrow. Obey my orders and live to fight again." We splashed across the narrow burn and continued to run, now climbing steeply. My side began to ache. Moments later we entered the draw where I sought to set our ambush.

"Not a footprint left," I ordered. "Not a broken branch or a torn clump of heather. So soon as I signal, make your every shot count for we are badly outnumbered. Fight in silence, that they have no idea how few we are." I watched as my men, panting heavily, climbed to the shelter of rocks and small caves. I could hear the indistinct rustle of the approaching enemy so I climbed to a broken jumble of boulders where I crouched and notched an arrow.

Moments later the Pict came at a fast pace. The leaders had passed almost beyond bowshot when the rear-guard rushed into the narrow slash.

Still breathing heavily from our rush to this place, my blood raged at the sight that met my eyes as the trailing warriors approached. Two men, my men, with hands severed and belly's slashed open, dragged by ropes around each ankle, leaving a bloody trail behind.

Barely did I quell my own battle-cry of rage over the obscene brutality. My arrow took a huge man between the shoulder blades. Even before the cry of alarm echoed in that narrow defile, twenty of the Pict lay dead or dying. A second flight of arrows cut off the screams of many more. Yet again they proved themselves a formidable enemy with measureless courage. The survivors charged into the very shadow of our hiding places, while the wounded dragged themselves to any cover they could find and prepared to sell their lives dearly. An hour it took, but our rage gave no room for survivors. And though we had evened the numbers and held the high ground, a long and bitter fight we had before the last Pict lay dead.

Two of my men lay dead and nine of us bore wounds.

Fifty-four Pict did we number among the dead.

I sent one of my men to signal the watch with his burnished shield, then looked to the wounds of my people. A battle-axe had struck my shoulder, bruising badly through my leather jerkin, but doing no permanent damage. An arrow had again pierced my left leg.

We stripped the dead of anything of value, finding little beyond a few gems they had doubtless stolen somewhere. An indistinct noise caught my attention. Barely had I bid my men to silence before all could hear it.

"Tis a vast number." I spoke softly as my men gathered around me. "Feel the ground tremble."

I gazed upon my small group. "Those of us who cannot run, into shelter. Let them pass. Stay unseen. We will pick off stragglers and harass them. To the Keep, the rest of you. Run and do not stop running. Draw their attention if you will, but put the Keep wall between you and them before you stop to give battle."

"But Sire," one of them remonstrated.

"Go!" I shouted. "The odds are impossible, but I will not countenance defeat."

Chapter Eighteen
God of Fire and Ice

EIGHT ABLE BODIED MEN SHOUTED as they broke into a run, even as the signalman burst into sight madly shouting and waving his arms.

"Run with them," I commanded. "Defend the Keep to the last man." I then ducked into my own shelter as the swift tramping grew louder. A savage battle-cry burst from many Pict throats, for they had heard the shout. Multiple trumpets sounded their cruel call as well.

The first of the Pict army entered the narrow gorge at a run. Seeing the dead of their own people and the last of my runners at the far end of the gorge, they howled their fury.

Our small group remained unseen, but my alarm for the Keep increased. We did not have enough warriors to face such numbers, even with the incredible strength of the Keep.

When the main army had passed I gave instructions to my men. "We must stop their supplies. They cannot long fight on empty bellies. We are ten, wounded all, against a thousand. Think what songs will be sung. Proud I am to lead such men."

For the next six hours, with battle sounds sometimes reaching us faintly, we cut off wagons one at a time, killing the small group of guards, releasing and arming the drivers, usually thræls. Thus our numbers had grown to 32 by the time a group of Pict warriors came back looking for supplies. Four of the thræls died before we had overcome that small group. The others, having tasted both freedom and victory, fought like veterans.

Broken carts and dead bodies choked the narrow gorge. We reduced supplies to a trickle, spreading confusion and panic. The number of Pict dead continued to rise as the evening faded into night. Wounded and exhausted we fought on.

As the shadows deepened I encouraged my men, then crept toward the south end of the gorge and climbed the treacherous slope. I carried a Pict spear with me. My plan had more of desperation than of hope, yet I had marked a boulder that seemed to overhang the cliff face. My shoulder ached and my leg dragged. My fingers bled from scrabbling against rough stone.

I worked desperately, for the numbers of Pict warriors below kept growing and would soon overwhelm my small band. Blindly I stabbed the spear into every crack and crevice beside the boulder, clinging like a fly in the darkness. I pried and twisted and strained. Grit and small stones rained down. Shouts from below and the sounds of grunting exertion told of men climbing toward me. More and more men filled the hollow. Forays farther into the gorge brought shouts of outrage as Pict warriors fell before arrows from my unseen men.

Fog began to seep into the gorge, blanketing it thinly, then slowly rising. The grunting and gasping drew closer. A sliver of moon gave faint illumination to the eyes and gleaming teeth of a man barely a body length below me. I leaned hard on the spear and heard a strange, rending groan that seemed to come from the rock itself.

I relaxed pressure on the spear, then leaned into it again. My feet slipped from the narrow ledge. I felt the solid crunch as they struck the upturned face of the Pict warrior just below me.

My head smacked against the cliff face. I heard the screaming curse as a man fell. My head swam. Roaring filled my senses.

Blackness surrounded me. Dust choked me and every breath felt like the kick of a horse in my chest. Memory returned slowly, with the bitter taste of failure. I had obviously fallen and knocked myself senseless. That I still lived proved only the mockery of whatever god existed.

I heard boots scraping through loose rubble, a cursing Pict voice, then a shout. Something struck my foot. Shouting brought more voices, then the shifting of rocks, more dust and deeper pain. Torch light flashed around me as hands dragged from a hole in the rubble.

With eyes full of grit, I could not focus on the faces that loomed above me. I reached up—a futile defense against the spear that drew back in a great, muscled arm. My hands spread to ward the blow.

Cursing and shouting clamoured against my pounding head. I heard the clatter as the spear fell, the grunt of men striving, then felt myself jerked upright. My legs would not hold me and I collapsed, bitterly cursing the gods who had spared my life to give me to the Pict.

Hours—or days—passed in a blur of pain and confusion. Light and darkness traded place with capricious disregard for normal length of day. Whips razed my back. Leering faces spat questions in a savage language. Cruel hands grabbed my left hand and spread it, exposing the gap where the third finger ended in a stump. Chains about my wrists and ankles held me fast to a tree, then to the wheel of a cart.

A cruel dizziness mingled with choking dust. My body twisted and slumped, spinning, but moving slow as an ox-cart wheel turns. Every stone and hollow jerked me, rubbing wrists and ankles raw. The arrow through my leg added one point of hotter fire in a body that burned with pain.

The ox-cart ground to a halt. I hung, my left shoulder close to the ground and found myself staring up to the Keep wall.

As dust settled I heard the sound of men and beasts drinking from a stream. Pict still assaulted the wall, so the defense still stood.

The ox-cart lurched forward and my world reeled in slow-motion circles. The cart dropped into the shallow burn, plunging my face below the roiled water. I gulped and gasped, desperate both to drink and praying I might drown. Again the gods mocked me for the cart lurched up the other bank with agonizing slowness, then dropped with a bone-crunching jerk.

An hour later they released me from the ox-cart and tied me to a tree with a heavy weight of chain. A hunk of hard dry bread they threw to me. I found the weight of chain around my wrists almost too heavy in my weakened state to lift the bread to my mouth. Desperately dry from riding in the dust, I could barely swallow. A guard dashed a pail of water across me, then laughed as I fought to suck each drop cupped in filthy hands.

A cold fog settled on the valley and I shivered uncontrollably, amusing my captors. They built a fire, close enough that its light fell upon me, but too far for me to gain from its warmth. As the night deepened a cold rain fell. I leaned back against the tree, trembling. I tipped my head back and caught a trickle as leaves fed it down on my face. For long, weary hours I took in the life-giving liquid, slow as it came, and cruelly cold as I found it in my weakened state.

Rain still fell in the morning. My guards threw me a hunk of soggy bread. It had sat in a hollow soaking up rain. They did not want it. Life giving stuff and softened, I could eat it. I felt renewed strength, though I took care not to show it.

The ox-cart could go no farther. Cursing and sweating, my captors dragged me up the slope into the circle of stones. I began then to understand my fate and again bitterly scorned the gods I had prayed to. Worship would be renewed in the very Circle of Stones I had forbidden to my people. My blood would make the first sacrifice. The nine-fingered one they would offer to their gods, then renew their attack on the Keep. I searched desperately for some escape, but the guards laughed and mocked me. A sodden mist continued to fall. Too light to call rain, it yet soaked and chilled.

Despair settled on me as I watched. My captors tied me where I could not fail to see. Three poles they lashed together, then hung a rope from the centre. They raised the poles over the well itself, then took them down to adjust the length of hanging rope. A priest, hideous with tattoos of an eagle on his left breast and a raven on his right, both bowing to a figure that stood in a fire, danced about the circle with moans and chanting, shaking a rattle made from a human skull. He wore a necklace of human teeth, but nothing else. Deep scars made bars across his forehead and cheeks.

The battle continued at the wall. Hunger showed on every Pict warrior I saw, and with it exhaustion. I could not guess the reason beyond the impossible hope that my companions still held the gorge and barred them from their supplies.

The dull afternoon was darkening into evening when men began to gather within the Circle of Stones. A huge scarred man entered the circle. All except the priest backed away and bowed before him. Heavily tattooed and bearing the marks of many battles, he strode to the well. He sniffed disdainfully at the tripod, then turned toward me. His knife bit deep and hot as fire as the blade caught my chin and lifted my face. A cruel sneer twisted his face as he watched my blood trickle down his knife blade. My light-headed exhaustion gave way to dumb terror, then cold rage. I stared defiantly at him.

"You have killed many my people," he accused me. "A slide you make and close a valley. So starve my warriors and many bury. I make sacrifice. Your blood."

He pressed the knife deeper. The pain, fiery hot, almost wrung a scream from me. "Here. This well. This circle where many blood spilled once. You die." He spat the words at me.

"Nine fingered one." He pulled the knife back, laughing as blood dripped from it, then grabbed my left wrist in a massive and powerful fist. "Gift to Tlæchtgö. He hear me. Give victory."

"I would know before I die the name of the mighty one who dares Muninn's Keep." My voice sounded more a youth than a lord, but the words, I hoped, would feed his ego, though what that might gain me I could not tell. "You bring me good news to die with. But will a sacrifice at Woden's shrine bring you success if you honour another god here?"

"Woden? He big thunders make, and fills with dead his halls. But weak he is, for the stones fallen lie and none but I dare his circle. I, Kïncaid ap Tïrrèll serve Tlæchtgö, god of fire and ice. Living blood bring I to him. The nine fingered one give I, Kïncaid ap Tïrrèll, to him. And greater still will be my name."

I searched vainly for words, searching also for courage to face the death that so swiftly approached.

Shouted orders had me roughly removed from my bonds and dragged to the well. Swiftly and savagely, ropes twisted about my ankles and I dangled head-down over the well itself. The priest approached, shaking and mouth foaming, a ceremonial knife held in one trembling hand while the skull rattle gave off its deathly music in his other hand. He screamed and moaned, making slashing motions with the knife, yet even in his 'trance' kept a measured distance between himself and the savage leader of the Pict army.

Kïncaid ap Tïrrèll sneered as he stared at the broken arrow sticking out of my leg. He grabbed and jerked it free, wrenching a groan from me. Blood gushed from the wound, a hot stream flowing down my inverted body, then dripped into the well.

Kincaid then leaned over the hole, his chest almost against my body. He drew the knife he had cut my chin with, then slashed a great X across his scarred chest, laughing with his head thrust back as blood streamed from the cuts and dripped into the blackness of the well. A great shout rose from the worshipers, while trumpets sounded their strident calls. I understood no words except the oft repeated "Tlæchtgö, Tlæchtgö, Tlæchtgö," as they beat on their shields.

A moment later Kïncaid ap Tïrrèll did the same to me, the knife biting like a serpent across my chest, my blood streaming down my chin and face, running into my hair and dripping from there into the well. It took all my will to suppress a scream.

"A living sacrifice you offer," I gasped the words, a last desperate fragment of a plan beginning to take shape. "You are wise, mighty one, for never did a true wyvern choose dead meat over live. The gods cannot be less discriminating than a dragon." I struggled to draw sufficient breath, the blood, in seeming impossible volume, streaming into my mouth. "Cast me whole and still alive then, or pass me the knife and see the courage to face death like a man."

Kïncaid ap Tïrrèll snorted a derisive laugh, thrust the knife into my bound hands and stepped back. With all my remaining strength I curled my body up and slashed at the rope above my feet. I heard the scream of the priest and caught a glimpse of him charging, open mouth and knife outthrust as the rope parted.

The plunge, my body still curled into a ball, wedged me in only a few cubits down, back raked by the stones. A groan escaped as I shifted. I plunged the rest of the way, my bound hands jerked above my head, my body battered as I fell. Cold water exploded around me. I fell back and fought the encroaching blackness.

Shouts and cursing, distant and distorted, penetrated my consciousness, then a quick darkening and the strange gulping sound of a body descending a throat of cold stone. A blast of water burst around me as someone else struck the bottom of the hlaut-bolla. In the faint light that penetrated from the surface I saw the priest, face twisted in a grimace of rage and hate, belly opened from navel to breastbone. The eyes blinked once at me, then stared sightlessly.

Groping among the spilling entrails sickened me, but I found a blade. I quickly cut my bonds, then staggered clear of the hlaut-bolla. Drained of strength I left the body where it lay, then began a painful shuffle in the blackness of the tunnel. Weakness beyond words made my left leg drag. The cold penetrated deeper.

The stone door, when finally I reached it, proved almost beyond my strength to open. In the darkness I found the skill of my stone workers rather too great and feared I would die on the dark side of their workmanship. Its opening defied me for long weary moments.

I dragged myself against the gate while I strained for the rope that rang a bell where the watch stood far above. I heard pounding feet and shouted orders. A grim and heavily armed group of warriors approached the gate, arrows notched and gaze searching every shadow.

No breath had I for speech, but held my left hand where their torchlight would show a missing finger.

"Milord. You live," a voice gasped, breathless after the swift descent on the stairs.

"Aye," I responded wearily. "If you use the word carelessly."

As they lay me in my own bed I struggled against great weariness. "Let not the enemy know that I live still. But a little while ago they made a living sacrifice to their god. My presence might lead them to know the well gives entrance to the Keep." The bed enfolded me. Sleep was swiftly winning the battle.

"Rest, Milord," Dierdre's voice spoke softly from some far distance. "Already word of your return has given new strength to those on the wall."

Something splashed on my chest. My eyes flicked open long enough to see her dashing tears from her eyes. A soft warmth touched my lips, wholly new, wholly delightful. I fought against sleep, clinging to the moment, yet sleep claimed me.

I sank into endless, aching blackness. My fingers gripped the blade of

Gungnir. Blood dripped from my hand burning when it struck my chest. My fingers opened and the blade plunged toward my heart. Yet it was not the knife, but myself that fell endlessly down into Woden's Well. The tiny sound of blood-drops striking the water of the hlaut-bolla echoed and amplified somehow into the thunder of a waterfall.

Dierdre fell with me, her closeness bringing joy. Yet her face twisted into the hideous, leering features of the Pict priest. Cruel laughter pursued me to Mr. Gerhardt's dark lockup and endless hours of cold blackness. I wakened to the naked blade of a long sword reflecting light from an unseen fire. The tip dripped blood, black in the firelight, yet I knew I dreamed still.

From some great distance the noise of battle intruded. A sense of urgency, as of something almost remembered, brought me to the verge of full wakefulness, then a knife cut the rope that bound my ankles and I plunged again into Woden's Well, falling, falling, falling.

The water of the hlaut-bolla scalded the skin from my body. I fought to awaken, to escape the horror, but the dream repeated, over and over.

A trumpet sounded and I started up from my bed. A hand with a cool cloth pushed me back down. "He wakes," I heard a strange voice speak the words. Quick feet crossed the room.

"Milord?" Dierdre's voice questioned.

My mouth felt thick and dry. My head weighed heavily upon the bed. A gummy residue glued my eyes closed. The hand I lifted to my face felt heavy and weak. A cloth, warm this time, came to my assistance.

My head pounded and the room swam before my eyes. "How long?" I croaked the words.

"Three days, Milord," Dierdre answered. "Your fever was such that we despaired for your life."

"And the battle? The walls still hold?"

"Aye, Sir. They hold, though hard pressed."

My vision slowly cleared and I saw the marks of fatigue upon her. "And I have kept my bed all that time? A poor leader I am, Dierdre."

"Nay, Milord. For each time the watchers ask if you breathe still, and they determine the Keep will be yours when you awaken."

"They are a good people."

"Aye. And they have a good leader," Dierdre affirmed.

I struggled to sit up. Dierdre's hand behind my shoulders felt warm and strong. Again the room spun around me. I sat for a moment then, leaning heavily on her, aware of the warmth and softness of her body. I staggered to my feet. My left leg threatened to topple me, but I stepped hesitantly toward the rowan staff where it leaned against the wall.

"Prepare a mount for me," I requested. "I have not strength to walk the wall, but I would ride among my people." I unwrapped the Ring of Thorvæld and lifted the staff, appalled by its weight and my weakness.

I had to be helped into the saddle and sat for a moment while the world spun around me. The rowan staff proved too heavy for my weakness so Bertrm fashioned a support for it. I rode then, a long, slow circuit of the Keep wall, praising my people as they held the watch, thinly spread. Women and children formed part of the guard. Everyone who could draw a bow, and many who could only roll a stone off the wall took their turn. The wounded, wrapped with rags, crouched with whatever weapon they could still wield. The shout that followed me lifted my spirits and restored strength of will if not of body.

By the time we broke fast in the morning I had exhausted my small store of strength. Yet an hour's healthy sleep, no longer tortured by fever, brought a faint sense of vigor. My sword arm could barely grasp a weapon. I was no warlord leading my people, but it seemed none but me realized.

It is a strange thing that in the tales and songs war leaders either die gloriously in battle or rise from their wounds to fight on. They do not lie on beds of sickness or stagger to a horse needing almost to be tied into the saddle. It was my curse to know I did not measure up.

The stench of death rose from the Pict encampment. Ravens and vultures wheeled in the sky or fed on corpses. A few eagles joined them, though not the great numbers that old tales spoke of. The small number of enemies made no sense. Of the thousand who had rushed through the gorge, it seemed less than 300 remained.

Chapter Nineteen
Feeble Strength, Tormented Pain

My advisors gathered about me in the blacksmith shop. Pollard and Burleigh rebuilt swords and tipped spears. They reeked of sweat and the stink of the forge. They worked at the old forge, doubtless to be closer to the centre of the battle. Dark shadows under their eyes spoke of sleepless nights. Burns on arms and hands told of working glowing steel when too exhausted to exercise necessary caution.

To the ring of hammer blows I learned of the events of the last days.

With the enemy number so large, Erhard had called out women and children armed with stones and axes to watch the walls and cut ropes wherever the Pict attempted to scale them. Sling-stones from children had accounted for many fallen enemy. Other children recovered arrows as the Pict launched them recklessly over the wall.

The Pict had fashioned a crude catapult and launched stones and burning balls of pitch. Yet the fires did little damage and few injuries resulted. We had even roofed with stone, though not by choice. Burning pitch guttered out harmlessly. Only once had a stone struck a building with damaging force.

Under Erhard's wise direction, cries of outrage and threats of vengeance sounded when stones or pitch fell on an empty field. The Pict had continued to aim at that imagined target.

Arrows shot from the walls with deadly accuracy had convinced even the most foolhardy that Muninn's Keep would not be easily breached. Yet the trees that crowded the slope offered much shelter to the enemy.

The fog during the first night of battle could have worked to their advantage. But they had launched their attack during the early phase of the moon so faced increasing light each of the succeeding nights.

"No help from Drahæm?" I questioned my advisors.

"None, Surra," Erhard replied. "But if smoke tells a true tale they fight their own battle."

"How many have we lost?" I asked, dreading the answer.

"Too many, Surra," Erhard responded. "If those with you in the gully still live, 42. If they have perished, 51. Durward has not been seen since before the battle began, and six children and two women be among the dead. Many who continue to fight be wounded."

I groaned. I then struggled to my feet, appalled by my weakness. "Help me to the wall," I commanded. "Bring my longbow."

For hours I crouched at an arrow slot and gazed across the enemy encampment. I chose the northeast where the ditches joined the steep-walled valley. From there I could see much of the valley and the circle of stones.

The stink of death seemed a visible shadow that shifted and changed beneath wheeling vultures and croaking ravens. Great birds fed wherever I looked.

It lacked two nights of a full moon, but clouds overshadowed the sky while tendrils of fog drifted up the valley from Greystone Burn.

Some movement of men showed among the Pict. "Do they mount one last effort, or do they retreat?" I questioned the exhausted warrior who stretched upon the stone a few cubits away. The battle had lasted nine days and he looked to have never slept during that time. His sunken eyes showed red and bloodshot above great dark shadows. His lips had cracked. Filthy hair matted against his skull. Broken fingernails and bleeding, scabbed knuckles marred the hand that lay across his bow. A wooden drinking cup sat empty beside him, a fly crawling along the rim. A clay jar lay tipped and empty nearby.

The man was slow to answer, his brain fogged by weariness. "The Pict never retreat," he spoke the words like a curse, his voice cracked and dry as his lips.

"Erhard," I called. "Choose five of the children to carry water to every warrior. Keep every cup full. Command those whose hands shake to hold the cup, to sleep an hour—longer if no alarm is sounded. Let them also, one at a time, bathe and wash their garments. It will give renewed strength."

I longed for the comfort of the scroll of *Isaiae filii Amos.* Though it rebuked more than encouraged, I needed wisdom beyond my own.

Two vultures croaked their disgust and heaved themselves into the air when disturbed close beneath my watch. The fog thickened, but a group of five appeared for a brief instant.

"To arms," I called softly. "Their war leader, Kïncaid ap Tïrrèll, is within bowshot below. Take him first, then any of the others."

Forms looking so like corpses that vultures circled and sometimes landed came to sudden life. I notched an arrow on my longbow, the only weapon of its power and range along this section of the wall. The moment stretched long and the fog seemed to grow thicker even while we watched.

A bowstring twanged to my right, followed an instant later by another from even farther right. Shouts and curses burst from below us. A form appeared indistinctly through the fog and I drew back and released, groaning at my feeble strength and the pain. Crowding into the arrow slot the man beside me leaned far out with his bow fully drawn. He drove an arrow down the face of the wall.

Some sounds in battle impale the mind. The sound of an arrow striking flesh and bone, the grunt wrung from the victim, the almost silent slipping of fingers losing their grip on stone, the rush of air and the thump of a body falling, the crackle of broken branches and heather tearing from its anchorage in the rocks—they are almost worse than screams and battle cries.

A gust of wind tore a rent in the fog. Two men struggled to drag a third out of bowshot. My longbow sounded its fatal shuuuttt a second time.

The fog closed in again, but cries of outrage spread. A swift and reckless charge, like a rogue wave breaking on the ocean shore, drove the vultures from their grisly meal. Screaming Pict burst through the protective fog, naked blades and bodies exposed to our relentless arrows. The wave broke and shattered on the rocks. The fog itself seemed to take on the colour of blood. The cries of the dying ringed the Keep—and a first in my hearing—cries of panic.

A trumpet sounded its strident call and Pict battle-chiefs fought for order. Through gaps in the fog we saw fleeing men cut down by their own leaders. But they were spread too thin, their losses too high, and the panic had taken hold. The wheeling vultures and harsh cry of ravens sped them on their way.

Victory in battle must be celebrated, but the stink of death and our own great losses had left me feeling like a broken, weary child. Barely able to walk, but not carried away to die in glory, I felt less a leader than at any other time in my memory.

As dusk settled the fires burning in the valley glowed fainter through the fog, then one by one winked out. Ravens and vultures heaved their heavy, bloated bodies up, circled briefly, then roosted in trees and on rocks.

I ordered a cask of wine opened, sipped from the cup brought to me, then offered a cup all around.

"The children too?" someone questioned.

"They have fought like adults," I responded. "Offer a sip, but a sip only."

I sent one of the youth to bring Burleigh to the forge. I named three other men who battled with drink and asked them to join me also. "A bitter task I have for you if you are willing," I informed the four men. "The people make merry with a cask of wine newly broached. I will not forbid it to any of you for you have proved yourselves men many times over in these days. Yet I would offer a task if one cup should awaken a thirst for more."

"Ah—and a whole barrel I have dreamed of this last sen'night," one man confessed through cracked lips. "What task, Sir? For the barrel had best be empty afore the cup be put in my hands."

My eyes misted as my gaze swept the small group who nodded their agreement. "At least one body lies in the hlaut-bolla beneath the circle of stones. The Pict priest. . ." The memory of those grim moments choked me. "Others may have been cast in, either dead or alive. I convinced their war leader that a living sacrifice would better honour his god."

One cup of wine does not erase the horrors of more than a sen'night of battle, yet feet stamped to a thrumming harp as I limped to the threshing floor. Loud laughter and bleary-eyed grins greeted me. I praised my people, then gave instructions that the watch be relieved and for others to get all possible rest.

The black form of wheeling vultures greeted me when I left my bed in the morning. I had slept the sleep of exhaustion and the sun, which gave a sickly yellow glow through the fog, already showed above the eastern wall. A horse stood saddled and ready when I limped outside.

I found more than half the watch dead to the world, sleeping with hands still on weapons, flies crawling across faces while vultures circled above.

The huge number of vultures feeding in the valley gave confirmation that the enemy had in truth abandoned the battlefield. In a number of places I marked a disturbance among the carrion birds. I doubted not that a wounded Pict warrior lay there, battle-axe close to hand, and probably a bow also.

Noon had nearly arrived before we broke fast. As the temperature rose, so did the stench. Haggard, sleep-wrinkled faces greeted me with embarrassment and shame, yet I too had slept long.

The watch was but poorly kept that day, nor could I fault them. However, I sought to bring order and discipline back, for though the Pict had suffered a great defeat, they would not easily turn away from a fight.

The afternoon shadows had lengthened before the first heaps of Pict dead began to burn. We killed the wounded Pict where we found them. Two more of my people suffered wounds and one died before sundown, a bitter aftertaste to our victory.

We stripped weapons and meager treasures from the bodies. I did not command it, but my people brought many gems, rings and armbands of gold to me. A golden torc appeared among the treasures, perhaps the richest of all the booty. I gave it and a ring to Dierdre as payment for the two gold pieces she had given. The torc had the value of several gold pieces. Yet she had given an extravagant gift to me also—half of all her wealth when she had a bairn to care for. The ring, a plain gold circlet, could be used for anything gold could buy.

The ring of axes sounded as bodies burned. Trees which had sheltered the enemy fell. I remembered well Erhard's caution against cutting trees, but would not face another battle with such benefit to the enemy. Horses laboured to drag logs up the steep slope at the northeast. The slow-moving, stolid oxen dragged them from there within the Keep itself.

Five days after the conflict had ended the smoke from piles of burning bodies had finally thinned. Every gust of wind coming out of the west brought relief from the all-pervasive stench of death. The plague of flies had thinned and the sky no longer bore the shadow of thousands of carrion birds.

We mourned our dead, having hastily buried them in the catacomb during the battle. Those who had died outside the wall had lain too long, exposed to weather and vultures, but we gave them a funeral pier separate from the Pict dead.

When a group of my warriors stumbled on a pocket of Pict survivors two more of my men fell in battle. One, coughing blood from an arrow wound, lived long enough to return to the Keep, but died shortly after sundown. On that bitter reminder that the enemy remained deadly even in defeat, the watch renewed their vigilance.

I retired early. For the first time in months I wept as I lay on my bed. Good men had died, and I wondered to what purpose. A blackened face bending over me woke me shortly before dawn.

"I have succeeded, Sire, though the timing was ill chosen."

Stupid from sleep I sat up. "Durward?" I questioned. "Durward Morton? What do you here?"

"Crossing the wall, Sire, though the guards would have shot without hesitation this night."

I rose and pulled my robe about me, then reached for the rowan staff. I leaned on it as I limped from the house. "We had given you up for dead," I confessed. "Show me where."

Other shadows merged into warriors who quickly approached. "Our wall breaker has succeeded again," I informed them quietly. "We will see this breach and learn how it may be closed."

Murmurs of astonishment met my announcement, and more than one angry mutter demanded the man step into the light.

"Durward Morton has now twice succeeded. He came unchallenged to my bed."

I heard the schick of a sword sliding clear, and suppressed snarls of rage. "Hold!" I commanded. "Under your very noses he slipped, with every one of you alert to danger. Had he been false, no better opportunity could he have found than just moments ago. That I live still is evidence of his honour. That he succeeded is evidence of his skill."

"Tis the evil eye," I heard someone mutter.

"Aye. No mortal could do such."

"And where was he through the battle? A traitor he is, skulking somewhere when every man's strength was needed."

"He is a man of flesh and blood—and no traitor, else I am much mistaken." I cut off the talk. "With great skill and great patience, he has done what one in a thousand might dare attempt. With his face blacked, even his teeth, and the very stealth of a shadow, he has moved among the shadows. It is well he is our friend and not our enemy. Now let us see this weakness and seek to make it impossible, even for one with skill such as his."

More men gathered, armed and prepared for battle.

"Dawn approaches, Sire. The shadows soon change." Durward urged me toward the wall. Where a slight curve followed the natural edge of the cliff-face, a deeper shadow seemed to swallow him. His voice suddenly spoke from six cubits above my head.

"This is the most difficult point, Sire, and the guard now stands but two paces from me, drawn by the commotion. He did not hear me before and was some distance away when I made my crossing."

"Who goes there?" The guard's angry voice challenged the invisible speaker almost at his feet. "Halt! I have an arrow notched."

"Do not shoot." I commanded. "You have the unfortunate honour of being the one on whose watch the crossing has been made. Yet standing here, with several watchers beside me and the man barely gone from my presence, I cannot now see him, impossible though that seems."

"Mr. Thorvæld, Sir. None has crossed on my watch. That I swear." The man leaned over the wall and gazed down at our growing group.

"Will you swear it still?" The voice of Durward came now from across the wall, muffled and indistinct.

I moved into the shadow and attempted to climb, without success. Even with torches, the hand and foot grips gave barely sufficient purchase and my wounds made me too weak to reach the top of the wall.

"It is no shame to you that it happened on your watch. Such skill I have never seen, nor believed when I have read of it. But one in a thousand of the bravest enemies could do the same, yet come daylight we will seek to close this gap against that one." I gazed at the men around me, then called. "Durward, return to us, having proved your prowess and exposed a weakness."

With the entire Keep astir by now, Durward found himself surrounded with back-pounding youths and grizzled old warriors alike, all eager to hear of his exploits. We broke fast with the sun barely above the horizon and mist lifting through it over the Circle of Stones. After we pushed back from the board, I set a team to block Durward's every skill in climbing the wall, both on its inner and outer surface.

"Tell us, Durward," I asked at board that night, "How did you escape the Pict?" Naturally lean, his face had a pinched, starved look to it. Deep shadows under his eyes told of a long and weary time. He ate like a starving man also. I set the saltcellar before him and he grinned his thanks before dipping his fingers into it and sprinkling some on his food.

"I harried them, Sire, picking off stragglers," he spoke between mouthfuls. "The hunters returning with game—I ate better than most of the enemy, though that is not saying much. I have some skill in creeping unseen—as you know. They were desperate for food, starving. Four times tipped cooking pots led to fights—with one or more of the enemy dead. If they are credited as my victims, more than a score have I slain in the very midst of their camp.

"I harried them further as they withdrew. I never thought to see the day the Pict would retreat, Sire. Bodies lie spread for two days north. Little enough honour there be in such battle, though at the end they had found their courage again and began to die as warriors."

"Warriors? They be animals—less than human!" a voice bitterly cut in.

"Mothers, wives and children will grieve the dead among them," Durward responded in a quiet voice. "Savage they be in battle, with reckless courage, but men still." His weary gaze swept us. "Every life I took left a mother without a son, a child without a father." He pushed back from the board and strode from the room.

I stared after him. I felt again the wonder of the caliber of people I commanded. Calling the potter to me, I gave instruction that a saltcellar be made and placed at each corner of the great room, that none of my people should ever again sit below the salt. We had little enough to put in the cellars, but it would be shared by all.

I rode with a heavily armed guard to Mr. Gerhardt's farm. The watch had seen smoke during our battle, but it had been impossible to go to his assistance earlier. The most able of my men were battle weary, led by a cripple who struggled to sit a horse.

Four mangled bodies hung from the oak tree along the east fortress wall. We found the stable a burned out shell, every animal slaughtered and eaten, and the well filled with stone and charred timbers.

The great stone walls of the house still stood, but the Pict had battered down and burned the heavy doors. Little would burn within the house, though we saw evidence of many attempts. Neither Mr. Gerhardt nor his daughter appeared among the bodies riddled with arrows and mutilated with axes. The child's nurse lay across the threshold of the nursery, her naked body showing the abuse she had suffered before her death.

The stairs to the cellar collapsed as I tried to descend. Grabbing an unburned timber, I pushed the wreckage clear so more of my men could join me. We checked the cells and the dark hole. "Search the rest of the cellar," I instructed my men. "Under the kitchens, the wine cellar. See if you can get into the old tower. There is a hiding place somewhere. Mr. Gerhardt may be living still."

A locked door had always guarded the wine cellar. Now, smashed clay jars and a sticky residue of spilled wine and beer stained the floor. Great casks lay smashed. Two sections of shelves stood, stripped, along the north wall.

Chapter Twenty

The Salamandríne's Hoard

A SLICK SCUM COVERED THE FLOOR of the kitchen cellar, with destroyed shelves and smashed pottery jars. With the stairs destroyed, I struggled to get back to the main floor and then the second floor. The door to the shrine room hung crookedly from its hinges, but the Pict had left the room itself. Even the scrolls still rested in their clay jars in the lattice wall.

I could not banish the child's talk of a dragon from my mind. Something seemed to have changed since I had last gazed on the shrine. The bucket forming the 'well' sat higher. When I grasped it, it shifted under my hand, exposing a hole a grown man could scarcely pass through. Stale air rose, with a hint of dust freshly disturbed.

"Mr. Gerhardt," I called. I reached a foot down into the dark opening, feeling for the ladder. The rungs sagged, but I forced myself to descend.

"Check the wine cellar again. I will hope to come out that way." I struggled to squeeze my shoulders through the opening, then reached for a torch. The skittering of rats sounded, though my mind seemed to hear huge scales sliding across a stone floor.

It seemed a great depth, the wound in my leg adding to my difficulty. The air burned my lungs and the torch gave a weak and sickly glow.

I found a low opening I had to stoop to pass through. A rat's eyes glared at me from the back of a dry reservoir. Its teeth gleamed yellow in the light of my torch. Footprints and drag marks led left. Rats scurried into a jumble of fallen rock.

Dark puddles soiled the floor. Ancient beams sagged. Slabs of rock seemed to interlock and provide strength more timeless than oak. Drag marks led to a door. Still mindful of the child's talk of dragons, I pushed against the door. The hinges shrieked the cry of the damned.

A narrow passage reached before me, turning to angle left. The air was even worse here, with a hint of rotting flesh. I forced my feet to take the passage. A doorway of sorts stood in front of me, the smell of wet ash coming from it. It opened into the well shaft. Faint light reached from above.

Another door opened into a small, cluttered room, barrels and shelves taking much of the space. The stench of rotting flesh assaulted me. A groan sounded as torchlight spilled into the room. The red eyes and yellowish teeth of rats reflected the torchlight, then shrank into a crack between stones. One of three heaps of rags stirred.

A water jug lay tipped on its side, empty. Glazed eyes stared from a face barely human. A hand grasped at a sword, but failed to lift it.

The shafts of two arrows protruded from the shoulder.

"The Pict have been defeated, Mr. Gerhardt. They've fought a bloody war, but they've been beaten." I spoke to the figure. "For a time you can let your sword lie."

I knelt beside the man and drew the water skin from my belt. A few drops only I squeezed and let run across his lips. His hands trembled as he tried to clutch at the bag, but his weakness proved too great.

I pulled the cloth back from the second pile. A moan changed to a wail, thin and dying, sounding the very suffering of Hades. A young girl still breathed, but seemed in agony. She lay on her side, her face and the remnants of hair showing the ravages of fire. Rot had begun to consume her flesh. Sorrow too deep for expression weighed me down.

No life remained in the third pile where rats had fed on the corpse.

Mr. Gerhardt, by sheer stubbornness, continued to draw breath. I gave more water, though he spilled most of it. I then checked the rest of the small room. A stair led up behind a stone wall. It turned to the right, then stopped at a wood wall. Faint light showed through cracks and I caught glimpses of my men on the other side.

I thumped with my sword, then called. "The shelves hide a door just through this wall." It took but a short time for them to tear the shelves apart and open the wall.

Several of my men made the sign against the evil eye as they descended. We drew Mr. Gerhardt out, burned flesh peeling away under our hands.

I knew more of the healing arts than any of the men with me, but held little hope. We cut off the arrow shafts, then forced the tips through the rotting flesh of his back and pulled them clear. Mr. Gerhardt fought us feebly for a moment, then became senseless. A thick putrid fluid poured from the wounds. I could do little beyond pouring wine on his wounds. For reasons no one knew something in the wine could stop the wasting and rotting of flesh if applied early enough. We had not brought the leech with us. He worked among the wounded at the Keep and could not be spared.

We poured wine on his daughter's rotting flesh as well, but she ceased to breathe within moments of reaching the clearer air in the main cellar.

We built a funeral pier for all except Mr. Gerhardt's daughter and put torch to the remains. Her we buried in the family crypt outside the main fortress walls. The Pict had not defaced it for they feared places of the dead. Strangely, the names carved on enclosed platforms included Thorvælds and Thorvlds as well as Gerhardts.

Almost nothing could be salvaged from the wreckage, although we found a few scattered sheep and one calf that had somehow escaped the Pict's desperate search for meat. I marked the animals as Mr. Gerhardt's and tied them so we could take them with us when we returned.

I found the hearthstone with the House of Thorvæld inscription. I wished to return it to the Keep, yet hesitated to claim it while Mr. Gerhardt lay dying on a litter beside me.

I searched the sub-cellar, wishing the brief portion I had read while still a thræl in this house had given more information. In the main room I found no silver and only the rusted remnants of a few inferior weapons. The great barrels had once held foodstuffs, but rats had gnawed holes and emptied them.

Three days we spent and to the amazement of all, Mr. Gerhardt clung to life. We carried him to the Keep on a litter behind a horse. He spoke no words in that time beyond a bitter reproach to the gods for forcing him to continue to breathe.

The wound that healed so slowly made me feel a burden. I longed for Dierdre, but she worked long hours among the wounded. Death approached for two, their flesh rotting where arrows or battle-axes had bitten deep.

I returned to Mr. Gerhardt's farm with another crew armed for battle, but carrying tools to harvest forage wherever it could be found. Anything left of his harvest must be saved. We had need for more than his and our own combined. There appeared to be none left alive of his household, and how he clung to life no one could tell.

The scrolls from the shrine room we gathered to take to the Keep. Mr. Gerhardt had no use for them, but they seemed to me true treasure.

Because my leg wound limited me, I searched the sub-cellar again while my men harvested. Behind the barrels I found another opening. A loose stone in the wall gave entrance to a cavern. More suited to a serpent than a man, it sloped into a gaping throat in the natural rock. Soot and scorch marks from torches—or something else—marked the ceiling.

Alone and calling myself a fool I crept into the dark opening, holding a torch before me. The opening widened and leveled out, though still descending slightly. The cavern stretched back some dozen paces and widened to as much as eight. Grey stone with steaks of coloured rock formed the roof, walls and sloping floor. To my left a hump of rock rose to meet the ceiling. A strange, serpentine formation snaked across the floor, twisting around a jumble of casks and barrels, like a dragon guarding its treasure. Of strangely coloured rock, streaked with brown and green, the formation rose two cubits from the floor, with a spiny ridge along its back. I had read but little of salamandríne, the wingless dragons of tales so ancient that few had been put to parchment. The child had spoken of singed hair and I knew some claimed they lived in fire.

The noise of my entrance would have wakened any normal living creature. I stood for long moments and stared at it. In the flickering light of my torch the sides seemed to move as if it breathed. What might have been the head faced away from me.

Near the neck of the creature—just visible from where I stood—shards of pale, mottled blue lay in curved pieces. "Nest" and "eggs" forced their way into my thinking. I did not carry the Ring of Thorvæld. No fabled blade hung at my side. Wounded and barely able to walk, it seemed I stood in the lair where dragon eggs had hatched. The sword my hand gripped—when had I drawn it?—had barely lost the reek of the forge.

For long moments I stood as if frozen. I became aware of slow dripping and water that oozed from a crack in the wall and left a darker trail until it disappeared in a narrowing tunnel. Water dripped from a mottled white cone that hung from the ceiling.

I had read too much of dragons it seemed. My own breathing echoed and seemed the hiss of a wyvern or some other beast. The tunnel that led farther into darkness would not allow passage of a great dragon, but a serpent of deadly size could have used it, or a salamandríne like the creature that lay on the chamber floor.

Barely could I force my feet to move beyond the head. What seemed a foreleg reached toward the shell fragments. The barrels and casks lay behind. Tiny points of dull red glared, like unblinking eyes. The head seemed less a head from this side, but I felt myself sweating. No sound but the slow dripping of water and my own breathing could be heard. No creature smells mingled with wet stone and mud. No heat radiated from the beast of stone.

I lifted the lid of one barrel. A silver plate lay at the top, with a scattering of copper and silver coins upon it. A gold coin showed among those of lesser value. The other casks also stored a rich treasury, though not so rich as dragons in the tales guarded. No flames consumed me. No serpent hissed from the recesses.

Mr. Gerhardt still lived, however, so I left the cavern as I found it. I wormed my way back to the entrance where I hid the door once again. I then returned to the Keep with my men. I wondered if taking so much as one coin would have wakened the beast.

The Lay of Thorvld spoke of the rightful lord waking the wyvern. It also told of the rotting flesh of the steward and the death of the daughter. Though the exact words eluded me, it made reference to the worm still living and the steward being no more.

My mind searched for answers it could not find. Could the flow of water have formed such a shape? Was there in truth a salamandríne there, dead or in sleep so deep that it seemed dead? If so, what would waken it? The warning, "Beware the torch, Fire gives birth to fire," did not seem a warning to take lightly.

The agony of Mr. Gerhardt's slow dying tempered my hatred for him.

If somehow he survived I would inform him of what I had found. Some part of me also feared there might be more than some ancient pattern in the stone. I hesitated to claim the treasure while Mr. Gerhardt still drew breath.

A heavy snowfall in late October gave hope that the last of the Pict would withdraw and we would be free of attack for another season. Clashes had claimed three more lives in the weeks since the battle. Two other wounded had died.

My people brought in an old man from the trail south. His horse had gone lame and he had made effort to pitch camp beside an ancient oak, but snow had smothered his fire. Cold, wet and near death, he did not speak for several hours, though given wine and hot broth.

I sought moments alone with Dierdre, something in me drawing ever more strongly to her. The moments came rarely, though little Ilsa would run and hold up her arms to be lifted when she saw me.

As the early snow dwindled my people ranged ever farther north. Some fortunate groups returned burdened with meat, but most did well to bring back more than they consumed during the search.

The old man survived, but remained weak and apparently mute.

None chose to rebuild the village, though I did not forbid it. The tavern had been destroyed, although the keeper recovered a hoard of buried coin. The brothel continued with only a brief interruption during the days of battle. Two families surrendered their dwellings to the brothel-keeper in exchange for a few coins. Battle-weary men beat a path to the door. I had no grounds for complaint, yet it seemed a shameful thing that desperately needed coin should be so used while starvation threatened us.

"Milord," Erhard, drew me aside one evening. "It be Sheridan, the bard."

"What? Who?" I questioned.

"The old man stranded during the storm. The one we thought could not live."

"Can it be?" I questioned. "Why did no one note a harp on his saddle?" I mused for a moment. "If it is him he deserves a higher honour than has been given."

"Tis refreshing, Sirs, to be treated just as an old man—a foolish old man doubtless—to be out in such a storm."

I turned to see the bard who had so stirred my emotions when I had heard him two years earlier. "Sir," I bowed respectfully toward him. "You do us great honour."

"Nay," he responded. "Tis selfishness brought me here. I would meet the young lord, now he has broken his chains. Would that I had strength to sing one last Lay before I die."

"Shall I gather the people? Almost, I would pull the watch, that even the guards in the lonely hours might sit at your feet."

"Nay. My wisdom grows old like my body. Life lies ahead for you and your people. Do not abandon the watch."

Chapter Twenty-One
A Name of My Own

WHEN WE GATHERED THAT NIGHT, nearly 200 strong, Sheridan sat near the forge fires. Pollard lay his hammer aside. To my surprise, Sheridan knew of my readings from the *Isaiae* scroll. It seemed he knew the writings better than I, and it took me some time to find his choice. I read:

> *"Where they walk in darkness, a great light has shone.*
> *Where the shadow of death falls, light rises.*
> *The nation has grown and overflows with joy*
> *as when the harvest is abundant,*
> *as when they have plundered their enemies,*
> *broken the yoke from their shoulders,*
> *and the rod of those who oppress.*
> *The warriors garments dipped in blood,*
> *will be burned.*[v]

"Admirabilis consiliarius Deus fortis Pater futuri saeculi Princeps pacis.[vi]

For a child is born for us.
A son is given for us.
The rulership will be on his shoulders.
He will be called wonderful counselor,
mighty God,
everlasting father
prince of peace."[vii]

"I am no priest of the Christus." Sheridan's voice reached out with surprising strength after I had read the passages. "But many the years I have seen. Gods have risen and fallen. Teachers have drawn people after them. Yet one god has stood. The learnéd seem to be in agreement that the Son is this Christus, though much has been done in his name that violates his own teaching."

He mused a moment, then continued. "Wisdom beyond all I have dreamed lies in that scroll. The Son, the Christus, spoke with similar wisdom, then defeated death."

His gaze swept the crowd, then came back to me. "Do not cast away thoughtlessly the old gods. But look long—look well to the claims of this god, and his son, the Christus. My days are over. My search comes to an end. Could I trade all the wisdom gained across the years for one hour spent at the feet of the Christus, t'would be folly to refuse."

It seemed a long quiet time, with just the sputtering of the torches. A restless stirring showed among the people. "You spoke of one Lay you wished to sing, honoured Sir," I finally prompted him.

"Aye," he responded. "But I'm an old man and weary. Many tales find their way south from Muninn's Keep, and oft beyond belief. But old men are not so easily fooled, except by their trust in their own wisdom. That can put them on a lonely trail where they would perish in their foolishness except someone rescue them."

His fingers played across the harp strings. He leaned back against the warm stones and raised his face to the ceiling, staring into the shadows. "Tis a tale you know. It sits fresh and raw on your memories."

Dierdre approached with a cup of ale. He received it distractedly from her hand, then turned sharply toward her. "A storied warrior." His voice fell silent for a moment. "One will come from your womb, Milady, who will be worthy of his father." He sipped the ale and continued to regard her. "My vision grows week, both within and without, but this much I still see." His head sagged then, and it seemed he slept. Dierdre stood like one stunned, then quietly withdrew. The harp fell from Sheridan's hand, sounding a discordant note as it struck the floor.

"Old men think they will live forever." It seemed Sheridan spoke to the floor itself. "Almost, they are as foolish as young men who think the sword only devours others." He raised his gaze and met mine for a moment.

"It cannot be tonight." He sighed. "Another will sing the Lay of Muninn's Keep. Tis a tale to endure a hundred generations." Sheridan continued. "Aye. And tis victory true. But yet the dead are still dead and victory comes at high price." He sighed deeply. He sipped again from the cup, leaned against the wall and let his eyes close.

"The one you called master has but few days left. He dares not believe your claims." The bard spoke in a faint voice, seemingly to himself. "We each fight our battles and come to the close of our days. Wise man or fool we die. And who will say one is better than the other?"

Sheridan breathed his last sometime in the night. He left a note written in a shaky hand:

Sheridan, to Theodoric Thorvæld

Some will foolishly think my bones a treasure. Let my body be burned, therefore, that it feeds not their folly.

Whether or not the god of Isaiae and the Christus his son are true gods I know not, but do not give up your search.

Delay not to take the woman to wife.

I stared at the note a long time,

We built a funeral pier and burned the body of the wisest man I had known, though I had only twice listened to his wisdom. It seemed wrong that the stench of burning flesh should accompany the loss of such a great man. As I watched the flames, portions from the scroll passed through my mind:

I am the first and the last.
I laid the foundation stones of the earth and set it on its
pillars.

My right hand spread out the heavens and held them.

If only you had paid attention and listened
your peace would have been like a river,
your rightness like the waves of the sea.

They won't hunger or thirst.
The sun won't beat on them.
One who cares will lead them by springs of water.

He carried our diseases and took our sorrows upon himself.
Yet we thought God did it, punishing him.
But it was for us he was wounded, beaten and pierced.
It was for our healing that he was whipped.
The Lord laid our wrong-doing on him.[viii]

If these words spoke of the Christus, and Sheridan had expressed conviction that they did, then more and more I found reason to consider him a true and worthy god.

Because of our losses, numbers had dropped below 300 souls, yet I despaired to feed 100 of them unless now, at the most bountiful time of the year, we began to ration severely.

I thought often of the treasure at Mr. Gerhardt's house. It might buy supplies enough that my people could remain. But Mr. Gerhardt still lived. Facing the salamandríne and taking its hoard raised other questions. Were the broken fragments egg shells or pieces of pottery?

Was the salamandríne reality or deception? The child had spoken of singed hair. Should I take her word? Did the Lay of Thorvld speak of the salamandríne in that cavern, or something other? And did salamandríne eggs even have hard shells or were they leathery? Unanswered questions surged through my mind.

After consulting Erhard and Bertrm I called my people together in the great hall. "Stores are in desperately short supply for the winter ahead of us," I informed them bluntly. "Two bitter choices do we face. Begin even today to ration severely while hunters continue to seek to stretch our meager supplies—or—as many as can and will—move south of the great wall. For you who have resources with which to buy, or skills for a trade that would earn your winter's bread, such a move may save you from starvation and ease the burden here, saving other lives as well."

"We wish to stay under your leadership, Sire," a woman's voice called. Many an *aye* sounded from the crowd.

"You honour me, a young leader of a great house." I called back. "Yet a house that has not had years enough to put stores by for such a time as this. My leadership cannot put food in your bellies this winter. But if some of you will go south, yet return bearing weapons and ready to work the soil, you would grant a boon to the one you seek to honour and save lives also."

Muttering and grumbling swept across the crowd, punctuated by loud cursing. I felt their despair as my own. I limped from the great hall. At the base of the stairs to the watchtower I sat and stretched my legs, easing the ache from my wounds. Dierdre came to me, bringing biscuit and a hunk of cheese. I took comfort in her presence. "You care for your people and they know it, Milord," she finally said. "I have the gold you have given me. Shall I take Ilsa and go?"

"Ah, Dierdre," I groaned. I stared at her bleakly, searching for words. "How can I let you go?" I whispered the words. "I need you here. I. . ." My voice fell silent.

I bit into the cheese and stared out across the Keep. "They deserve better," I said softly. "You also deserve better. Would that I could buy supplies to feed them all."

Her hand touched my arm, warm and soft. "You have done all living man can do for them. Do they deserve better than that, Milord?"

A few moments later she excused herself. I felt somehow more desolate with her absence, yet more free than before. My arm felt warm where she had touched it.

Three days later a funeral spirit prevailed as 140 people prepared to leave. With the rationing started they had seen that my word held true. Even as they gathered and began to pour in disorderly fashion out the gate, the watch reported a lone rider approaching from the south.

The tavern keeper complained bitterly when I refused to sell extra food-stuff to him. In disgust he packed what belongings they had managed to salvage after the Pict attack. With his wife heaping abuse on him and on me, they left with the others, rudely pushing through the crowd.

The exodus took much of the day for they left as people going into exile. I gripped the arm of most, or tousled the hair of children, trying with little success to share my thanks and encourage them, hoping most would fare well and return in the spring. It was a futile hope for some.

The rider, when he drew near, carried a longbow slung loosely across his shoulders. A sword hung at his side. His clothing and features showed the weathering of a life beneath the open skies. He sat his horse with a latent vitality and intense alertness. Ruddy of skin, his black hair and beard showed flecks of grey. Some half-memory plagued me at sight of him and even more at the sound of his voice.

"I am Finlay, of the house of Kyle," he informed us. "I seek Erhard, the scrivener, and would have words with Theodoric Thorvæld, lord of this house." He swung down from his horse and stood before me.

"And do you come in peace or to our hurt?" I questioned. Something teased at the back of my mind at the naming of the house of Kyle, but like so many fragmented memories, I could make nothing of it. His name however, struck me as amusing, for *fair-haired little soldier* did not fit him.

"I bring news that will doubtless be of interest, Sir—news of the nine fingered one who bears the ring." His glance swept both my hands, coming to rest for a moment on my left. He stared at me as if expecting something, then shrugged "And do I have the honour of speaking to the Lord himself?"

"Aye, Surra, you do," Erhard responded for me. "And I be Erhard. What would you with me?"

The man glanced at the people shuffling despondently away from the Keep. "You face an exodus. You have fought a costly battle with the Pict. Do your people abandon you now?"

"Nay. They be a good people—deeply loyal to their leader," Erhard replied. "They leave of necessity, not choice—to stave off starvation for themselves and us who remain."

Finlay's glance swept Erhard's face, then my own, watching as I gripped the arm of an old man who walked with a cane and would probably not see spring. "None have been ordered to leave," Erhard stressed quietly. "Those with ability to buy, or a trade that will earn their bread—have been asked to go, that our supplies might stretch enough. Some few, like old Cameron here, give too much." Erhard's voice fell silent.

"Too much?" The old man questioned. "What good's an old goat like me? Jist one more mouth to feed." He waved his cane at Erhard. "Don't you worry none about me. I'm too stubborn to die easy. I'll be back come spring."

"I hate to see you go, Cameron," I broke into the conversation. "And I'll hold you to that promise. Besides, who's supposed to teach a young buck like me if there aren't a few grey-beards around?"

"Some youngn's never learn, but you'll do fine, Laddie." He poked me with his cane. "I'll 'spect you to be married to that Dierdre lass and working on some bairns of your own come spring. So don't you disappoint me." He turned and marched purposefully out onto the trail.

I turned to Erhard. "Go Erhard." I said quietly. "Hear what your guest has to say. I will join you at the evening meal."

Erhard nodded. "Pretty good advice, I'd say. Old Cameron's not in his dotage yet. And I'll remember that about grey-beards too." He grinned, then turned and strode away from the gate. Finlay followed, leading his horse.

A deep melancholy settled over me as the last stragglers moved south. I found myself limping badly as I came to board that night, with little appetite, rationed though the meal was.

"Remain if you will," I requested of Erhard and the stranger. "If you are able to share news, I would hear it now."

"He brought a letter," Erhard told me. "Addressed to me it was, though I know not who wrote it." He drew a tattered scrap of parchment from his clothing and spread it before me.

> *Litle lrning wit letrs I got frnd. Yet I sed this writn in the fir Sense words what is wrot is presius und scrolls tresure lik gld I mslf brn to hit savn The nin fingrd un hit taks aboot Thinks I my frnd mit make undrstndin of hit*
>
> *I send hit you with un I trust my lif Dangr I make him und myonself so be with care*
>
> *Yer frnd*

It proved simple enough to decipher, though the spelling presented a challenge.

> *Little learning with letters I got, friend. Yet I seed (saw) this writing in the fire. Since words what is wrote is precious and scrolls treasure like gold, I myself burned to its saving. The nine fingered one it talks about. Thinks I my friend might make understanding of it.*
>
> *I send it you with one I trust my life. Danger I make him and my own self so be with care.*
>
> *Your friend.*

"The letter then, is of a sensitive sort," I observed quietly as Dierdre approached. She asked if I wished ale or barley cakes for our guest.

"Thank you, Dierdre. No," I replied. "We will share of our best, but will not break rationing to impress him." She bowed slightly and withdrew.

Erhard then placed the other letter before me. Charred and bearing a broken seal of dark red wax, marred and half melted so the device and name could not be deciphered.

A friend to Erhard—Greetings

Not everyone has forgotten your father's service. Oft have I read the scroll he died to save and regretted the small-minded treachery of the priest who left him to die. Much would I give to hear your father's understanding of the words I dare not here repeat.

But a whelp myself at the time, I was witness to your flogging, though not to your sale. I held the priests in high regard before that time, and could scarce conceal my contempt after.

Guard well these words. If wisdom so guide you, let them be reduced to smoke and ashes. The religion of the Christus has weakened the priest's power, yet do they wield a heavy hand and bear much influence among the people. The time will come, but is not yet when I must confront them. So let these words not fall into evil hands.

The genealogy is sure. The nine-fingered one is no impos-

ter, though he knows it not himself. Thorvæld the Conqueror is his direct forbear, as I knew while he was still within my household.

His loss in the clan raid and subsequent sale at auction would prove a great embarrassment were his pedigree known. That he had been beaten bloody before he stood on the auction block and knew not his own name would yet avail me little should he learn of my part in his rearing. Yet gave I him every advantage except horses. The prophecy of horse killer I would stay. But tales from Muninn's Keep suggest he has earned the title in spite of me.

Do not oppose him. If the prophecies be true, he were a better friend than enemy.

As to the prophecies themselves—A bold and reckless man watched as four men toured Muninn's Keep. Only three of them returned, the fourth horse bearing a burden, but not a man. Yet a wild man clad in a raw boar skin and carrying a rowan staff made the weary trail on foot just days later. A nine fingered man he was, the watcher swears. The tales of the ring you know from that day forward better than I, and the boar skin that covers it on the rowan staff you have seen with your own eyes.

The man's learning and his skill with weapons I can attest to, though tales of the battles he has fought sound to have grown in the telling.

More proof at this time I cannot give, for in the wrong hands it might be his undoing, and mine.

Farewell

Slowly I read the words through, then a second time. I had family, a past. The name I had chosen actually *belonged* to me.

Chapter Twenty-Two
More Dangerous Than Wyverns

I RAISED MY GLANCE TO THE STRANGER. "Finlay, of the house of Kyle, how got you this letter?" I questioned.

"I was the watcher, Sir," he said slowly. "When four men toured Muninn's Keep some seasons past—and only three returned. I was watcher also at other times. I would doubtless have died in the raid when you were taken, but was away at the time. I am rather too reckless a fighter. It would seem from the tales that I. . ." His voice fell silent for a moment. He seemed to gather his thoughts, then continued—"that *your* teacher modeled recklessness."

He paused again as though groping for words. I thought he had said more than intended and wondered at the 'I' so quickly changed to 'your'.

"My master sought to know how you fared. The raid did much damage and we were weakened beyond taking you back. But he sent me often to watch from a distance. You saved my life that day, when you gave no sign that you recognized me as you stood, beaten and bloody on the auction block."

"Do not give credit greater than is due me, Sir. I have no memory of any auction. Even the dark lockup at Mr. Gerhardt's farm and the whipping that preceded it escape my memory. I know of it only from what I have been told and from the scars my body bears. Injured badly I was and totally ignorant of horses." A weak laugh escaped me. "One of my oldest clear memories is standing beside a horse in Mr. Gerhardt's stable, trying to take a saddle off and not knowing how. My mind recognized writing and my hand recognized a sword, but I have had only glimpses of a past before that date—until this letter—and your words." I sighed. "I have feared what I might learn. I had been branded as a thief and flogged for crimes I have no memory of."

Abruptly I stood. "Much you have told me. Much there is yet to hear. Since it was drawn from the fire, someone has read and sought to destroy the letter. On that too I would hear your thoughts." I paced painfully. "Will you stay some days?" I asked. "News you bring of Erhard's father and he will doubtless wish to know more. I also, like a starving man, will wish to taste all the secrets that you may share."

"I will stay if I may be permitted," He replied. "Winter will not be long in coming and will be harsh, else I am but a poor judge. I have some skill as a hunter. Meat for my own mouth and several besides can I provide."

I nodded, then left the room.

Long before I reached the base of the stairs to the watchtower I regretted not having brought the rowan staff. The wound pained me badly and a bitterly cold wind had sprung up. I ached for my people camped along the trail.

I had been reduced to a crawl before I gained the stone ledge beneath the watchtower. The tower itself I could not manage so leaned against the ledge and stared to the southeast where glimmers marked lonely campfires. The exertion and pain had slowed my raging thoughts, yet questions clamoured for answers. At least the tavern keeper was gone and the brothel no longer within my walls, though I felt a shameful hunger for the pleasures promised.

At the late night change of the watch they found me crouched in the lee of a rock, chilled and shivering badly. They brought a jug of ale heated over the coal fire in the tower. I gulped it eagerly. To my shame I needed help down the stairs. Stiffened by the cold I could not walk.

At board the next morning Mr. Gerhardt shuffled in. Bent and wasted, he looked an old man now, with health and spirit broken. "Mr. Gerhardt," I greeted him. "Tis not a happy occasion that brings you to my hall. I would that I could welcome you with all your household healthy."

"They tell me you are a very warlord, Thræl," he choked the words out, his voice raspy and dry, ignoring my offered friendship.

"No longer am I thræl, Sir, though had you not dealt treacherously with me I might be. Yet that is behind. What assistance is in my power to give, you will receive." I paused, then continued. "Warlord? I fight like a foolish youth who thinks himself beyond death. I would rebuke any of my people who so fought."

"The hearthstone be yours. Git it out of my ruins." His voice broke and he coughed weakly, then spat blood on the floor. "The farm too. Take it and be damned! I care nothing for it any more.

Would to all the gods that I had died."

"The hearthstone I will recover, Sir," I responded quietly. "For here it belongs. The farm I will work for you so long as you live. Have you no one left? Is there none at all to give it to?"

"I told you it was yours—fool thræl." His voice rose and his face turned deep red, then his tormented lungs convulsed him.

"I'd as soon give it to my dog," he gasped the words, then spat again. "But the Pict devils killed even him."

Nothing I could say would make his pain less. I turned to leave.

"Thræl! Fool!" Mr. Gerhardt's harsh voice stopped me. "Send me the scrivener you stole from me."

Refusing to speak to his accusations, I left the room. Harsh laughter died into strangled coughing.

"Theodoric." The word reached me as the door closed behind me. Again I stopped.

"Proud as a lord born, you always were. I should have flogged you harder." Again his voice died into coughing.

I found Erhard. "You are a free man, Erhard. You are not in bondage to me or to Mr. Gerhardt, though he knows not how to treat anyone as other than thræl. He desires a scrivener. If you are willing I request it of you. If unwilling I will seek someone else."

Mr. Gerhardt did not come to board again. I went to his room once and found myself cursed so did not see him again. Three days later he breathed his last.

Erhard brought the document he had written under Mr. Gerhardt's instruction.

I told the imposter, Theodoric, that he could have the farm. But for five generations past has it been held in trust to the true heir of the House of Thorvæld. No joy could I or my heirs know if one from that house appeared, yet I am without heirs and my final hour approaches. May it come swiftly.

A curse on the lying one who claims leadership of the House of Thorvæld. May the flesh rot off his bones and his lungs rage with fire. May the true heir win and hold this place against the Pict and every imposter.

Let my body be burned, not buried, that my bones might never lie beside the thræl, Theodoric.

Though my hands weep blood and my life drains from me so that I cannot put my mark on this parchment, I, Holt Gerhardt, have spoken.

If Theodoric be the true heir may the curse come back on me.

May it be even so.

"What does he mean—*held in trust?*" I questioned Erhard and Bertrm. "It sounds as though the farm was never his."

"Aye, but that he would not confess while hope of life remained," Bertrm responded.

"And someone he had purchased as thræl could never fit his idea of who the true lord must be." Erhard added.

"Tis a grim curse," I mused darkly, my mind seeing the rotting flesh and smelling the stink.

"A grim curse indeed," Erhard agreed. "Much on his mind for that be how he died. I did not tell him that Finlay brought the very proof he thought could not be found."

"Finlay?" I questioned.

"Finlay, of the house of Kyle—in the letter he brought." Erhard spoke slowly, searching for words. "It be confirmation that you be the true heir of the House of Thorvæld. The name you claim be your own, Surra, and this Keep and Mr. Gerhardt's farm."

"But the curse?" I questioned again.

"Look you at this line, last but one. *'If Theodoric be the true heir, may the curse come back on me.'* Master Gerhardt lived and died the very curse he uttered."

I stood and paced, painfully aware of the wound in my leg. Several times I started to speak, then stilled my tongue again.

"Finlay has been three days on the hunt. He will be back soon, Sir," Bertrm assured me. "Insight he will have, and understanding that we lack."

I ordered a funeral pier prepared for Mr. Gerhardt. I took no part in bearing the body or in lighting the fire. He held me in contempt and would have counted it a dishonour. Yet so far as I had influence, I saw that he received a fitting tribute.

Finlay returned as my people lit the fire, his horse heavily laden under three young wild pigs.

I would have gone even then to recover the treasure from Mr. Gerhardt's house, but duties pressed and winter drew close. Nor did I know even yet, if the salamandríne was more than a rock formation, or if the shell fragments meant other creatures hid in the recesses of the cavern.

Little had I seen of Dierdre and several sleepless nights had plagued me, but I spoke carelessly of a wedding feast—the flesh of wild pigs bringing bounty we had not known for some time.

She stopped and stared long at me, then breathed words that once again set my mind whirling. "I feared you would never ask again, Milord." She fled to the kitchen then.

"You look like you've jist been swallowed by a wyvern," Erhard said with a chuckle.

I finally questioned him in a halting voice. "Erhard, how does a man know when he is ready for marriage?"

"Ah—more dangerous than battling wyverns be that one." Erhard grinned and continued. "The wild boar chomps till his mouth foams white, daring all comers. The stag rakes the trees with his antlers and clashes with any who oppose him. I know not how the raven and the hare choose their mates, but doubtless feathers and fur fly—yet even then the lady-love sometimes plays them false. A dangerous game indeed, Surra."

I pushed back from the table. Dierdre worked with three older women. Ilsa toddled beside her. My gaze followed, warmed by the knowledge that Dierdre had somehow become Mistress of Muninn's Keep.

"There be no falseness in that one, Surra." Erhard's words drew me back. "The heart that beats neath that breast be noble as any high-born woman. More—tis a heart bought and paid for."

I felt the sharp bite of jealously at his words, and a sense of loss almost bottomless in its depths.

"None have I seen pay court to her." My voice broke, shaming me. "Who—is this man? Though little can we spare, we must make a worthy wedding feast."

"Then you admit yourself ready, Surra?" Erhard questioned.

"I. . . ?" I stammered. "I must give her up or betray her. For thoughts of her torment me, though I never thought it torment till now, knowing she is promised to another."

Erhard stared at me like I spoke some foreign language. "Never before have I thought you mad, Surra. To give her up *would* betray her."

"But you said . . ." I stopped, bewildered.

"I said, 'tis a heart bought and paid for,—paid as far back as the day of your proving against Erskine's sword."

I sank back onto the bench. Emotions beyond understanding or control turned my mind to a tumult. "Flattery does not become you." I finally choked out the words, failing to give them the sternness I desired.

"Tis no flattery, Surra. Never did I learn to give such," Erhard answered—and he spoke true. Flattery was foreign to his nature.

"A lesser woman would have crawled to your feet, Milord—or to your bed."

"But I know nothing of women," I confessed.

"Aye, Surra. Women have ever baffled the male mind. Though oft, and to his own hurt, the man thinks with other than his mind, so wars are fought, blood be spilt, and children are born that the fight might continue for another season. Tis the joke of the gods, Surra, and of greater mirth to watch than to live."

"But may a man who leads a house, whose life is not his own, take a wife of his own choosing? Little have I read of such. It seems the marriage bed buys a neighbour's army, not love."

"Your life is not your own?" Erhard stared at me. "Mayhap you speak true, Surra. For never yet have I found falseness in you. Why, then, does everyone lust after the power of the master?"

"Because they are ignorant," I said with some disgust. "Yet you choose not to answer my question." I spoke quieter now. "Is it to the good of this house if I take a wife of my own choosing?"

"Rare it be, Surra, else I am much misled, to find one to birth your heir who also holds you in the highest esteem and stirs that most dangerous part of you to its depths. Great be the danger to a household when the lord be so stirred by another man's wife. Great be the security of a household when the lord's own wife so stirs him."

Finlay stood to one side, a faint smile playing on his weathered features. I struggled to pull my thoughts from Dierdre and turn them to him. "What of my past?" I questioned.

"Little enough I know, Sir," he replied. "I reported to my master, who, I think, trusted me deeply yet never took me into his confidence. He feared for your safety, though why he never said. It was another, not my master, who wrote the letter. Yet my master sent me with it after it was pulled from the fire." He gazed at me thoughtfully. "It really is true that you have no memories before Mr. Gerhardt's farm?"

"None that I can make sense of," I answered quietly. "My hands knew the feel of a sword. My eyes knew writing. But I cannot tell how they knew."

He stared at me pensively for a moment. "Very strange it is, Sir," he finally said. He remained silent for some moments, then spoke again. "Your eyes don't lie, though you should know me well." He shook his head, then continued. "It is no boast to say my skill with weapons was as great as my master had seen. Yet a youth who came to our household—not yet a man and lacking a man's growth and strength—proved himself my better, though he had much to learn. It may be that none but me knew his skill exceeded mine, for he had not yet his full strength."

He drew his sword then, sparking an instant alertness among my men. A circle swiftly formed, with every man grasping something usable as a weapon. "Ah," Finley commented, running his fingers along a blade a man might have shaved with, then slowly, without threat, lifting the sword aloft with both hands. "For all my skills it would be a swift death if I proved false to you. You have learned well and taught your men the same skill. Women too, I see."

I followed his glance and saw Dierdre had lifted a spear from the wall. She stood in profile, very much a woman, and yet a warrior. I knew she stood ready to fight and to die—for me. I knew also that she handled the spear as well as most men. If I had doubted my love for her before that moment, I did so no longer.

Those thoughts passed in a second, emotions held in check as I gauged the response of my warriors. Finlay posed no threat, but he might die if my people did not agree. "Try her skill with your hat," I suggested.

Finlay glanced at me, bowed slightly, then sheathed his sword in a swift, fluid motion. Ever the warrior, his glance swept the circle that surrounded us. He tossed his hat toward a gap among the watchers.

The spear took the hat out of the air between two men who stood scarcely a pace apart. It struck the stone wall a ringing blow, striking sparks.

Finlay bowed toward Dierdre, a slow smile spreading on his face. "A warrior maiden, true, Milady. A fitting bride for the lord of the House of Thorvæld, methinks."

Stepping over to the wall, he picked up the spear. "The mothers of your enemies will mourn their sons should they come between you and your lady, Milord." He stooped again and picked up his hat, then stared ruefully at the hole torn by the spear. "It was a good hat, Sir." Then he grinned and turned toward Dierdre. "Ah, but it was well thrown, Milady. And well earned my lesson. You are a prepared people."

The ring of watchers relaxed and drew away from us, a subdued excitement stirring among them. I sat still at the bench. Erhard and Finlay both took their places across the table from me.

"I was your teacher, Sir, with weapons," Finlay said after a brief silence. "Another taught you letters. Every skill we could impart you gained—every skill except horses. That we were forbidden to teach. I never was told who I taught, or why. The letter I carried here is my first knowledge of your true identity. Doubtless my master knew."

"What can you tell me of the House of Thorvæld?" I asked.

"Little, Sir. I had but small love for writing. I thought your time with scrolls, parchment and ink a waste. It seemed you were born with a sword in hand. Your mother died in childbirth. Perhaps that is why. My master knew my skill with the sword and vowed that skill should be yours as well." He paused a moment, then continued.

"The house of Thorvæld sparked small interest in the taverns, though tales of old battles and a ring of gold said to be heavy enough to anchor a ship were sometimes told. I weened the ring's size and weight to be somewhat exaggerated. More rarely, and whispered over their cups, were tales of a nine-fingered one."

"So in truth you know little more than I do?" I reluctantly voiced the question.

"Aye, Sir. Except that you were trained as a lord is trained, except for horses being forbidden. I never understood that and thought it always a grave error." Finlay paused again. "Perhaps had I been more attentive to books I would have known the prophecy of horse killer. My master knew, somehow, that you had a destiny, and sought to prepare you for it."

"Why, if he trusted you, did he never take you into his confidence?" I questioned.

Finlay stared at me for a long moment, then spoke with a rueful, almost defiant air. "To my shame he knew my tongue was prone to wag overmuch at the taverns."

The rebuke that rose to my lips died there. Many a valiant warrior is overly fond of the beer jug.

My gaze turned toward the kitchen, my mind drawn back to Dierdre. "And marriage, Sir? Did my training also equip me for that?"

"My thoughts on marriage did not meet the approval of my master," Finlay confessed. "An ale-wife, Sir. I always swore I would marry an ale-wife or never wed."

"So you are the father of sons then?" I asked.

"No Sir," Finlay admitted. "Ale-wives are in short supply with more than enough men willing to drink their beer and sire their children."

I pushed back from the table. "I am sorry, Finlay, that this house boasts but little of the brewer's art." I nodded to my companions and walked to the kitchens, limping, but feeling a new strength that somehow lessened the pain.

"A hawthorn branch, Sir, at her door. Tis the fitting way to ask." Finlay spoke the words softly as I walked away.

Ilsa ran to me and I caught her and swept her up in my arms. Her mother leaned back from the oven where she worked, brushed hair from her eyes, then walked toward us. The flush on her face seemed more than the heat of the oven should cause.

"Do you think, Ilsa, that you could stand me for a Da, if we could talk your mammy into considering it?" The little girl in my arms squirmed and giggled. Dierdre stared up at me and blushed.

"I think," she whispered softly, "the mammy might be persuaded—that a little girl needs a Da."

"And could the mammy be persuaded that a little girl also needs a brother?" I whispered into Ilsa's hair.

Dierdre blushed deeper.

"I have need of a harpist's skill and a poet's tongue. I possess neither." I stumbled over the words as I tried to speak my thoughts. "I asked once before, and ill-timed was my asking. Not much smarter have I grown in the way of women in the months since."

"Well?" she questioned, mocking, yet the mockery held no sting.

"More dangerous than battling wyverns, Erhard says." I murmured the words, feeling the heat rise in my face.

"The leader of a house should have a wife. Only one there is who stirs my desires, who stretches my mind toward verse and makes my arms ache to hold her." I groped for words. "If I left a branch of hawthorn outside your door, would you leave it, or replace it with a weed? It should be the Feast of Beltane for such an experiment, but . . ." My voice faltered. "Could you be persuaded to be my wife, Dierdre? Could you share the good and the ill of your life with the good and the ill of mine?"

"You are more a poet than you know, Milord," Dierdre responded, her lips trembling a bit. She reached a hand to brush Ilsa's hair from her face. "The kindness you have shown this fatherless bairn would have earned my answer, even if you showed no love for me. Yet you have always treated me with respect, something I have no memory of before you came to Mr. Gerhardt's farm." Her eyes brimmed with tears as she stared up at me. "Will it be all thorns?"

I shifted Ilsa to my left arm, then reached toward Dierdre. "This time of year, it will be a challenge to find a branch with a leaf left on it," I said softly. "But I hope I can offer something more than just thorns."

Dierdre leaned against my arm for a moment, her body warm against me. She twisted slightly away from me and drew something from her bodice, then turned back. The gold torc I had given her, she spread and placed around my neck, pressing the ends close.

"If the lord of this house is to be my husband he must wear this torc." Her voice fell silent as she stared up at me with brimming eyes. She leaned into me then, seeming to mold her body to mine. "I have decided I cannot settle for less than a lord," she whispered, "so you must look the part." She grinned through her tears.

Not trusting myself to speak, I pressed my lips into Ilsa's hair as my arms squeezed both mother and bairn. Beyond words—at least beyond my skill with words it is—to describe my feelings in that moment.

Chapter Twenty-Three
Of Joys and Sorrows

THE FUSS OVER WEDDINGS COULD ALMOST make a man regret the asking. With food so scarce the feast would be small, yet men clapped me on the back and women gathered around Dierdre like so many hens squabbling over one chick. They tormented Ilsa also, till she toddled away in tears. We finally stood before our people. Dierdre and Ilsa wore gowns of pale wool. Ilsa looked a true princess, though she had played by the fire and stained her gown with ashes. Dierdre looked a queen and my pulse quickened at sight of her.

Torches in the great hall threw a smoky light as Erhard nervously faced us. "I be neither bard nor priest," he declared as he stood within the circle of stones laid out on the floor. "The man who stands before you be the man who won my freedom. Like a son he be to me." He paused and cleared his throat, nervous, but somehow triumphant. "We have seen him, as a husbandman making wise decisions about crops," Erhard continued. "We have seen him as a warrior, defending his people, mighty in battle. We have seen him defending justice, protecting the least of us and holding the powerful to a high standard."

He turned then to gaze on Dierdre, and his smile widened. "The woman who stands before you was also set free by this man. We have eaten—all of us I suppose—of that which her hand has prepared. Free, no longer a thræl, she has yet served, given of herself, shown that beauty and strength go together. Could a more fitting bride for the Lord of Muninn's Keep be found?"

He stepped forward then and took a scarlet cord that Ilsa carried and toyed with as she stood beside her mother. "Since I be neither bard nor priest, my words will be few." A ripple of laughter swept though the crowd. He nodded to us and we crossed our wrists, one above the other. He bound them with the cord. He turned then to a boy standing by my side, carrying a sword. It had proved too heavy for the lad and he fought tears when Erhard took it from him.

I looked on an elaborate weapon, encrusted with gems, beautiful, but unfit for battle. Erhard laid the flat of the blade on my right shoulder, then Dierdre's right shoulder, then on our bound wrists. He did the same with our left shoulders, and then with the tops of our heads. A triple triad with the sword. He spoke old words, well known to most of my people, blessings from the east and the west, the north and the south. He did not call on the goddess Brighid, though tradition dictated he should. Instead he proclaimed. "Milord and Milady, may your union be blessed. May many bairns come from your joining. May the Christus honour you and through you, all your people, as you have searched—and begun to honour him."

Erhard turned from us, raised the sword high and swept the crowd with his gaze. "People of Muninn's Keep," he shouted. "Theodoric Thorvæld and his lady, Dierdre." A cheer rose and swept through the hall.

Finlay, a skilled hunter, had brought down two stags and a wild boar, so we feasted far better than I had dared to hope. As Dierdre and I left the celebration, men offered to "show me" all I needed to know. Laughing, I drew the sword they had insisted I wear. I threatened death to anyone who disturbed us before we broke fast in the morning.

Ah, but winter nights, long and cold even with fires burning, were a different experience in a shared bed, the warmth and the joy of a strong, but soft body beside me. I will not speak of other joys, but ere spring approached I had more reason to rejoice. Sheridan had spoken of a 'storied warrior from Dierdre's womb.' I confess my pride swelled even as Dierdre's body swelled.

In early spring, before we could put plows to the land, I left Erhard in command at Muninn's Keep and returned to Mr. Gerhardt's house with a small party, heavily armed. I removed the hearth-stone with the inscription, *Se Hus of Thorvæld,* and prepared to take it back with us. Then I took my men into the sub-cellar, to the room where we had found Mr. Gerhardt and his daughter.

Fear showed in the eyes of some, mockery in others, when I spoke of the salamandríne shape in the cavern I had found. I ordered my men to stand on each side of the opening, shields at the ready. If the creature breathed fire, they would have some protection.

"Morse, Peyton, you have both been beneath the circle of stones outside Muninn's Keep. Accompany me now if you will." I gazed at the men who stood about me. "Swords will be of little use in the cavern, except as comfort to the hands that hold them. If the creature is more than stone and our entrance awakens it, well. . ." What more could be said?

With my own sword sheathed and a torch in hand, I squirmed down the narrow hole and stood once again in the cavern. The air burned my lungs and eyes. Muttered curses sounded as Morse and Peyton joined me. The half hidden sneer Peyton had sported disappeared. With three torches burning, the creature looked more alive than before. The voices from above, distorted through the entrance tunnel, fell silent.

"By the gods, Sir. You did speak true," Peyton sputtered as he fumbled with the torch and hastily drew his sword.

"Have I been in the habit of mistruths, Peyton?" I asked.

The flush drained from his face. "I meant no offense, Sir." He dropped to one knee as he apologized, but his gaze did not leave the creature and he continued to grip his sword. "I never believed they was real."

I picked up one of the mottled blue shell fragments. "There may be more than one, if this is as it appears."

Morse had stepped close to the creature. He stood among the barrels of treasure and probed gingerly with his sword. "Tis just behind the forelegs, Sir. The breast of the creatures be not armoured if the tales have told it aright."

He lay his torch on one of the barrels and gripped his sword with both hands, drawing it back.

"Stay your hand, Morse," I commanded quietly. "You are a brave man, but all you will do is shatter your blade." My gaze searched the full length of the creature, trying, in the flickering torchlight, to see any sign of life. "If it moves, strike with all your strength. Though I think it stone and not flesh and blood."

"Aye, Sir," Morse reluctantly agreed. He continued to stand with sword held at the ready.

I rested my torch against one of the barrels and lifted another, surprised at its weight. "This may be the waking of it," I warned. My gaze again swept the creature as I stumbled to the cavern entrance. "The smell?" I questioned. "Is it not the same as where coal is gathered? Where I have been warned against torches?" I received no answer, though both Morse and Payton had helped bring coal from the depths.

I turned back to my task then and grunted as I pushed the heavy barrel up the tunnel, till the men above could pull it free. Six barrels and several smaller jars of clay we removed while the creature lay unstirring. With just a few jars left to move, I saw that Peyton had left his place of watchfulness and with torch in hand searched the deeper reaches of the cavern.

A man at the top of the entrance tunnel reached for the next jar when some deep rumble shook my body while a boom to absorb all other sound seemed to crush my very skull. The mouth of the man leaning towards me opened in a scream I could not hear. Something massive drove against my feet and thrust me farther up the tunnel. Flames surrounded the man before me. Then, as if launched from a catapult, he hurtled backwards. Only then did I realize that flames surrounded me as well. I could not draw breath. Then silence reigned again—a penetrating silence, as if all sound had fled.

The mouths of my men worked. Arms waved wildly. Eyes stared

at the hole. Finally someone grasped my hands and pulled me clear.

Burned hair has a peculiar stench. I struggled to my feet. My men crowded around, mouths clamouring. "I cannot hear," I said, and they backed away, mouths gaping.

"Peyton? Morse? Are they still inside?"

Terror continued to twist the faces of my men. They could face the Pict with their hideous tattoos of woad and cruel battle-axes, but this defied comprehension.

My head throbbed and my chest ached. My face burned and one hand bled. "I must go back inside, get the others." I could hear my voice now, as from a great distance. A ringing sounded in my ears. I forced myself to squirm back into the hole, but found I could not breathe and had to re-emerge. "Death is in this air," I gasped.

With eyebrows and the sides of beards gone, my men looked strange, misshapen. I raised a hand to my own beard and knew I looked as bad.

The torch would scarcely burn when I entered some time later. My men argued, but I would not risk more lives. Nor would I abandon in the darkness ones who might, by chance, be still alive. Too well I knew that pain.

The torch gave but a sickly glow. The creature lay unmoving. Two remaining jars still sat behind the foreleg. Morse lay against the wall beyond the creature's head, though it seemed he had dragged himself some distance from it. No breath moved his chest. With his beard burned away, his face showed red and blistered. Payton lay, twisted and broken, against the hump of rock.

My breath came in shallow gasps. This air, with the smell of burned hair heavy on it, was without life.

It proved almost beyond my strength to push the bodies up the tunnel where other men could draw them out. I gazed then on the salamandríne, hating it and hating the treasure for what it had cost. I left the remaining jars untouched and squirmed back up the hole.

The dead men had no wives, so we built a funeral pier and set flame to it. A somber company, with beards shaved and hair clipped, we returned to the Keep. We bore the treasure with us, though I could not make myself look on it.

Long I held Dierdre in my arms that night, aching over the needless deaths, drawing strength from her.

In the late morning, the people who had left for the winter began to arrive. Food was still scarce. We had not yet begun to plow, yet their return brought some measure of healing to my ache. Many were the tales shared over a jug of ale, and the salamandríne had somehow grown, though no living eyes but mine had seen it. The cavern could not have held it now, and the blast of fire could melt stone. That I had gone back into the lair elevated me in the eyes of some of my people, confirmed my foolishness to others.

I held my own council, remembering The Lay of Thorvld.

Near The North Tower Gainst The Well

Worship was wont to be Made

A Worms Lair is There.

Enter At Thy Peril.

Beware the Torch

Fire Gives Birth to Fire.

Though The Wyvern Sleep An Endless Age
The Rightful Lord May Waken Her.

I had not forgotten the smell that burned lungs and eyes, the same smell that in coal gathering has the wise extinguish their torches and grope in darkness. They claim the very air will burn with a fierce and swift fire, and few who know that fire know daylight ever again.

"Cameron has returned, Surra," Erhard broke into my thoughts. The old man stood beside him, leaning on a cane. "I feared the winter would not be kind, but he lives and thrives."

I stood and gripped the old man's arm. "Welcome, Cameron. Tis good to see you back. Never again, I trust, will I have need to make such a request."

The man snorted. "Make no rash promises, young'n 'cept to continue to care for your people. If an old goat like me has to come home, you gots to be doing something right."

"Maybe it's all the she-goats that brung you," Erhard broke in with a laugh.

"Them's why I carry this stick." Cameron waved his cane at Erhard. "To beat them off."

Glossary

ale-wife—A woman who keeps an ale-house, expert in brewing ale and beer.

Alf-blot—An offering to the elves.

Athelings—Members of a noble family.

Below the Salt—The position of the Salt Cellar on the table gave indication of rank. The farther *below the salt* a person sat, the lower they ranked among those at the table.

Beltane, Feast of—Celebrated on the day the hawthorn begins to blossom, traditionally May 1st, often dedicated to Bel, the Shining One.

bladder-pipe—An instrument predating bag-pipes, often used at funerals and during battle.

braw—handsome, fine.

Brighid—Goddess, patron of lore, protector of women in childbirth. (Not to be mistaken for *Bridget of Kildare* who later filled a Christianized role of the festival.) Celebrated during the first days of February as part of the Feast of Imbolc.

burn—A brook or rivulet.

carnyx– A war trumpet used by the Pict, with a wooden tongue that gave it a strident, undulating tone.

cubit—A measure of about 45.5 cm (18 inches), the length of a man's forearm.

darkle—To appear indistinctly with a rippling effect.

faerie folk—Little people of great wisdom and power, often mischievous, but rarely malicious.

fealty—Faithfulness, loyalty.

flædg-stafir—Deception runes. Deliberately misleading, thought to have magical powers.

flagellum—A whip with multiple thin strands and bits of lead or bone attached to tear flesh.

Freya's Tears—Pieces of amber (tree sap), especially small tear-shaped drops. Highly valued, some thought them to give magical protection, like a talisman.

gibbet—An upright timber with a crossbeam projecting at right angles from its upper end, used for hanging criminals condemned to death.

Gungnir—Name of Woden's Spear; also the sacrificial knife made from a boar's tusk.

hlaut-bolla—A basin for catching the blood of sacrifices made to the gods.

hrœfn—(raven) Large black carrion bird; similar to the crow, but larger.

Imbolc, Feast of—Celebrated during the first days of February. See *Brighid.*

jarl—A warrior of noble birth.

Keep—Fortress—especially the inner refuge where a last stand can be made, or a larger fortress with exceptional defensive capabilities. See *Muninn's Keep.*

kelpies—Water Sprite, demon; a malicious spirit that would drown and devour.

knucklebones—An old game played with the knucklebones of sheep or goats. Has some similarity to the modern game of jacks.

Lay—A ballad or narrative poem, especially as told by a bard.

leech—A physician; one who sometimes uses leeches to blood-let.

Muninn—The name of one of Woden's ravens.

Muninn's Keep—The massive and highly defensible fortress Theodoric rebuilds from the ruins.

peat—Dense, partially carbonized moss, often cut in blocks, dried and used for fuel.

Pict—A warring people from the north, noted for their blue (woad) tattoos and their savagery in battle.

polecat—A skunk.

portcullis—A heavy lattice-work gate that can be dropped to close off an entry to a fortress, usually with sharpened spikes at the bottom.

portend—To warn of, as an omen.

portent—An indication or sign of what is to happen, ominous significance.

pulse—Leguminous plants, such as peas, beans etc., and their edible greens.

rowan—A small tree native to Europe; Mountain Ash. The staff is a symbol among the Druidic priesthood.

salamandríne—A mythical lizard said to live in fire; a wingless dragon.

sark—A shirt.

scrivener—A clerk or scribe.

sen'night—Literally "seven-night," a one week period.

skep—A beehive made of straw in the shape of a small rounded thatched dome.

stone—A unit of weight, about 6.35 kilograms (14 pounds).

thræl—Literally "slave" one in bondage.

Tlæchtgö—Name of the god worshiped by the Pict.

tor—A high rocky crag; a hill, quite rugged.

torc—A collar made of soft twisted bands of gold. A symbol of rank.

trencher—A shallow wooden plate.

Valhalla—The great hall into which the souls of heroes fallen bravely in battle were received and feasted by Woden; the hall of the worthy dead.

wench—A young serving girl; an unmarried girl labourer.

woad—An Old World herb of the Mustard family. The blue dye-stuff obtained from the leaves.

Woden—The chief Norse god. Wednesday is named for Woden. Many ancient and modern documents spell the name, *Odin*.

Woden's Nine—The circle of nine stones surrounding a well in a grove dedicated to Woden Worship.

worm—A word commonly used for dragon, although *wyvern* was also frequently used.

ween—Understand.

wraith—A spirit or ghost.

wyvern—A winged dragon, sometimes called a worm.

Author's Notes on the Research

Behind the Writing

The research for this story both fascinates and frustrates. Documented history for the period and location is patchy and often contradictory. Much of it comes from Christian scholars recording Pagan oral traditions centuries after the events occurred. Less interested with 'history' than with 'conversion,' it still carries a wealth of information, but has often been "Christianized," at least in part.

Medieval chat-lines have proved a rich source of information—though nearly impossible to authenticate. Research has also explored many occult and New Age sources where a more intense commitment to historical authenticity seems evident. Those sites have also yielded a rich source for agricultural practices, wedding and funeral customs and festival celebrations. The symbolism of the hawthorn is a striking case in point, both for the many references and for the often contradictory information. It is described variously as a good luck and a bad luck talisman, a fertility symbol and a chastity symbol, a danger and a protection. Among a myriad of traditions surrounding hawthorns is the rather intriguing one of a man proposing by leaving a hawthorn branch at the door of his intended bride on the day the hawthorn first bloomed, traditionally May 1st. Leaving the branch there indicated acceptance of the proposal. Replacing it with a half-spoiled vegetable from the cellar indicated, in a rather unsubtle manner, refusal.

The number 'nine' holds a cult-like significance only partially explored in the story. Triple triads, or three groups of three appear with surprising frequency in ancient documents, usually without explanation. Where explanations have been offered, there seems a danger of modern invention as much as ancient belief. Where used in this story either the characters are grappling with the questions themselves, or they appear without explanation. The author ascribes no significance to the number nine. He has simply used it where it suits the purposes of the story.

A Word About Weapons

Evidence indicates the longbow existed before the end of the 9th century. Longbows would have been more powerful than the regular bow, but the resilience of the heartwood of a yew tree had not yet been employed, so they would not be the quality of weapons made famous by the British in the battle of Crécy in August of 1346. The crossbow, though known to the Romans from 400 AD, does not seem to have appeared in England before a Norman invasion of 1066. Even the poorest people could make spears and lances, but good swords demanded rare skills and costly materials to produce, so few people owned them. Armour came at high cost also, so a leather jerkin and a leather covered wooden shield was the norm. The metal shields that gleamed and reflected light were used almost exclusively for signaling rather than for battle.

CALENDAR DATES ASSUME THE PRESENT-DAY CALENDAR.

The best educated people at the time would have used the Julian calendar with its astonishing mathematical precision of a calendar year that came within 11½ minutes of the actual solar year. Considering those calculations were made in 45 BC, that accuracy is almost beyond comprehension. Yet the 11½ minutes per year over the centuries (with several corrections imposed) had accumulated an error of approximately four days by the year 892 AD. What present calculations show as January 4th or 4 Janus, would have shown on calendars of the time as December 31, 891. Paradoxically, the less educated people would have measured their year from the vernal equinox (about March 21), so would have no accumulated error. For simplicity I have disregarded the error in the actual writing.

A WORD ABOUT BELIEFS CONCERNING DEATH

A striking absence in documents studied is any reference to reincarnation. Ancient Celtic beliefs about eternal life differ strongly from Christian beliefs, yet have no commonality with wide-ranging beliefs in endless cycles of lives so common to many other traditions, time periods and areas of the world. In Woden's Hall or Valhalla, the heroic dead fought epic battles eternally. Only the most worthy and courageous gained such a "reward."

A WORD ABOUT HISTORICAL AUTHENTICITY:

This work does not pretend to be a historical document, yet much historical research has shaped the writing. The author will dare to claim a conscious and deliberate effort to be authentic to the period of history. It is a fascinating time and place, and the weaving of a story around some of its elements has been a delightful and rewarding process. The general region in which the story takes place is factual, but the farm itself, the Circle of Stones with the well and Muninn's Keep are all purely fictional—although drawing on a composite of actual sights and ruins that can be visited today.

Arthurian legends have been researched. They play no direct role in this story, but the research has yielded many rich details. Stonehenge was already an ancient structure at the time, but far to the south and little known to the characters of this story. Burial mounds, sacred groves, wells dedicated to Woden worship (often spelled 'Odin' in ancient documents) and a multiplicity of Pagan practices, many of which endure in some measure to this day, provide a vast collection of word-pictures and traditions. They make a rich palate for the artist to dip his brush into, and of necessity, demand that he focus on a small part of the total picture, trying to bring that part to life.

A WORD ABOUT THE LANGUAGE

For the time and setting of this story, far more French than English influences would have been known in the spoken language, with a mixture of Roman, Gaelic & Norse words as well. Little would be recognizable as present-day English.

A WORD ABOUT DRAGONS, WYVERNS, WORMS & SALAMANDRÍNES

The terms, dragon, wyvern and worm appear interchangeably in both ancient and modern literature. Tales abound in northern England and many other parts of the world with surprisingly similar physical attributes, of a fearsome winged creature. In only a few of the tales did it breathe fire. There are compelling reasons to ask if an actual creature existed behind the tales, though the author has not attempted to answer that question. That the legends were part of everyday conversation at the time of the story seems a safe assumption. That there was mixed belief even at that time also seems a safe assumption.

Interestingly, the older the stories, the more likely there was an attempt to subdue and tame, rather than kill the dragon.

Stories of salamandríne (*salamander* in more conventional spelling) seem to predate most dragon stories. A more serpent-like, wingless creature said to dwell in fire, it is not so well established in ancient literature. Where it does show up, layers of occult or religious belief seem to overlay the physical descriptions. Usually described with lizard-like scales, rather than the smooth-skinned amphibian it is named for, the ability to regenerate body parts has found its way into a number of dragon-slaying tales.

For the purposes of this story the author has confined himself to the beliefs of the period so far as he can determine them, without trying to say whether or not those beliefs were valid. A number of the tales of the time period originated from events within a half-day's journey of the setting of this story. They would therefore have been part of the cultural consciousness, believed in firmly by some and scoffed at by others.

The author has hinted at a methane gas explosion in the cavern in Chapter 23, but left all characters but Theodoric convinced the salamandríne was the source of the fire.

A WORD ABOUT WILDLIFE

Hares, Red Deer, Fallow Deer, Roes, Wolves, Foxes and Wild Pigs were common in England in the ninth century. There seems to be no evidence of wolves after 1680 within England, although they survived somewhat longer in Scotland. The ferocious nature of the wolf in many ancient tales does not fit with the animal well known in Canada and the U.S., except where it has interbred with domestic dogs. References to bears can be found in some ancient literature, but with little evidence of their existence in England at the time of this story. Many smaller creatures did not find place in the sketchy documented history that has survived. Probably the most dangerous animal to hunt or to stumble across accidentally was the wild pig, yet it was highly valued for its meat—and for the skill and courage required hunting it.

A WORD ABOUT THE POEM

Woden's Nine, with apologies and tribute to Robert Service. The influence of "The Cremation of Sam McGee" is obvious in this poem. One of my favourite poets, I frequently see his stamp on my own work, though rarely his singular skill and genius.

Woden's Nine

Neath the old dark beams of a tavern dim
that has seen four hundred years,
a tale half told can get a hold
of imaginings and fears.

In the long, long night by a peat-fire's glow
and a tavern's somber cheer
the stranger told bits of the tale
I had journeyed far to hear.

He sat in the pub and he nursed a mug
of some Old-Country Ale.
He'd start to speak but some memory bleak
would cause his voice to fail.

Muninn's Keep

Now I sought the truth of a diff'rent world
beyond an ancient wall
where the hills are high, the valleys deep
and ageless memories call.

Where Muninn's Keep and Woden's Nine
are lost in a misty age
and the stones hold silent council
o'er the wisdom of the sage.

The old man mocked my questions
though gently—with a laugh,
said the dark oak beams, four hundreds old
could not count the half . . .

of the years I hoped to understand
and the tales so dimmed by time.
Then his cup he lifted once again
and his gaze locked firm to mine.

Now a peat-fire's glow gives a meager light
and his age I cannot say.
But beneath his cap showed a fringe of white
and his beard was mostly grey.

Years of sun and wind and rain
had deeply lined his face,
while his great build told a wordless tale
of some long forgotten race.

"North of the wall is a barb'rous land
that is cursed and cruel—but free,
with rugged hills and valleys steep
where burns rush to the sea.

"Woden worship—still practiced there
in the dim and failing light
of an ancient grove where the fog lies thick
and the oak trees guard the night.

"The nine-fingered one," he said to me,
"from out that ancient age,
bowed not at Woden's Alter,
risked the god's fierce rage.

"Long sought in blindness groping.
Searched a scroll that bore no name
of a god who seemed more worthy
than the one of bloody fame."

Then his voice grew harsh and raspy
as he spoke of blood there spilled
to the god of war and thunder,
and my spirit coldly thrilled.

Then I seemed to see a fire
beside an ancient well
and my mind saw a nine-fingered man
and a god who screaming fell.

How I trembled at the courage
to defy so fierce a god.
And I wondered who he worshiped;
wished to walk the self-same sod.

So I questioned, *"The nine-fingered one,*
bore he any son?
Does his race endure? Did his courage last?
Did he find that holy One?

Did he worship one still nameless?
Or had he given up the quest?"
The questions burned inside me.
I could not let them rest.

But the man gave me no answer,
as he raised his cup again.
In the dim and flickering fire-light
I felt something much like pain.

For the left hand I saw—a massive hand
with a tale of years of toil,
and a missing finger—broad the gap
t'ween nails deep grimed with soil.

And he spoke not even one word more
though his hands clenched into fists.
And it seemed to me that memories deep
bore him through timeless mists.

He lay his money on the bar.
He left me quite alone.
Broad shoulders scarcely fit the door
and I sat still as stone.

And I searched my mind for answers
in the things he didn't say
till the tavern keeper brought my bill
and sent me on my way.

Neath the old dark beams of a tavern dim
that has seen four hundred years,
a tale half told had grabbed a hold
of imaginings and fears.[ix]

Endnotes

[i] Anonymous. Excerpt adapted from *Beowulf*. Gummere, F.B. *trans.*, Eliot, C.W. *ed.*, Harvard Classics, Vol. 49. (PF Collier & Sons: New York, 1910). Public domain e-text obtained via the Online Book Initiative.

[ii] Isaiah 1:2 Latin Vulgate 405 A.D Public Domain

[iii] Isaiah 1: 5-6 Paraphrase

[iv] Isaiah 57:15 Paraphrase

[v] Isaiah 9:2-5 Paraphrase

[vi] Isaiah 9:6 Latin Vulgate 405 A.D. Public Domain

[vii] Isaiah 9:6 Paraphrase

[viii] Isaiah 48: 12-13, 18, 49:10, 53:4-5 Paraphrase

[ix] Adapted from the poem *Woden's Nine,* Self-Distributed in Let Heaven Weep 2009 Audio CD. Used by permission.

About the Author

Brian C. Austin and his wife live on a small acreage at Durham, Ontario, Canada. They have three grown children and seven grandchildren. Besides writing Brian serves as church librarian and serves on the Board of Directors of the Canadian Mental Health Association, Grey-Bruce Branch.

Austin's published work has appeared in local newspapers, *ChristianWeek, Fellowship Link, The Interim, Faith & Friends, Our Family Magazine, Relate Magazine,* and *The Shantyman,* as well as in the anthology, *Hot Apple Cider* and in the books of poetry, *Laughter & Tears, Let Heaven Weep,* and *I Barabbas,* published in Trade Paper and/or Audio CD editions.

www.UndiscoveredTreasures.org

ALSO BY THIS AUTHOR:

A contributing author to *Hot Apple Cider,* a best-selling Canadian Anthology published by *That's Life Communications.* ISBN 978-0-9784963-0-2.

Laughter & Tears Trade Paper, published by *Word Alive.* ISBN 978-1-8949286-6-3.

Laughter & Tears Audio CD, distributed by *Word Alive.* ISBN 978-1-8949286-7-0.

I Barabbas DVD and Audio CD. Self distributed.

Let Heaven Weep Audio CD. Self distributed.

www.undiscoveredtreasures.org